The biplane sailed across the sky

It circled about, the buzz of its engine coming and going on the warm breeze, as it zipped in for another bombing run.

Leaning out the window, Krysty fired a single round from the M-16 at the sky. Yanking the steering wheel back and forth, Ryan sent the Hummer zigzagging down the riverbed. After a few moments, he hit the gas and raced straight for a while, before braking hard and swinging randomly left and right again. Speed was their only armor.

Suddenly, Jak roared past the Hummer on the motorcycle, then swung past in front of the wag.

Running was something Ryan hated to do, but dying was a lot worse.

Other titles in the Deathlands saga:

JAMES AXLER

DEATH LANDS®

Sky Raider

A GOLD EAGLE BOOK FROM

WORLDWIDE®

TORONTO • NEW YORK • LONDON
AMSTERDAM • PARIS • SYDNEY • HAMBURG
STOCKHOLM • ATHENS • TOKYO • MILAN
MADRID • WARSAW • BUDAPEST • AUCKLAND

For Melissa, as always

First edition June 2007

ISBN-13: 978-0-373-62588-8
ISBN-10:   0-373-62588-X

SKY RAIDER

Fear is sharp-sighted, and can see things underground, and much more in the skies.
—Miguel de Cervantes,
Don Quixote de la Mancha (1.3.6)

THE DEATHLANDS SAGA

This world is their legacy, a world born in the violent nuclear spasm of 2001 that was the bitter outcome of a struggle for global dominance.

There is no real escape from this shockscape where life always hangs in the balance, vulnerable to newly demonic nature, barbarism, lawlessness.

But they are the warrior survivalists, and they endure—in the way of the lion, the hawk and the tiger, true to nature's heart despite its ruination.

Ryan Cawdor: The privileged son of an East Coast baron. Acquainted with betrayal from a tender age, he is a master of the hard realities.

Krysty Wroth: Harmony ville's own Titian-haired beauty, a woman with the strength of tempered steel. Her premonitions and Gaia powers have been fostered by her Mother Sonja.

J. B. Dix, the Armorer: Weapons master and Ryan's close ally, he, too, honed his skills traversing the Deathlands with the legendary Trader.

Doctor Theophilus Tanner: Torn from his family and a gentler life in 1896, Doc has been thrown into a future he couldn't have imagined.

Dr. Mildred Wyeth: Her father was killed by the Ku Klux Klan, but her fate is not much lighter. Restored from predark cryogenic suspension, she brings twentieth-century healing skills to a nightmare.

Jak Lauren: A true child of the wastelands, reared on adversity, loss and danger, the albino teenager is a fierce fighter and loyal friend.

Dean Cawdor: Ryan's young son by Sharona accepts the only world he knows, and yet he is the seedling bearing the promise of tomorrow.

In a world where all was lost, they are humanity's last hope....

Chapter One

A hot, listless wind blew across the expanse of dried earth to form little dust devils that swirled around the group of armed men. An old weathered oak tree stood nearby, its gnarled trunk strong in spite of the constant flash floods that swept the river valley. The bare branches offered the men little shade from the scorching sun, and high overhead a pair of eagles soared on the thermals, calling their defiance to the storm clouds darkening the distant horizon.

Tied to the tree with a length of dirty rope, an old mule snorted in annoyance and shuffled its hooves on the hard ground. The animal was heavily laden with bulging canvas sacks and leather water bags. Nearby, old wooden planks had been laid across two big rocks to form a crude table.

"Look, ya wanna trade or not?" Digger snarled, leaning forward to rest his palms on the table.

Sitting behind the table, Baron Jeffers said nothing in reply. But the two sec men flanking the baron instantly worked the bolt on their longblasters, ready to start firing at the slightest hint of trouble. If Digger noticed them, he gave no sign.

The three men from Indera ville were dressed in rough clothing, the usual mix of predark cloth and home-cured leather. The baron also wore a fancy jacket with a military design, and had a big-bore long-blaster slung across his back.

Only fifty or so yards away a gigantic mesa rose straight from the ground and dominated the valley in every direction. Its sheer rock sides were impossible to climb, but at some point in the past, a big section of the mesa had collapsed to create a large hollow with a rock overhang. Indera ville had been built directly below the overhang. A tall semicircular wall sealed off the ville from the hostile desert, along with the brutal men and muties that prowled the shores of the desert river. The rock overhang gave the population precious shade from the hot sun, and vital protection from the deadly acid rains that swept across the landscape every spring.

Crossing his arms, Baron Jeffers studied the skinny trader standing across the crude table. Indera ville was at the crossroads of a pass through the Diana Mountain and the sluggish Ohi River, so they had a lot of outlanders passing through. Which is why they had established the dealing tree.

Some of the newcomers wanted to stay in the ville. That was forbidden, even if the person owned a working blaster or was a healthy young woman. The ville was full and had plenty of homie weps, mostly crossbows and such, but more than enough to defend the ville. Most outlanders just wanted to get past the walls to see what they could jack, or to recce the ville for a raid. If they did and were caught, they were crucified, nailed to the dealing tree so that others would know better.

Jeffers scowled. And then there were a scant handful who came to trade, bits of predark metal for a bowl of soup, seeds from a nonmutie apple tree, and once, a whole box of predark meds! Of course, that had been many winters ago, when the Trader had stopped by in his armored war wags selling tech and books, and giving away hope for free. His deals were honest, his blasters always primed. The Trader didn't steal, and killed faster than summer lighting if somebody else even tried. Nobody crossed the Trader and lived.

Baron Jeffers sighed at the memory. But the Trader was long gone, vanished into the glowing mists of the western desert, and now there were only men like this Digger, usually on foot, occasionally on horseback, and sometimes riding in wooden carts pulled by chained slaves. Their deals were rarely fair, and they always stole whenever possible. Still, the ville needed whatever it could find in the way of tools. Life was hard.

"Okay, show me what ya got," Jeffers growled, sitting back in his chair, making it creak slightly. As he adjusted his position, the dark green canvas coat swept back to expose the brace of pistols jutting from his lizardskin belt.

The sec men standing on either side of the baron scowled menacingly, but their blasters packed only air. However, the razor-sharp bayonets attached to the end of each rifle barrel were real enough, and sharp enough to end the life of anything that made a move toward the baron. The real danger came from the sec men standing on the ville, wall-armed with crude cross-bows, the powerful hand-built weps more than capable of putting a barbed arrow completely through the chest of an invader standing near the wizened tree. The plant thrived on the blood spilled there.

"What, right here?" Digger asked, squinting his eyes at the guards along the wall. He licked dry lips. "I was kinda hoping we could talk biz inside. Out of the sun, ya know." He gestured vaguely. "A little shine, a couple of sluts…

"Not going to happen," Jeffers said, scratching at his belly, his hand closer to the checkered grip of his pistols. Unlike the rifles, his deadly blasters weren't just there for display. The brass was old, but the black powder was fresh and the split-lead bullets could blow a man in two. Weps were at a premium in the ville. Always had been. The armory had less than a hundred rounds of live bullets, and those were being saved for a dire emergency.

Digger smiled innocently. "Hey, there, I was only—"

"Nobody goes in but ville folk and sec men," the baron stated gruffly, placing both of his dusty boots on the ground as if about to stand. "And you ain't either of those, outlander."

"Okay, okay," Digger said hastily, raising both hands, the fingers splayed to show he held no weapon. "No corpse, no crime, right? Let's talk."

Grudgingly, the baron took his seat once more, and Digger exhaled in relief. Outlander, damn. Well, at least the baron hadn't called him a coldheart thief. That was something, at least.

Digger headed to his mule. On the ville walls, crossbows followed the trader as he flipped back the top of the lizardskin pouch and pulled out a wide rusty can. Returning to the barter table, Digger placed it in front of the baron and carefully removed the clear plastic top. The baron tried to hide his excitement, but his eyes shone. He could read just enough to know that military label on the predark can said coffee. Had the outlander found a food store buried under the mud somewhere and recovered a stash? Coffee was more valuable than predark liquor. Shine could be made these days, but no matter how carefully they were planted, coffee beans never grew.

Reaching inside the can, Digger pulled out a wad of greasy cloth and laid it on the table. The contents of the bundle gave a metallic click as he folded aside the cloth to reveal a dozen shining rounds of ammunition.

His gut surged with adrenaline at the sight, but Baron Jeffers locked his face into neutral, trying not to show his amazement. Black dust. Each of the brass was spotless, and the lead bullet was jacketed with copper in the old way that no wep-man could duplicate these days. Even more, they were long cartridges, designed for rifles, not pistols. Rifle cartridges! The sec men standing behind the baron shuffled their patched boots in the dusty soil at the incredible sight.

Reaching out, Jeffers lifted one of the rifle cartridges and weighed it in his hand. The brass felt as good as a woman's breast, delicious and heavy in his palm.

"So, mebbe we can go inside now, Baron?" Digger said in soft tones, lifting one of the perfect cartridges and turning it to catch the harsh sunlight.

In spite of his intense longing for live ammo, Jeffers felt suddenly suspicious at the remark. Now why did the fellow want inside so bad? The sun wasn't that hot, there was no chance of acid rain this late in the year, and a clay jug of water sat on the table. So why so keen about getting inside the ville? Only usual reasons were to jack supplies or recon the defenses. That kind of info would bring a big price from the enemies of Indera.

"Of course," Jeffers said with a smile, feeling his shoulders tense. "But your mule has to stay out here."

Digger turned to glance at the old animal tugging at a tuft of dried weeds sticking out of the ground. "Sure thing." He laughed, turning back. "No prob—" The trader stopped smiling at the sight of the baron holding both of his pistols level and pointing forward.

"H-hey n-now," Digger started as the baron thumbed back both hammers on the big wheelguns.

"Shut up, feeb," the baron snarled. "Cory, Abraham, get his blaster, and watch for tricks! There's something wrong here."

As the two sec men started around the baron, Digger hawked and spit on the table.

"So you're going to jack me, eh?" Digger snarled hatefully. "This ain't the rep of your ville!"

"You'll be paid in full," Jeffers said, holstering his handblasters, then sliding the rifle off his back. "If these are any good."

"Whatcha mean?" Digger shouted as one of the sec men grabbed his arm. He tried to shake the guard off but failed. "Just look at 'em! That brass be perfect!"

"If he moves again," Jeffers said, opening the breech of his empty rifle, "chill him."

"Yes, sir," one of the sec man answered, shoving the point of his bayonet against the trader's neck.

Digger went pale at the touch of steel, and made no further comment as a single drop of ruby-red blood welled with the point of contact. Slowly, the blood began to trickle down the man's neck, going into his tattered shirt.

"Ya gonna waste a brass just to make sure it's okay?" Digger said hoarsely. "That's crazy!"

"Better here than with a howler charging at you," Jeffers replied, sliding the round into his rifle. "We'll pay for this brass, too, trader," he added gruffly, working the bolt, closing the breech. "If it's any damn good, that is."

"Hey!" Digger cried, reaching for the ammo.

The two sec men nudged him hard and Digger went still, lowering his head as if braced for a blow.

Clicking off the safety, Jeffers leveled the rifle at Digger. The outlander opened his mouth to speak but nothing came out. Jeffers held the aim for a moment, then shifted the barrel toward the tree and pulled the trigger. There sounded a hard click and nothing else.

"Son of a bitch!" a sec man snarled, and slammed the wooden stock of his rifle into Digger's side. Ribs audibly cracked from the impact, and Digger slid to the ground, shaking all over.

"Nuking hell…" Digger gasped, starting to tremble. "Why'd ya do th-that? There's nothing wrong…with the brass…something busted…your rifle…"

"Oh, yeah? Let's see." Placing the rifle on the table, the baron worked the bolt to eject the cartridge, then yanked an eating knife from his belt. Carefully running the edge of the blade around the bullet, the baron separated lead from brass and emptied the cartridge onto the table. The wind blew the contents around as dry white sand poured from the brass.

"Dums!" Jeffers snarled, slapping the garbage aside. "Trying to buy his way past the gate with dums!" The baron strode around the table, pulling out one of his handblasters.

"Who ya working for?" he barked at the crouching trader. "Outies? Pirates? Thunder ville? Talk, feeb, and make it good, or you'll see the inside of my ville nailed to the front of the nuking gate!"

"Please, I didn't know!" Digger wept, trying to cover his face. "Please! I only…," A double explosion cut off his words and the two sec man screamed in pain as their knees were blown apart, bone and blood spraying onto the ground.

Snarling a curse, Jeffers fired his wheelguns just as the trader came up with two tiny blasters in his hands, the little weps almost completely hidden by his dirty fingers.

Derringers! The old word flashed through Jeffers' mind as he dived to the side, firing once more at the traitorous coldheart. One of his pistols jammed, but the other roared, blowing smoke and flame. Hitting the mud, Jeffers rolled to the side and came up with only a smoking hole in his jacket. The baron went to fire the second blaster again, but there was only a soft chug and a puff of gray smoke. Misfire!

Laughing in contempt, Digger aimed the two blasters at the snarling baron when white-hot pain lanced into his back and the barbed tip of a crossbow bolt thrust out of his chest. Dropping both of the little blasters, he clutched his chest, blood dribbling through his dirty fingers.

"Ch-chill me, and your ville dies," the trader rasped, pink saliva drooling down his chin.

Pulling a knife, Jeffers started forward when another feathered bolt stabbed into Digger's hip before a third went completely through his belly, pulling a ropy length of intestine out the other side.

Spasming from the pain, the trader gurgled horribly and slid to the mud, still whispering a warning.

Kneeling on the ground, Jeffers slashed his blade across the men's throat, then stood and waved at the archers on the ville wall. One of them waved back in acknowledgment, and made a gesture of coming out. But Jeffers waved that off. There was something wrong here, and he didn't want those ville gates open until he knew for sure that it was safe. The hairs were standing up on the back of his neck, exactly the same way they did when muties attacked in the night.

Striding to the fallen sec men, the baron saw that they were both chilled, and he closed their eyes with his fingertips. Damn it, they had both been good men, his brothers in battle killed by a jacking coldheart. A boiling rage built inside the baron, but he forced it down. Getting angry wouldn't bring them back. More's the pity.

Kneeling near the body of the trader, the baron retrieved the derringers and searched his clothing to find more ammo that fit the little palmblasters. He reloaded them both and tucked the blasters into his pockets. Now why hadn't the damn feeb tried to sell him these? Nervously pulling out a handblaster, the baron purged the spent chambers and started the laborious reloading process while he studied the landscape. Nothing was in sight but flat ground all the way to the Ohi River, and only the soft whispering breeze of the Indera desert…

The man went stiff. The eagles! Looking skyward, the baron gasped at the sight of the clear sky. Not a bird in sight around their nest. The eagles were gone.

"Oh, fuck, no," Jeffers muttered, scanning the rest of the blue sky. Not again!

Suddenly a whistling sound cut the air and Jeffers spun just in time to see something plummet out of the thin air and hit the ground halfway between him and the ville. The blast seemed to rock the world, and Jeffers went flying backward. He hit the ground with a sickening crack and felt fire erupt inside his chest as a rib snapped. Nuking shit!

He lost consciousness for a moment from the pain, but came abruptly awake as a second blast sounded.

It was farther way, and sounded odd. Higher some-how, as if the explosion happened in the air.

Cold adrenaline forced the man to his feet, and he weakly pulled out both derringers and fired at the sky as yet another detonation occurred directly on the overhang of rock above Indera ville. There was a moving dot in the sky, but if the weps hit anything, it was impossible to tell at this range.

Dropping the spent palmblasters, Jeffers started hobbling for the ville as a double explosion rent air, closely followed by a crackling noise. In growing horror, the baron watched as the rocky overhang started to splinter along its base.

"Get out!" Jeffers screamed at the top of his lungs, waving both arms. "Get out of the ville, you fools!"

The sec men on the wall began to ring the alarm bell, just as sunlight moved across the ground to touch the ville. People started to scream as the overhang sagged lower and lower from the side of the mesa, and then came free.

With his heart pounding, Jeffers insanely stag-gered toward the doomed ville and saw the colossal slab of granite impact.

The walls crumbled like sand, the alarm bell went instantly silent, and the frightened screaming abruptly stopped. Having trouble breathing, the baron kept walking as he watched a billowing cloud of dust rise around the edges of the rock slab covering his home.

Chilled. They were all chilled. It was impossible! Unthinkable! Indera ville had been destroyed by its main source of protection.

Slowing to a halt, Baron Jeffers cradled his aching chest, and now felt a trickle running down his left leg. He glanced down to see a spreading red stain. Blood. Digger had to have shot him. He touched the wound, inhaled at the rush of pain. But that was a good sign. A major wound would have gone numb. Pain meant it was minor damage. There was hardly any bleeding. He could have it stitched by the ville healer....

Raising his head, the man looked with uncomprehending eyes on the crushed debris of the ville. There was no more healer, or sec men, or anything. He was the baron of a graveyard. An outlander standing alone and wounded in the open.

Just then, a soft buzzing noise came from above, and Jeffers squinted into the sun to see a small black shape moving through the sky in a lazy circle around the broken mesa.

"Tregart," he muttered, raising a bloody fist to shake at the sky. "Damn you to hell!"

As if in response, the black shape swung away from the mesa and started directly toward the man. The dried mud in front of him kicking up dirty plumes as there came the faint sound of a rapid-fire blaster coming closer and closer.

Chapter Two

As the swirling mist in the mat-trans chamber faded, the six people standing inside the unit lay limply on the floor, gasping for breath.

After a few minutes Ryan Cawdor brushed the curly black hair out of his scarred face and tried to focus his good eye on the chamber. Every mat-trans chamber was identical, and this one was no different. At the far end was a closed vanadium-steel door, with a lever. The portal had to be closed and locked before the mat-trans would operate, which was some sort of an ancient safety feature.

Only the colors of each chamber's armaglass walls changed, each location decorated in a different color for ease of identification. Unfortunately, those color codes were unknown, as were the commands that would let the companions control a jump between one underground redoubt and another. Each journey via a mat-trans unit was a random leap into the unknown.

"Everybody okay?" Ryan asked, slowly forcing himself to stand.

"No permanent harm, lover," Krysty Wroth said, brushing the red hair from her face. Her green eyes flashed as they moved around the chamber, her wild mane of animated hair flexing unhappily from the aftereffects of the jump. The walls were orange with black stripes. That pattern was unknown to her. The companions had never been to this redoubt before, which was both good and bad.

Standing without effort, Krysty straightened her clothing, redoing a few of the buttons on her white shirt. It was a touch too small for her full breasts, but it was all that had been available at the last redoubt. The military-issue bra was a tad snug but with any luck, she might find something more serviceable in this redoubt.

Sweeping back her heavy bearskin coat, Krysty checked the knife in her left cowboy boot, then pulled the Smith & Wesson .38 revolver from the gunbelt around her trim waist. Far too many times the companions had arrived at a redoubt only to find they weren't the only ones there.

Busy checking his own weapons, Ryan merely grunted at the beautiful woman.

"Dark night, it's cold in here," J.B. Dix said, adjusting his wire-rimmed glasses. The small man exhaled slowly, and his breath fogged slightly. "Must be thirty degrees, mebbe less."

Still lying on the plastic floor, the man with the

silvery hair used an arm to lever himself up to look wearily around at them. Tall and thin, he appeared to be sixty years old, or even more, but his bright eyes sparkled with intelligence.

"Indeed, you are quite correct, John Barrymore," Doc Tanner intoned in his deep stentorian voice. "Something must be wrong with the life support system."

"I hope not," Krysty stated, holstering her blaster. "That's all there is between us and suffocating to death."

"Quite so, madam," Doc whispered hoarsely. "Quite so." The jumps through the mat-trans units always hit Doc and Jak Lauren the hardest. For Doc, it was probably because of the horrible experiments performed by Operation Chronos.

Fumbling to locate his ebony swordstick on the floor, Dr. Theophilus Algernon Tanner wrapped both hands around the silver lion's-head crest and levered himself erect. Dressed as if he were from the nineteenth century, the scholar wore a gentleman's frilled shirt and a long frock coat that had seen better days. But there was also a huge LeMat .44 pistol at his side, the grip of the massive double-barrel revolver worn from constant use.

"You okay, Jak?" Mildred Wyeth asked, swinging her med kit around to her front for easy access. Short and stocky, the black woman had once been a twentieth-century physician. During a relatively simple operation, something had gone wrong, and Mildred had been cryogenically frozen, only to be revived a hundred years later by Ryan and the companions. She had been traveling with them ever since.

In the savage wastelands of the early twenty-second century, her skills as a trained physician were beyond price, even though Mildred had virtually no instruments or medicine. The med kit hanging over her shoulder was merely a patched canvas bag salvaged from a U.S. Army M*A*S*H unit. The bag was filled with strips of boiled cloth to be used as bandages, a small plastic bottle of homemade liquor called "shine" for disinfectant, a pack of razor blades found in a bombed-out supermarket for her scalpels, and similar crude items. She sometimes felt like a photographer without a camera. Dr. Mildred Wyeth had the skill to save lives, but the tools of her craft were only items of legend in these dark days.

"F-feel fine." Jak Lauren spit, using the back of a hand to wipe the drool from his mouth.

Turning away from the wall where he had just been sick, Jak stood carefully, as if afraid his thin body might break from the effort. He was trying to keep it hidden from the others, but their travels through the mat-trans had been hitting the teenager hard lately, and it was taking longer and longer for him to get back on his feet after each jump. It was a strange condition for the albino teen, because he was normally as strong as a horse.

As he checked over his .357 Magnum Colt Python revolver, Jak privately wondered if maybe the effects of the hundreds of jumps they had made were wearing him down. That would be bad news if true. The mat-trans units in the redoubts were the only safe way to traverse the burning deserts and rad-blasted hellzones of the Deathlands. It would be a triple-damn shame if he had to abandon using that method of transportation. Worse—he'd have to quit traveling with his companions.

"By the Three Kennedys!" Doc roared, pulling at the lion head of his cane to extract a shining steel rapier from the ebony shaft. "Dean! Where is Dean!"

The rest of the companions paused at that, and exchanged sad glances.

"Sharona took him. He's no longer with us," Ryan said quietly. "Remember, Doc?"

The time traveler arched both eyebrows in indignation, then slowly his features softened as he recalled the events of the past.

"Ah, yes, my condolences, my dear Ryan," Doc muttered in embarrassment, sheathing the blade once more and locking it tight with a twist of the handle. "I had forgotten. The jump, you know...."

"Hey, anybody see my hat?" J.B. asked, running stiff fingers through his sparse hair.

Ryan kicked the battered fedora across the chilly

floor and J.B. scooped it up and tucked it back in place in a single move.

"I could use one of those myself," Mildred said, buttoning the collar of her denim shirt. "Damn, it really is cold in here."

"Mebbe everybody died leaving the air conditioner on," Ryan said in a touch of rare humor as he went to the wall and placed a hand on the vent.

"No, it's working," he reported, thoughtfully straightening the patch covering the ruin of his left eye. "And it's warm, too."

"Warm?" Jak said, frowning as he tucked away the Colt Python. "Colder than doomie's tit in here." Shivering slightly, the teenager zipped up the front of his jacket. The garment was covered with bits of metal and mirrors, as well as razor blades. Razor blades also lined the collar. If anybody was foolish enough to try to grab the teen around the throat, the person might lose a few fingers.

His combat instincts instantly alert, Ryan pulled out his SiG-Sauer and racked the slide to chamber a round.

"J.B., check the door," he ordered brusquely. "Everybody else, back into the mat-trans unit!"

Quickly the others did as ordered.

Gingerly touching the door, J.B. hissed with shock and pulled his hand back to suck on his fingertips.

"Dark night! The bastard thing is freezing!" he mumbled around the fingers.

Rotating the cylinder of her Czech ZKR .38 revolver as a prelude to possible battle, Mildred snapped her head around at that comment. "Impossible," she said, starting forward. "The reactors in the basement of a redoubt should keep the base warm even if it was at the North Pole! And the only thing colder than that would be…" Her eyes went wide. "Ryan, check for a draft!"

Frowning darkly, Ryan paused, then holstered his blaster. Walking over to join his friend, he pulled out a candle, and very carefully lit the wick with a predark butane lighter. Manufactured by the millions before skydark destroyed the world, the lighters were now worth more than a man's life in trade. The only thing more valuable was a loaded blaster. The friends had found several in the past.

As Ryan moved the candle along the frame of the oval doorway, J.B. reached into the munitions bag at his side and unearthed a bit of a candle and a butane lighter from the array of homemade explosives and predark grens.

Slowly, the two men moved the flickering flames along the edge of the jam of the burnished steel door. The flames stayed steady until nearing the concealed hinges of the portal, then both wavered and went out.

"Fireblast, there are holes in the seal," Ryan said, tucking the spent candle away. "Some sort of draft sucking out all the warm air."

Doing the same with his candle, J.B. glowered at

the door as if it were a ticking mine. "Gotta be one hell of vacuum on the other side," he said, pushing back his hat. "Think we're in space again?"

"Mebbe," Ryan returned. The companions had once found themselves in a "redoubt" that was orbiting the moon. They had been forced to leave almost immediately, but that redoubt had been safe and warm. If this one was in orbit and leaking air, then their wisest move would be to leave.

"Let's go," Ryan stated, turning for the mat-trans unit. "No way we're going to chance opening the door."

Hunching his shoulders, Jak muttered a curse. Another jump so soon wasn't something any of them wanted to do.

Going to join the others, Krysty moved past the vent and paused. The breeze was gone. Spinning, she placed a hand on the disguised vent and said a quick prayer to Gaia when she felt warm air, just a lot weaker than before. The life support of the redoubt had to have started working once they arrived, but was now running out of power. Soon, there might not be enough to operate the mat-trans!

"Into the unit!" Krysty commanded, starting to run across the chamber. "Now! We jump right fucking now!"

Not wasting a second, the rest of the companions jammed into the small chamber and as Krysty squeezed in with them, Ryan hit the LD button.

Nothing happened.

Fireblast! he raged silently. They had to have been here too long! The Last Destination option lasted for only thirty minutes! The LD button was no longer active and couldn't send them back to the Arizona redoubt they had just left.

With no other choice, Ryan hit the jump buttons hoping he'd randomly key a sequence that would take them *somewhere*. Almost instantly a new chill seeped into their living bones that had nothing to do with the vacuum of space. A swirling white mist rose from the solid floor and ceiling to fill the chamber, then lighting crackled in silent fury and the floor seemed to disappear as they all began falling into the artificial void that stretched from unit to unit across the planet, and beyond...

RISING STIFFLY from his throne, the old baron limped across the dais in front of the blockhouse.

The entire population of the ville filled the courtyard, as Baron Hugh Tregart hobbled down a short flight of stairs and headed for the pyre.

Reaching twice the height of a man, the stack of wood was bound together with strong rope that had been carefully dampened to prevent it from burning through too quickly and disturbing the pyre, and its sole occupant. Wrapped in stiff canvas, the body lay on top of the flammable mound, a few relics from childhood placed alongside the trophies of manhood. The hide of the first griz bear he had ever killed, his gunbelt. Only the precious blaster was missing.

Accepting a crackling torch from a sec man, the baron shuffled closer and blinked away some tears as he touched the pyre as if bestowing a benediction. Soaked with shine, oil, grease and even a few precious ounces of condensed fuel, the wood caught instantly, and the flames made a low roar as they spread over the pyre, meeting on the other side and then rising to the crest to engulf the still body of his son.

A dark plume of roiling smoke soon rose to hide the corpse of Edmund Tregart, and all across the courtyard people began to openly weep or to bow their heads and mutter prayers as the flames began to consume the young man.

"Ashes to ashes, dust to dust," Baron Tregart said in a loud, clear voice, tossing the torch onto the growing bonfire. Tears were on his cheeks, but his face was as impassive as stone. Only the whiteness of his hand grasping the walking stick showed his inner emotions.

"It is done," the baron said, turning to face the crowd of ville folk and sec men. "My son is gone. Now, bring forth the killers!"

There was a commotion at the rear of the crowd, and the people angrily parted to allow a group of grim sec men through with their two prisoners.

Wrapped in chains, the captives were wearing only bloody rags, their exposed skin covered with red welts from endless whippings. One man had a badly broken nose, the other had an eye swollen shut and bulging with contained fluids.

The ville folk cursed at the prisoners as they passed, several spit at the men, and a few raised sharp pieces of stone to throw. But the sec men got in the way, and the stones were reluctantly dropped to the dusty yard.

In the background, armed guards walked along the top of the wall around Thunder ville, and while the men desperately wanted to watch the coming execution, they forced themselves to face outward. Funerals, weddings, births, any major event involving the baron was a good time for enemies to attack. The sec men clenched their fists in frustration and kept watch on the desert river outside the ville. The muddy waters of the Ohi helped to keep the ville alive, but the river also brought outlanders from the distant mountains, and those were always trouble.

Returning to his throne, Baron Tregart sat heavily and cast a furtive gaze at the chair alongside. His wife, Hannah, was dying of the black cough, and now this. For a moment the old man thought his heart would break from the weight of his sorrow, then he inhaled slow and sat upright. A baron could never show weakness to his people, his father had always warned. Nor grant favors to an enemy. If he followed those two rules, his ville would prosper.

But it had been a lie. Thunder ville was dying. Food was so scarce that the women couldn't produce enough milk for their babies, and many of them "accidentally" dropped newborn infants on to stones to save the poor things from the endless days of painful starvation until sweet death finally set them free.

The crops were dying, and the stores of predark cans all gone. Many of his people were eating cactus from the desert, or the little green lizards that came out at night. One lad had even somehow caught a stingwing and eaten it alive. He died soon afterward, but the act itself had been incredible. Stingwings moved faster than arrows. That a starving child caught one alive was seen by many as an omen. The question was whether it was a good omen because he caught the food, or a bad one because he died afterward. Some had tried hunting, but any portable wildlife was too far outside the small ville for the starving, weak hunters to carry back. Even in pieces. And the scavs would have quickly devoured the carcass left behind.

A breeze shifted the smoke from the pyre and the baron flinched slightly from the smell of his burning son. Edmund had been on a scav run in the distance ruins, and miraculously found a cache of predark canned goods. The cans that bulged from internal pressure they didn't touch, experience teaching them that those were deadly to eat for man, beast and mutie. But there had been many more in good condition, fifty cans of food! Fifty! A bounty beyond imagination.

The cans had all been mixed with clean water, and then boiled for the length of a new candle to kill any rust-formed poisons. When done, the contents would have made enough soup for the whole ville. In this time of famine it was a godsend, his son hailed as a savior by the famished people.

"Then you tried to steal some!" Baron Tregart roared, standing and shaking a fist at the trembling prisoner. "You stole soup and spilled the rest! All of it!"

"Mercy!" a thief cried, raising his bloody hands.

A sec man alongside the prisoner thrust down his longblaster, the wooden stock ramming into the man's face, the bones audibly cracking. His chains rattling, the criminal fell to his knees, a thin arm thrown across his face as protection. Blood flowed down his cheek and dribbled onto his filthy clothing. The other thief burst into hysterical tears, a mad laughter mixing with the sobs into an unnerving noise.

"Make soup of them!" a thin woman screamed from the crowd. "Cook the fools over the young baron!"

Others in the crowd took up the cry, and Baron Tregart frowned until they raggedly ceased. Had they come to that at last? To eat their own dead to stay alive?

Once more, the baron stared in open hatred at the cringing thieves. He wasn't a brutal ruler, and might have forgiven them taking the food, but they had clubbed a sec man to do it. The sec man on guard that night was his own son, standing in for a childhood friend who was too weak to be near the food, the smell of the cooking soup making him too dizzy to stand.

All through last night, Edmund had burned with fever, the ville healer doing what she could, but even her herbs and poultices had been consumed during the famine. His daughter had cut her wrist and tried to feed her dying brother some of her own blood to give him strength. But in his delirium, the man refused. By dawn, Edmund was dead.

The child had foretold of this, Baron Tregart remembered bitterly. Food would destroy the ville. He had thought the doomie was talking about poisoned food, but apparently not. Just starvation. The one enemy the sec men couldn't stop with a million blasters.

"Captain Zane?" the baron said, turning to the side.

Looking up at the throne, Zane Dolbert gave a salute. "Yes, Baron?" he asked in a deep baritone.

"After the funeral, kill Edmund's dogs," Baron Tregart said softly.

"Baron?" the sec chief whispered in shock.

"You heard me, Zane," the baron repeated more forcefully. "Kill the guard dogs. There is no other food."

"I…" Zane swallowed, and tried again. "Most of my men will refuse."

"You will not kill them?" the baron began in a low voice, his eyes flashing with the force that had made him baron in the time of chaos.

"No! Of course, not that, my lord," Zane decried, vehemently shaking his head. "If you order it, Baron, I'll ace the dogs myself. But my men will not eat them. The dogs are looked upon as fellow sec men. They stood by our sides against muties and cold-hearts, and even the machines that came in from the high desert. The animals are buried in the Iron Yard with the sec men who have died in battle."

"Then let them refuse, and there will be more soup for the ville folk," Baron Tregart said softly. "But save half of the broth. Your men will eat when they get hungry enough."

"That won't be necessary, Father!" a voice called out loudly from the rear of the crowd.

As the people quickly moved aside, a young woman strode forward to stop at the bottom of the stairs leading to the dais. She would have been beautiful, but her cold eyes ruined the effect of her flawless skin and sensuous mouth. A cascade of long blond hair fell to her waist, bound by a rawhide net into a thick ponytail. As she opened her ancient leather jacket, a gunbelt was exposed with a shiny blaster riding at her hip.

The baron blinked at the sight. A blaster? Where had Sandra found a blaster?

"You're late, Daughter," he said in stern disapproval. Sandra Tregart looked at the raging bonfire across the courtyard for only a moment, then faced her father once more.

"There was business to do," she replied curtly, loosening the blue scarf around her neck.

"What kind of business is more important than this?" the baron demanded, gesturing at the crackling pyre.

"See for yourself!" she shouted. Pulling off a glove, she put two fingers into her mouth and shrilly whistled.

Suddenly there was a commotion at the back of the crowd, and people began to gasp, then cheer as a line of men marched into view carrying bundles and baskets.

"I have gotten us twenty dead horses, one mule and fourteen dogs," Sandra Tregart shouted. "All butchered and ready to be cooked into jerky. Plus, a hundred pounds of flour, fifty pounds of dried vegetables, thirty of rice, twenty loaves of bread, ten cans of fruit, and enough corn seed to plant half our cropland!"

Food! The cry went through the crowd like a shotgun blast, some of the wrinklies falling to their knees and openly weeping in relief. Baron Tregart could only gape at the sight of the baskets being placed at the foot of the dais. Food, endless food, spread in front of him, the salty smell of the fresh meat driving a knife of hunger into his empty belly.

Sandra took a small round of bread from a basket and tossed it to her father. He made the catch and stared at the golden-brown crust cradled in his bony hand as if it were the first bread ever made in the history of the world.

"There are also twenty bottles of shine," she said brusquely, as if throwing challenge at her father. "I claim all of it for myself, and the Angel. Agreed?"

"Yes, yes, of course, whatever you want!" Baron Tregart panted, waving the trivial matter aside, the other hand still holding the wondrous bread. "Zane! Get ten strong men and gather all of the wood you can find!" the baron ordered. "Build a cooking fire on the other side of the ville. Far away from here."

Looking at the towering flames of the pyre, the sec chief frowned. "Upwind from here, you mean, Baron," he corrected.

Slowly placing the round of bread into his lap, Baron Tregart nodded in assent. "Yes, good thinking. Use an entire horse, and twenty pounds of vegetables for soup. Then get five women to start making bread. Use half of the flour, the rest goes into the armory for safekeeping."

"Have the guards make sure that everybody drinks a bowl of thin broth before getting any meat," Sandra commanded sharply. "Or else they'll just vomit it back up. Whip the first person to get sick, and the rest will eat slower. That is all the food there is. We make it last, or we die this winterfall."

"Yes, my lady," Zane muttered, the sec chief placing a fist to his heart.

Both the baron and Sandra raised an eyebrow at that. Such a salute was reserved only for the baron and his wife. Sandra held the sec man's gaze for a long moment, then regally nodded. Turning, Zane started shouting orders, and people rushed to obey. The line of men picked up the baskets from the dais and started marching around the blockhouse. An old woman burst into tears of happiness, and from somewhere a man started to sing a working song.

"So it appears you are finally in charge, dear Daughter," Baron Tregart said slowly, leaning back in his throne. "Your brother still burns, and he has already been replaced."

The woman said nothing, her thoughts dark and private.

"Shall I jump onto the funeral pyre next?" the baron asked, lifting the round of bread and shaking it at her. "Or do you wish that pleasure for yourself, *Baron?*"

"I do not want to rule," Sandra said slowly. "I never have. You know what I desire."

"Bah, foolish dreams." The baron snarled. Unable to restrain himself any longer, the old man chewed off a small piece of the bread. The first swallow was without taste, and the baron had to command himself to stop to let the yawning pit of his belly accept the food before swallowing any more. His gut roiled at the invasion, then finally settled down, and he tried another small piece, and then another.

As his hunger slackened, the baron found he could now taste the bread. By the blood of his fathers, it was delicious! Sweetened with something, honey perhaps, or maybe a pinch of predark sugar. Food fit for a baron's table, and not the sort of thing that was traded away for a few live rounds of ammunition.

"All this food. There's too much. It is the wealth of an entire ville," the baron said, masticating each bite to make the food last. "Jeffers would never give so much for what we had to offer in trade."

Taking a round of bread from the basket, Sandra pulled out a knife and cut off a slice. "Oh, but he did," she said with a private smile.

Scowling, the baron lowered his repast. "Did you bed him for this wealth? Did you trade your honor to save the ville?"

"There are blasters, too, Father," she said, tossing the bread back into the basket. Reaching into a pocket of her leather jacket, Sandra pulled out a wad of gray cloth. Walking up the stairs, she placed it on the arm of the throne with a muffled thud.

Taking one more bite of the bread in his hand, the baron placed it aside and chewed thoughtfully as he folded back the oily cloth to expose a wheelgun. The metal was unblemished, without any sign of rust, and the barrel shone with a blue tint like winter ice. Now,

Sandra pulled out a fat leather pouch and laid it next to the blaster. With trembling fingers, the baron pulled open the top and saw it was filled with lead shot and a clear plastic jar of black powder.

"So, you did it," the baron accused in a hollow voice.

"Yes," she replied simply.

"So that mule you mentioned, it was Digger's," he ventured.

Over by the stone well, a group of laughing sec men tossed a rope over a bare tree branch normally used for hanging outlanders, and hauled the dead mule into the air. Even before its hooves left the ground, a child slid a plastic basin underneath and big woman started skinning the beast with a sharp knife.

Smiling slightly, Sandra shrugged. "He didn't need it anymore."

So the trader was aced, eh? he thought.

"Were there any survivors?" the baron asked hopefully. "I know about the power of the Angel, but surely you could not have… I mean, an entire ville?"

She laughed, and he received his answer.

"It was them or us, dear Father." Sandra chuckled. "There was no other way. One ville died, so another could live."

"But you took all of their food."

"All that I could find," she corrected, clenching her teeth. "Some of it was…inaccessible."

Slumping in his throne, the old baron tried to come

to grips with the idea of jacking the dead. More, Jeffers had been a friend. Long ago, the two villes had fought together in the Mutie Wars. Was that bond of honor to be broken over loaves of bread?

For a time there was only the sound of the funeral pyre and the happy singing of the butcher doing her messy task. As the meat came away from the bones of the animal, children took the huge wet slabs and awkwardly carried them around the blockhouse to the cooking fire. Staying close by the littles, armed sec men guarded the food and carefully stayed between it and the starving crowd who watched the preparations with near madness in their gaunt faces.

Hitching up his loose pants, a burly sec man approached the dais and clumsily saluted, his right hand not quite touching his temple. "Baron?" he asked hesitantly.

Sandra frowned at the man, but the baron turned to look upon the man with patience. Gedore was a new sec man, recruited just before the crops failed. He was strong and obedient, but lacking in any imagination. A grunt, as the baron's grandfather would have said. Just a blaster with feet.

"Yes, what is it?" Baron Tregart asked.

Gedore gestured to the chained men shivering near the funeral pyre. They kept casting furtive glances at the flames as if expecting to be tossed upon the conflagration at any moment. Plainly written on the faces of the sec men holding the chains of the two prisoners was their opinion that they would have heartily approved of such a command from their chief, or baron.

"What about the thieves?" Gedore asked.

Stroking the round of bread for a moment, Baron Tregart scowled at the two men in open hatred, his face contorting into a feral mask of fury. Releasing the bread, the old baron grabbed the blaster on the table and started loading the chambers.

"Bring them closer," Baron Tregart whispered hoarsely, both hands busy with powder and shot. "I shall do this myself. Myself!"

"No, Father," Lady Tregart interrupted, stepping in front of the elderly man.

Snapping up his head, the baron stared at her as his hands continued their work. After fifty years of being a baron, the man could load a weapon in the dark while drunk.

"They killed the son of the baron," he reminded her, closing the cylinder with a satisfying click. "The punishment is death."

"And why should we waste precious ammo on scum such as these?" Sandra asked soothingly, then smiled at the chained men. She could see a flicker of hope come into their faces.

"No," the woman continued. "Don't shoot them, Father, and there shall be no burning today to mar the funeral of my brother."

"Thank you, lady!" one of the prisoners cried, dropping to his hands and raising both hands.

"Gedore!" Sandra said loudly, motioning him closer.

The big sec man rested a boot on the dais and leaned inward. She could see the folds of loose flesh around his neck and guessed he had been giving some of his rations away. A lover, perhaps? That would end today.

"Yes, ma'am?" Gedore asked.

"Cripple them, and throw them alive to the dogs," Sandra said calmly, savoring the panic that grew in their eyes. Fools, did you think to ace a Tregart and live to tell the tale? "I see no reason to waste all of the meat. Today marks the passing of my brother, and the salvation of the ville! Everybody eats their fill!"

Her eyes sparkling with amusement, Sandra grinned at the stunned prisoners. "Even the dogs," she added softly.

"No!" a prisoner screamed, shaking all over. "Mercy, mistress! Chill us, please! It was an accident! An accident! I swear!"

A guard cuffed the man silent, while the other prisoner slumped his shoulders and began to softly weep, his tears falling unnoticed onto the dusty ground.

"Take them away," Sandra commanded with a flip of her hand. "Oh...and, Gedore?"

The sec man had already started across the courtyard, so he stopped to look over a shoulder. "Ma'am?" he responded.

"If I find them with cut throats, you will be next. They go into the pens alive."

Turning slightly pale, Gedore nodded, and started directing the other guards to herd the shuffling along the street toward the dog pen near the front gate. As if sensing the coming meal, the dogs began to howl in eager anticipation.

"Justice must be swift," the woman recited, "if it is to be fair."

Looking up from the bread and the blaster in his lap, Baron Tregart tilted his head at the beautiful young woman.

"So you do remember the stories I used to tell you and Edmund at bedtime," he muttered.

"Yes, I remember," she said, facing the bonfire. The figure on top of the woodpile was reduced to only bones at this time, and as she watched even those crumbled away and the tongues of red fire lapped at the darkening sky. It was done. Edmund was gone.

"Now, there is only you, Daughter," Hugh Tregart said softly.

"That was all you ever had, old man," she whispered with a snarl. "Except that you were too drunk to notice before."

But the desert wind carried away her dark words and nobody heard.

Chapter Three

Sucking in a lungful of warm air, Ryan struggled awake and looked around the mat-trans chamber. So soon after the first jump, the second one had hit them like a gren. He dimly remembered their arriving, and then nothing.

Shaking his head, the one-eyed man rose onto his hands and knees, shook his head to try to clear his mind. Fireblast! He had to get sharp. Had to make nuking sure they weren't in the same redoubt again. Repeat jumps were rare, but they had happened before. Brushing back his wild mane of hair, Ryan focused his eye and grunted in relief at the sight of the chamber walls. They were a lime green with horizontal red stripes. It was a redoubt they had never been to before.

As the life support system sent a clean fresh breeze of sterilized air into the unit, painful groans started coming from the rest of the companions.

"Green walls," Mildred said, fumbling to unscrew the cap off a canteen at her side. "At least we're someplace new." Letting the cap drop to the end of the little chain that attached it to the military canteen, the physician took a small drink from the contents. For quite sometime she had been trying to find an antidote to the jump sickness, but so far she had nothing more effective than a mix of coffee and whiskey.

Unfortunately, both of these items were few and far between. The current brew was an herbal tea laced with something called spike, a raw liquor distilled from cactus. The moonshine had a tremendous kick, but there was never a hangover the next day, and it was a wonderful neural inhibitor and painkiller. Mildred had traded a small fortune in .22 bullets for three precious bottles. This was the very last of the Spike.

Hesitantly, everybody took a sip of the brew, making sour faces. Giving back the empty canteen, Ryan started to speak when he saw Krysty staring behind him. Dropping the canteen, he spun in a crouch with his blaster out and ready.

That was when he saw the corpse.

Holstering his piece, Ryan shuffled over to the body leaning against the exit door, one of its desic-cated arms parched on the lever that opened the oval portal. The corpse was dressed in a predark military uniform, the patches and medals meaning nothing to the Deathlands warrior. But the flap was open on the holster at its side, and the handblaster was gone.

Scowling, Ryan noticed that the corpse appeared to be blocking the door.

"Bastard died trying to hold the door closed," Ryan muttered, glancing at the portal with growing unease. He wondered what was on the other side.

Staring at the closed door, Krysty rubbed her temples as if in pain.

Ryan noticed the gesture. "Got something?" he asked tightly.

The redhead paused, then shook her head.

That didn't reassure the big man much. The woman's psionic abilities were sometimes blocked.

Kneeling alongside the grinning corpse, Ryan checked the ammo pouch and found only one spare clip where there should have been three.

"Must have been a hell of a fight," J.B. said, moving closer. The Armorer clicked the safety back on his Uzi machine pistol and let it drop at his side.

"We better take it slow, just in case of a booby," Ryan warned, rubbing the scar on his cheek. He sure wasn't ready to do another jump. "If this guy was trying to keep folks out, whatever was on the other side might have had the same idea."

"Woman, not man," Jak added, pointing. "Ears pierced."

Tucking a strand of beaded hair behind an ear to get it out of the way, Mildred hid a smile. "That didn't mean a thing in the modern American Army, my friend."

Taking the corpse by the shoulders, Ryan gave a gentle tug and the withered arms broke off with a snap. They slid out of the loose sleeves and stayed attached to the rifle as he carried the body away.

Placing it against the wall, Ryan saw the identification tag on the chest. S. Jongersonsten. Damn name was too long for them to add the first. Mebbe it was a woman. No way to tell now.

Carefully breaking the fingers, Mildred got the ancient arms free and put them with the body.

Going to the door, J.B. pulled out some tools and checked for any traps. The rest of the companions formed a defensive arc behind the man, their weapons ready.

"It's clean," J.B. finally announced. He tried to move the lever. The mechanism worked smoothly as if freshly lubricated, the internal bolts disengaging with dull thuds.

"Ryan?" J.B. asked, tugging his fingerless gloves on tighter.

Working the bolt on his Steyr SSG-70 rifle, Ryan said, "Go ahead."

The Armorer pulled the door aside on silent hinges. He stayed crouched behind the door to give his friends a clear field of fire, ready to throw his weight forward to close it again fast if something tried to come through. But there were no blaster shots, only mutters of surprise.

Swinging his Uzi machine pistol to the front, J.B. clicked off the safety and stepped around the door just as Ryan and Krysty walked through into the antechamber beyond.

Following close behind, Doc, Mildred and Jak blocked his view. But as the companions spread out, J.B. saw the place was full of corpses. Old corpses. Dozens of them. And the floor was covered with the empty brass casings of spent ammunition. Most of the bodies were in pieces, and there was a smudge on the inside of the vanadium steel door suggesting that a gren had been used to try to blow it open, resulting in a spectacular and deadly failure.

"What the fuck went on here?" Ryan growled, sweeping the room with a stern gaze. The body in the jump chamber had been desiccated to the point of mummification, but these looked as if they were only a few years old! The wrinkled skin resembled leather instead of ancient parchment.

Careful of where they stepped, the companions moved through the antechamber and entered the control room. There were more bodies here, all of them showing signs of death by violence. Bullet holes, knives in chests, and one poor bastard bent over the control console with a fire ax buried in his back.

"Check the comp!" J.B. ordered. "If that's damaged, we're not going anywhere."

Holstering her weapon, Mildred went to the

control board while Ryan stepped to the master computer. The lights still rippled across its face as always, but he found a line of dents across the front of the machine. Somebody had fired a full clip from a machine gun, but the rounds hadn't gotten through the thick metal housing of the mil comp.

"The government really built these redoubts to last, that's for damn sure," Mildred whispered. "Well, the controls aren't damaged, aside from a busted monitor."

"Good show, madam, then we can still egress as desired," Doc said, checking a corpse slumped in a chair. The colonel had stopped in the middle of reloading a shotgun, but the body seemed to be without damage. Then he spotted the thin line that went from ear to ear. Somebody had slit his throat from behind as he'd thumbed in spare cartridges. Ghastly.

"They killed each other," Krysty said, walking among the slain soldiers. Every branch of the service was here, Army, Navy, Air Force, and a few that she couldn't recognize. Delta Force. Who were they?

"And when the ammo ran out," Ryan muttered, resting the stock of his rifle on a hip, "they kept fighting with whatever was available, handblasters, knives, table legs, bottles…"

Slowly turning in a circle, Jak frowned. "What cause?" he asked. "Mutiny?"

"Not on a U.S. base," Mildred stated as a fact. "No, a war plague seems more likely. Yes, that could be it. I had heard of such things. Rumors only, of course. Biological agents that drove the enemy temporarily insane so that they would slaughter each other, then our troops could march into the territory without opposition."

"Filthy way to fight a war," Doc rumbled, easing down the hammer on his massive LeMat revolver. "Although Tennyson would have been darkly amused."

"This is the way the world ends," Ryan said softly. "Not with a bang, but with a whimper."

Doc beamed at that. "You remember the poem!" he cried in delight.

"It's about war," Ryan countered gruffly. "And you sure as hell have repeated it often enough." He nudged a corpse with his Army boot. The clothing rustled like old leaves, the dried body rocking from the impact as if weightless. "Mildred, why are the ones in here fresher than the husk in the jump chamber?"

"I have no idea," the physician said, seemingly annoyed by the mystery. "The life support system keeps the redoubt constantly flushed with sterilized air. These bodies should be withered husks by now."

Ryan scowled, but said nothing.

Kneeling next to a mutilated corpse with the glass fragments of a busted bottle embedded into his face, Jak eased the dead man's service revolver from its holster and checked the load. Four spent shells, and one live round.

"Think safe stay?" Jak asked, pocketing the .38-caliber bullet. His Colt Python could use both .38 bullets and .357 Magnum rounds. Never made sense to him for anybody to carry a wep that only used one caliber of ammo.

"Yes, it's safe," Mildred said without hesitation. "There are no biological vectors that could survive exposure for a full week, much less a hundred years. But if anybody starts feeling dizzy, stop whatever you're doing and sing out fast."

"Fair enough," J.B. said, pushing open the hallway door with the barrel of the Uzi.

A single corpse slumped against the wall in the corridor, an automatic pistol dangling from his raised hand, the wall on either side and the front of his uniform stitched with bullet holes from an automatic weapon.

"There's a lot of lead to be salvaged here, if nothing else," J.B. stated in hard practicality.

Kneeling by the body, Jak tried to free the blaster, but the hand was locked in a death grip. Pressing the ejector button, he dropped the clip and thumbed out the intact shells. There were four 9 mm rounds, but they were the wrong size for his Colt.

"Here," the albino teenager said, passing J.B. two of the rounds for his Uzi, and giving the others to Ryan for his 9 mm SiG-Sauer. Everybody else used .38 rounds, except for Doc and his black powder Le Mat.

Pocketing the rounds, Ryan looked around for the

body of the shooter, but the hallway was empty. There were no other corpses in sight, just the double line of doors leading to the elevator and stairs at the far end. There were no other signs of violence, no blast marks or spent casings on the floor.

Nobody cared about the hallway, Ryan realized. These soldiers fought for access to the mat-trans-mat. But that made no sense. The blast doors on the top level of the redoubt were large enough for a tank to drive through. A hundred men could have walked out that opening. So why fight over something that could only hold a limited number of people? Ryan scowled. Unless something was wrong with the blast doors.

Walking past the water fountain, Ryan found the usual framed map on the wall. Almost every redoubt was exactly the same, so the companions knew the bases intimately. This one seemed normal in every aspect.

"Okay, we better do a recon of the whole base," Ryan decided, pulling out his SiG-Sauer and jacking the slide to chamber a round. "We go two on two. Krysty with me, Doc with Jak, J.B. with Mildred. Stay tight. You find anything still alive, blow its mutie head off and come running."

"Why do you think it would be a mutie?" Krysty asked, her animated hair flexing in harmony with her thoughts.

Frowning, Ryan loosened the panga in its sheath.

"'Cause nothing norm would have willingly stayed in this graveyard," he stated. "We meet in the garage on the top level in an hour. Let's go."

As the companions separated into pairs, Krysty and Ryan headed down the main corridor toward the elevator. The doors opened with a soft sigh, exposing a tangle of bodies, knives still thrust into throats and bellies. Bypassing the corpses for the moment, the man and woman shifted the dead out of the lift. The dried bodies weighed very little.

Removing a colonel with large wounds in his back, Krysty discovered a naked woman on the bottom of the pile. Her military uniform askew and ripped in places. Both of the female soldier's hands clutched a pair of automatic pistols with the slides kicked back showing they were empty, and there was spent brass everywhere. The black-rimmed glasses and rictus grin gave the face of the female mummy a demonic appearance that was unnerving even to the hardened travelers of the Deathlands.

Muttering a curse, Ryan looked at the male soldiers he had placed in the hallway, and saw that some of them had their pants unzipped and belt buckles loosened.

"Attempted gang rape." He growled deep in his throat. Looking at Krysty, the man had a brief flash of when he'd first met the redhead in a burning barn, a coldheart going after her. "What the hell happened to these people? From what I read, the predark military of America didn't do this kind of thing."

"Well, for some reason, these were about to," Krysty said. "At least the woman died fighting and took them with her."

"Small comfort."

"Agreed, lover. But better than the alternative."

"Guess so," Ryan stated as he took the woman's ankles and Krysty took the shoulders. "But the sooner we get out of here, the better."

"No argument there," Krysty said, her green eyes flashing in ill-controlled hatred.

Gently, they placed the corpse off by herself and got into the waiting elevator. Ryan hit the button for the basement, and the door sighed shut. The elevator car began to silently descend into the bowels of the subterranean fortress.

In the hallway, something stirred in a shadowy corner and sluggishly started shifting the corpses until there was a clear path to the elevator once more.

Chapter Four

Heading for the front gate, Sandra Tregart strode along the streets of the ville. Now that the food had been delivered, she had more important things to do. Much more important.

This was the day to try the Demon! she thought, feeling a tingle of excitement. After so many failures, this one had to work. It would work! Or heads would roll.

Cutting through the marketplace, Tregart smelled the aroma of cooking soup in the air, and people were already lined up with cups or wooden bowls, impatiently waiting for their share. As she passed, the people smiled and waved, and old folk too weak to wait in line joyously called her name from second-story windows.

"Bless you, lady!" an old man shouted. "All hail the Baroness Tregart!"

Several more people took up the cry, and Sandra smiled at that. How amusing. Baroness, eh? Did they think Sandra was her mother, or that she should take over the ville from her father? Either way, they would only have to wait a few more days and the matter would be settled. Permanently.

Turning a corner, Sandra saw a commotion near the front gate and spotted a couple of outlanders arguing with the sec men on guard duty. Then one of the outlanders passed over a bottle half full of amber liquid, and the sec men waved the strangers through. She stopped in her tracks, rigid with fury. A sec man took a bribe to admit an outlander!

"Hold it right there!" Sandra bellowed, starting forward again quickly.

The sec men blanched at her approach and cowered in fear. One of them threw the bottle away and it crashed on the street. However, the outlanders only drunkenly leered in frank appraisal of the woman. Her clothes were clean, and her blouse was open at the neck, exposing a wealth of rising cleavage.

"Nuke me running," the tall outlander said with a chuckle. "The gaudy sluts come to mee'cha right at the gate! Black dust, now that's what I call hospitality!"

"I'd give a working blaster for a ride on that," the short man agreed, slurring the words. Spitting into his palms, he smoothed back his greasy hair. "Yes, sir, a working blaster!"

The nearby people went silent, and the guards began to quickly move away from the outlanders. They had seen this all before and knew what was coming.

However, near the edge of the crowd, a teenage boy placed his cracked bowl on a windowsill and started forward. "How dare you speak like that to her!" he shouted angrily, grabbing a rock from the ground.

With a curt gesture, Sandra made him stop. Respectfully, the teen moved back into the line and dropped the stone.

"Shitfire, ya sure got him well trained!" The tall stranger laughed uproariously.

"How much?" the other man asked, jingling a pocket. "We got brass, for that ass."

"What was that again?" Sandra asked in a deceptively soft voice, crossing her arms.

"You h-heard me, bitch," the outlander hiccuped, rubbing his crotch. "My buddy and I have just spent a fucking month trekking through sand and rocks to reach the Ohí, and we ain't seen a gaudy house since Christ was a cowboy."

"So how much?" the short man added, staring at her breasts. "Come on, name a price!"

"Months, eh? So, have you two been using each other?" Sandra asked, smiling sweetly. "Or do you prefer muties? I hear there is a nest of stickies just to the north of here." She squinted as if trying to get a better view of their stunned faces. "Yes, several of their uglier young do resemble you two quite a lot."

"Fuckin' bitch!" the tall outlander snarled, pulling out a knife. "No slut talks to me like that!"

Weaving slightly, the other man started to add something, but finally noticed the fearful expressions of the neighboring crowd. What the hell, they were acting as if this gaudy slut was the baron! And for the first time, the outlander moved his gaze off the body and onto her face. Looked hard. Her beauty was without flaw, her full lips and dark eyes bewitching. But even through the drunken haze, he saw the raging fury behind those lovely eyes, and suddenly knew he was looking into the face of death.

Spreading his hands to show he wasn't armed, the short outlander rapidly shuffled toward the gate, while his snarling friend lumbered forward.

"Ya nuke-eating slut, I'm gonna cut you a new one," the tall man said, reaching for the woman's arm.

In a lightning-fast move almost too fast to follow, Sandra uncrossed her arms and leveled a derringer, the little blaster almost hidden in her closed fist. She fired, and the tongue of flame from the .44 Magnum round actually engulfed the outstretched hand of the outlander.

Recoiling, he raised a bloody hand, with several fingers missing, the shock masking the agony of the mutilation. The drunk was still reeling, the pain only starting to contort his features, when Sandra stepped close to slash across his face with a knife. The blade opened his face like wet bread and burst his left eye. Blood went everywhere.

Shrieking, the outlander fumbled for the rusty

wheelgun tucked into his belt. But Sandra slashed again, severing the tendons of his hand. Screaming in pain, he pulled the arm back with the hand flopping loosely at the end like a dead thing tied to a stick. Now the derringer roared once more, and crimson erupted from the man's crotch, the discharge setting fire to his soiled pants. Howling in mindless agony, the drunk toppled over, and the woman started to hack him to pieces with her sharp knife.

Staggering away, the short outlander was almost past the gate when he stopped, a rush of shame filling his belly like acid rain. That was his friend back there getting aced. They had traveled together for years, fought side by side, eating out of the same rusty cans, huddling under the same ratty blanket for warmth in the mountains, one of them holding a girl while the other had his fun. They were brothers in everything but blood, and he was leaving him behind to get aced by some feeb slut?

Blind fury filled the outlander. Yelling a battle cry, he spun and pulled out his blaster, then charged, shooting at every step.

With the first shot, the crowd vanished as if by magic, and Sandra quickly raised the twitching man as a shield. The mutilated drunk jerked as the incoming lead slammed into his chest, and his shoulders slumped into the sweet release of death.

Snarling, Sandra tossed the body aside and pulled

out a second derringer. Hot lead hummed through the fragrant air going past her head, and the baron's daughter fired both barrels in unison.

The running outlander's throat exploded under the double assault and, dropping his blaster, he grabbed his neck with both hands. Gurgling horribly, he fought for breath as Sandra threw the knife and it slammed into the man's chest. Going limp, the outlander took a single step, then collapsed upon the street.

Calmly, Sandra reloaded her little weapons and hid them away again, carefully pocketing the spent brass. Her father had taught her how to shoot, and her brother had instructed her to save everything. But nobody had trained her to kill; it was a natural talent.

"Wall guard!" Sandra shouted through a cupped hand.

An armed sergeant on top of the ville wall waved in reply.

"Have this drek fed to the dogs and place two new men on the gate!" she yelled loudly.

The sergeant gave a salute and rushed off to relay the command.

"You two, come here," Sandra ordered, pointing at the sec men near the open gate.

Glancing nervously at each other, the sec men walked closer and dropped to a knee in the street.

"Idiots and fools. Ten lashes for taking a bribe," she said coldly. "Plus, ten for not closing the gate before leaving your post. Plus, ten more for tossing the bottle of shine away! Everybody knows that every drop in the ville belongs to me. *Me!*"

"Thirty lashes? But, ma'am…" one of them began, looking down a side street toward the barracks. Directly in front of the brick building was a large wooden cross, dripping with leather straps. The punishment rack.

Setting her jaw, Tregart glared. "Forty lashes," she barked. "Or do you want to make it fifty?"

The sec men looked at the ground and said nothing. Letting them stay that way for a few minutes, Sandra snapped her fingers. "Rise, fools. Now leave, before I have you crucified for being cowards."

Turning pale, the two sec men gave a shaky salute and went back to the gate to wait for replacement guards.

"As for you, boy," the woman announced, walking over to the terrified teenager. On closer inspection, Tregart could see he was dressed like one of the pilgrims that had arrived a few months ago from the southlands, raggedy clothing covered with of patches, and sandals made from pieces of car tires held on with some rope.

"Ma'am?" he said, cowering slightly.

As Sandra stopped in front of him, the teen bent a knee in respect. She smiled at that. Respect given freely was twice as sweet as obedience though fear. Yes, he would do nicely. "You may rise, boy," Sandra said benignly. "I saw you start forward to help me in this." She gestured at the sprawling corpses.

"I live here, and you are the daughter of my baron," he muttered, turning red in the face as he awkwardly stood.

"Apparently you are the only man who remembered that!" Sandra said, her voice rising into a shout.

The other people standing nearby shuffled uneasily as if trying to hide behind one another. Sandra gave them the full weight of her stare for a few moments, then turned her back on them.

"I need a ground man," she said, running her fingers through the boy's mane of greasy hair, but finding no lice or other vermin. "To help with the Angel. The job is yours. Report to the barracks for a hot bath, a meal and a blaster."

His head snapped up at that, his young eyes going wide. "My lady?" he whispered.

"You heard me, lad." Tregart chuckled. "What is your name?"

"Brian, my lady."

"Nothing more? No last name?"

He shrugged. "No, my lady."

"Then I shall give you one," Sandra stated, glancing at the rock he had tried to use earlier. "From this day on, you're Brian Stone. Is that acceptable?"

Eagerly, the teenager nodded.

"Very good, Stone," she said, pulling out a handkerchief to wipe her hand clean. "Now get moving, and go get that bath, Afterward, you can claim what you want from the clothing of the outlanders. I can't have my guards fighting muties barefoot."

"Boots, too, my lady?" Brian asked, his voice rising a notch in disbelief. His bare toes wiggled at the prospect.

Sandra began to laugh. "Yes, boots, too, Mr. Stone. And don't forget a gunbelt for your new blaster!"

"Yes, my lady!" Brian cried, taking off down the street toward the barracks. "Blessings upon you!"

As the teenager raced away, Sandra turned in a slow circle to scowl at the rest of the people present.

"As for the rest of you!" she said, not shouting, but somehow her voice seemed to cascade along the street. "My thanks for your loyalty!"

Nobody dared to speak as a dry wind from the desert beyond the Ohi moved across the ville.

"It shall be remembered." She sneered, then turned on a heel and headed for the gate once more.

"She never would have acted like this with Edmund still alive," a bald man muttered, watching her leave. "Do you think she'll…you know…to Brian?" He made a vague gesture.

A toothless old woman nodded as the line shifted forward. "She did to all of the rest, so why not him, eh?"

"I'd rather be aced," another man stated.

"Ghastly," a young woman shuddered.

Just then, the breeze shifted direction to bring them the tantalizing smell of the cooking food, and the hunger in their bellies drove out any further thoughts of compassion toward the fate awaiting the new young sec man.

TAKING THE STAIRS, J.B. and Mildred climbed over the corpses littering the steps. A lot of the lights were out in the passageway, and Mildred decided it would be wise to use her flashlight.

Reaching inside her med kit, she pulled out the precious device and pumped the small handle several times to charge the ancient batteries inside. The survivalist tool had been among several items the companions had found in a looted hardware store, and it was irreplaceable.

Flicking the switch, Mildred was relieved to see a pale yellow beam from the device illuminate the stairwell in golden tones.

"Dark night!" J.B. cried, swinging up his Uzi as something moved in the shadows. But the man refrained from firing at the very last moment when he saw the rope wrapped around the man's throat. As a warm breeze wafted from the air vents in the wall, the body moved again, gently swaying back and forth.

"A suicide," Mildred said, tightening her grip on her revolver.

"Can you blame him?" J.B. answered as they climbed the steps rising past the dangling body.

At the top of the stairs J.B. found a Marine with an M-16 assault rifle by his side, an ammo pouch of clips over his shoulder. The sergeant had been shot in the belly and clearly bled to death, as evidenced from the pool of dried blood around him on the floor.

Checking the pouch, Mildred found only spent clips, but J.B. found the clip partially inserted into the M-16 was fully loaded. Easing the clip into the weapon, he flicked off the safety and worked the arming bolt by hand to cycle all thirty rounds through the weapon. Nothing jammed. Reloading the clip, he slapped it into the assault rifle and slung it across his back. There were hundreds of dead soldiers in the redoubt. If each of them only had a few live rounds on their person, this could be the biggest find of weapons in many a month!

"Sure hope there's some food, too," Mildred said, obviously following his train of thought.

"Gotta be," he said, easing open the door to the next level with the barrel of the Uzi. "This many mouths had to be fed."

Mildred clicked off her flashlight at the sight of the brightly illuminated hallway. Then she stopped in her tracks, and J.B. muttered a curse.

A sandbag nest had been built in the middle of an intersection of corridors, the dead men lying on top of the belt-fed .50-caliber machine guns. These soldiers had no obvious signs of violence, but more importantly, they were all wearing gas masks.

HEADING DIRECTLY to the galley, Doc and Jak found the doors barred with tables, bullet holes and spent shells everywhere, along with several ruined sections of the corridor that could only have been caused by grens.

"Like started doing wolfweed," Jak muttered, brushing the silky white hair from his face.

Pressing his face to the window in a door, Doc looked around the kitchen and recoiled in shock.

"They had somebody tied down to a table," Doc began, then his stomach rebelled and he turned to heave in the corner. But only bile came up. What food he had eaten that morning was long gone, purged from his system by the multiple jumps.

"Cannies?" Jak asked, peeking inside.

Wiping his mouth clean on an embroider handkerchief, Doc spoke softly. "Jak, my dear friend," he whispered. "I am fully aware that my mind is half gone from…the things that have been done to me by scientists and that madman Strasser, but if whatever befouled this redoubt starts to enact its virulent filth upon me, please…"

"Won't feel thing," Jak promised, patting the time traveler on the shoulder. "My word. But you do same for me."

Doc solemnly nodded, and the two men shared a moment beyond friendship, brothers in blood standing against the world.

"Then let us press on," Doc said, starting down the corridor. "There is much to do, and I yearn for the feel of clean air on the face."

"Hope blast doors work," Jak said, pushing open the door to a lavatory. The smell was long gone, scrubbed clean by the life support system, but the floors were smeared with ancient filth. "Else, why these not run?"

Doc tilted his head at that comment, and looked upward as if he could see the blast door somewhere above them.

"A very good question, my friend," he muttered. "That is a very good question, indeed."

THE REACTORS in the basement proved to be intact, the techies inside all killed by self-inflicted gunshots. It seemed clear to Ryan and Krysty that the techies had known what was happening inside the rest of the redoubt, and had chosen the fast way out.

With Krysty standing guard, Ryan did a fast sweep through the armory on the middle floor of the redoubt, but it was as he had expected. Every weapon case was either open or smashed apart. The shelves were empty of C-4 satchels, grens and Claymore mines. Only wrapping paper and warning labels remained. Dozens of longblasters and rapid-fires lay trampled on the floor, the treads of a forklift impressed into the plastic stocks and the bent barrels.

In the far corner, the floor and walls were charred black, and from the bodies on the floor it seemed that somebody had tried to operate a flamethrower on six other soldiers. He'd failed and they'd all died together in a fiery backblast of the erupting fuel tanks.

Trudging out of the room, Ryan noticed a cardboard box on a shelf and snatched it quickly, as if it might vanish into thin air. Peeling off the plastic wrapper, he saw it was a full box of 12-gauge shotgun shells. He tucked the box into a pocket for J.B. to use in his S&W M-4000 shotgun, and left the armory.

"Anything?" Krysty asked hopefully, lowering her wheelgun as he appeared.

"Not much," Ryan said with a growl. "They were fighting in here, too, and most of the stuff got busted bad. I saw a couple of crates of Stinger missiles in the rear, but the seals were broken so the electronics would be dead."

"We might still be able to salvage the C-4 from the warheads," she said. "Take a couple of pipes from the bathroom and we've got grens."

"Yeah," Ryan replied, removing the cap from his canteen and taking a swig. "Sounds good. We can do that tonight after chow. Now let's finish this sweep.

The sooner we get back together with the others, the fucking better I'll like it."

Her red hair flexing protectively around her face, Krysty gave a wry smile. "It's even getting to you, eh?"

The big man shrugged. "This hellhole would get under the skin of anybody. Makes the bug-infested redoubt in Texas seem friendly as a gaudy house in comparison."

As the couple left for the elevators, something stirred in the shadows of the armory and sluggishly started trailing after them.

Chapter Five

As the elevator doors opened on the top level of the redoubt, Ryan and Krysty saw that the garage was filled with row upon row of vehicles, all of them parked neatly within the painted lines on the concrete floor. Most were civilian wags, brightly colored cars, pickup trucks, vans, and about a dozen motorcycles. The bikes looked in good shape in spite of their flat tires.

On the far side of the garage some military vehicles were parked behind a wire divider that went from floor to ceiling. Ryan could see a couple of Hummers, several GMC 4x4 trucks, and even an armored half-track, the front tires flat on the floor, but the rear-looking treads seemingly intact. The half-track was armed with a .50-caliber rapid-fire, a belt of linked ammo dangling from the side. However, none of other vehicles showed any signs of damage.

"Odd," Krysty whispered. "There doesn't seem to have been any fighting up here."

"Mebbe whatever caused the madness never reached

this level," Ryan said, sucking his hollow tooth thoughtfully. "Or—"

"Or this is where it started," she finished for him. "Yeah."

A sharp whistle cut the air, and the two spun around, automatically taking a step to the side to throw off the aim of an enemy. Then they saw J.B. and Mildred coming out of the tool room near the fuel pumps. He was carrying a handful of road flares, and she was tucking a roll of duct tape into her open med kit.

"Any sign of Doc and Jak?" Krysty asked as their friends joined them, tucking away her weapon.

"Not yet," Mildred said, tying shut the flap on her med kit. "But knowing that old coot, he's probably grabbing a snack in the kitchen."

"Hope so," Ryan added, walking among the rows of wags. "We're low on food. Only got a couple of cans left."

"Find any MRE packs?" J.B. asked, tucking flares into his munitions bag.

Rattling the door to the pickup, Ryan shook his head. "Nothing. Even the armory was stripped bare." Then he grunted in remembrance and pulled out the box of cartridges.

"Here you go, 12-gauge," he said, tossing it over.

"Thanks," J.B. said, making the catch and placing the ammo alongside the flares.

"Well, we found some soldiers wearing gas masks," Mildred said, and then told them about the sandbag nest.

"But they went insane, too?" Krysty said, resting a cowboy boot on the fender of a car. In the bright fluorescent lights, the embroidered pattern of winged falcons could be dimly seen through the layers of dust and dirt. "So either they put the masks on too later—"

"Or else they didn't work. Yes, exactly."

"Gaia protect us," the redhead muttered.

"Amen to that," Mildred added grimly.

Stepping over a corpse in greasy coveralls sprawled on the floor, Ryan tried the handle on a sports car. Opening the door, he got hit by an exhalation of trapped air that sighed out carrying the smell of rotting leather and dust. He quickly closed the door. There was rarely much to scav in an ordinary wag.

Spotting the fuel pumps in the far corner, J.B. started maneuvering through the vehicles. If the pumps were still sealed, they might be able to get a few of these machines going again. If Doc and Jak didn't find anything in the kitchen or galley, they would have to go hunting outside, and wags would let them cover more ground in shorter time. With luck, there might even be a ville nearby where they could trade with the local baron. A single working wag and a can of juice would buy more food than the companions could carry in a week.

"Hell of a lot of wags here," Ryan stated, sounding suspicious. "It's as if everybody drove inside, parked their cars, then went downstairs to go insane."

"Come on, let's check the mil wags," Ryan suggested, getting back to business.

Going to a workbench, the three took some tools, then walked over to the wire fence. With a hammer and chisel, Krysty notched the padlock holding the gate closed, then Ryan easily smashed the lock open with a sledgehammer. The noise echoed loudly across the still garage.

As the chain snaked noisily to the floor, Mildred swung the gate open as Ryan and Krysty walked into the motor pool.

Separating again, the two circled the vehicles to make sure the area was clear, then started checking the machines. Choosing a Hummer, Ryan went to the back for the emergency kit. Sure enough, the box was there and still sealed. Forcing it open with his panga, he extracted a small first-aid kit, some road flares, a thermal blanket, three MRE food packs and a gun case. Opening the black plastic box, he found a Veri pistol coated with Cosmoline gel. The flare gun would need a good cleaning before it could be used, but it seemed in perfect shape, and there were six flares nestled in the soft gray foam cushioning alongside the pistol. Three of the aerial flares had split along the sides from age, but the others were intact, and the plastic tubes felt resilient when he gently squeezed. As a blaster, the flare gun was pitiful, but it made excellent trade goods.

Smashing open a locked window with the butt of her blaster, Krysty was already checking inside the cab of the half-track as Mildred pawed through the contents of another Hummer.

"Anything good in the first-aid kit?" Krysty asked.

"No." The physician sighed, tossing the open box back into the wag. "It's all useless. Just too damn old."

"Well, I found a few grens."

Excellent! Any ammo?" Mildred asked.

"No."

"Damn."

Just then, the concrete floor shook with a low rumble.

"Is that a quake?" Krysty asked, looking over a shoulder, her hair flexing as if stirred by secret winds.

"No, too weak," Ryan snapped as the sound increased in volume and strength.

"Mother of god…that's the blast door!" Mildred gasped in astonishment, dropping an ammo box. It hit with a crash, spilling brass rounds across the floor. "Somebody is coming inside!"

The startled friends turned to stare at the front of the redoubt where a wide tunnel opened in the wall.

The distant end of the zigzagging tunnel couldn't be seen, but there was no mistaking the sound of the powerful electric motors hidden inside the walls as they started to cycle open the massive nuke-proof doors that lead to the world outside.

THE CRATER WAS blisteringly hot under the sun, the hard stone ground seeming to reflect the solar heat until the temperature became almost unbearable.

Carrying a small umbrella, Sandra Tregart relished the meager shade it gave as she watched the almost-naked eunuchs toiling under the harsh sunlight. The lean men were wearing only sandals and loincloths, their sweaty skin burned to a deep, rich brown. The eunuchs were crawling along the rocky ground, removing every bit of windblown trash or sharp rock from the volcanic ground. The predark tires of the Angel were heavily patched, and every bump threw off their balance and shook the plane badly. Sometimes, it was difficult for her to gain enough speed for take-off. Thus every obstruction, no matter how small, had to be removed. It was a dirty job, inching along the strip that served as the runway, but Sandra refused to have slaves do the job. Slaves always wanted to rebel, and couldn't be trusted. The eunuchs were fanatically devoted to her, and so only they could perform the vital task.

That is, Sandra griped, unless the Demon worked.

Then all of her prayers would be answered. After which...

From the tent that served as the eunuchs' barracks, she could smell roasting meat and bread. After she had bombed Indera ville out of existence, her eunuchs had ridden the last few horses there to loot the ruins. In return, she gave them the first pick of the food. Naturally, the rest went to Thunder ville, but her men were fed before the ville folk. After all, they guarded her at night, and, what was more important, they protected the Angel. Although few enemies had ever gotten onto the impact crater that served as an airfield.

Jagged peaks of ancient lava formed an impassable barrier around the crater. There was only one break in the rocky walls, and it was closed with a barrier of tires filled with rocks and topped with rusty barbed wire. Flanking both sides of the small door were wooden sentry towers containing armed eunuchs who trained every day with their homie crossbows. They could ace a vulture on the wing at a hundred yards. Neither man nor mutie got close to the wall, and nobody had ever even touched the gate without her permission. Anything that headed in its direction was chilled on sight. Even her brother Edmund had been wounded once for coming too close. To her father and mother, Sandra had professed her most sincere apologies for the terrible accident. But in private, she had praised Digger for his marksmanship and promoted him to sec chief for the airfield.

Pausing on the barren field, Sandra frowned at the thought. Such a pity that Digger was gone. Perhaps Stone would take his place. After the teen had been properly altered, of course. She smiled at that, and continued her inspection tour of the airfield. Everything needed to be perfect this day. A lot depended on the success of her newest experiment. Black dust, the whole world depended on its success!

Glancing skyward, Sandra frowned at the orange and red sky, streaks of black ripping across the polluted heavens as endless lighting crashed amid the roiling death clouds. It was the same way almost every day. But on rare occurrences, the wind would shift direction and the cloud cover would break. That was when blue sky would show through, tempting her into the beyond, calling a sweet siren song of freedom. She turned and walked away. But it was a dream unfulfilled. No matter how quickly she got the Angel off the ground, the clouds would roll back in to the fill the momentary gap and steal away the blue once more. Her brother had often warned that even if she made it through to the clean air above, she would be trapped on the other side, maybe for days, or even weeks. Sooner or later her plane would run out of fuel and she would sail powerless into the roiling chem-polluted clouds to suffer a death beyond words. It would be unlikely that even her bones would make it through to fall upon the nuke-blasted soil below.

Sandra had quickly learned that flying was a matter of staying high enough so spears couldn't hit the Angel, yet low enough to avoid the deadly sky. It was a balancing act, but the results were worth the terrible risks involved. The freedom of flying! The incredible power!

Just then, an eruption of steam caught her attention, and she headed toward a group of swearing men. They were working around an iron van set on top of a brick hearth. A couple of bare-chested boys were shoveling scraps of wood into the banked fire under the vat, while a second group adjusted pressure valves. Coming out of the top of the vat was a large coil of copper tubing that arched downward to dribble a clear fluid into a fuel container. As it was filled, a man capped it tight, and slipped another container under the end of the tubing without spilling a single drop. Nearby, a lone man with a horribly scarred face was chopping up cactus plants and piling the juicy innards into a plastic bucket. With every burst of steam from the pressure valve, the disfigured man flinched as if to protect his scars.

Forming a semicircle around the still were eight large tents. One was for Sandra's ground crew to take shelter in during an acid rain storm, the floor raised high with rocks and old sheets of plastic to protect them from the runoff. The next was her home, with a bathtub for washing and a lockbox full of weapons and precious ammo. Two more tents were the workshops, another contained the Angel, and the rest were what Sandra called her lab, miscellaneous parts and bolts of cloth salvaged from ruins across the land. The last tent held the Demon.

"How is it going, Carter?" Sandra asked, stopping a short distance from the still. Between the crackling fire and the hissing steam, she couldn't understand how the men survived the awful heat. That was how Karl had been disfigured. He'd fallen asleep from the heat and caught a steam blast in the face. Incredibly, he'd lived, but never spoke again, and flatly refused to work the still again.

"Good afternoon, my lady," Carter said in a squeaky voice, grinning widely. Sweat poured off his hairless chest as if he were standing in the rain. "We just finished a new batch of shine. And Karl harvested enough cactus for a second batch. We'll start it fermenting tonight."

"Excellent," she said, mopping her forehead with a cloth. Already her white shirt was soaked, the thin material clinging to her skin. None of the men seemed to notice. "Take ten gallons and fill the tanks on the Demon. The wind is good, and I'm going to try again while we still have sunlight."

"But ten gallons is barely a quarter tank, mistress," Carter began in his child's voice. "How will you know if the Demon can be trusted until you fill the tanks completely?"

From under the shadow of her umbrella, the woman stared in growing anger at the giant.

"Yes, of course, you're right. Ten is more than enough," he burbled, cowering slightly. "I'll get them myself."

As the colossus lumbered away, Sandra allowed herself a private smile. She knew that Carter meant well, but the man was overly concerned with her safety. He was so large many believed him to be part mutie. The man stood almost seven feet tall, his wide barrel chest rippling with hard muscles. Yet his face was as smooth as a newborn infant's, his body completely without hair. Castrating the men working on the airfield had been her father's idea. And she knew that the main purpose of the mutilation was merely to keep her safe from the lustful advances of the sec men and to safeguard the ville throne from any bastards. But it was her mother who suggested using boys too young to notice her figure and face. Sandra had decided to do both, and the sexless youths grew utterly devoted to their female master.

Many years ago when she had first dragged the Angel to the crater, a coldheart had leaped out of hiding in a mountain pass and clubbed her to the ground. As the man started to rip off her clothing, the eunuchs leaped upon the man and literally ripped him apart with their bare hands. The story soon spread to other villes, and nobody had ever bothered Sandra again on her many journeys across the Deathlands.

Once, long ago and far to the east, she had found a graveyard of hundreds of predark planes, along with dozens of other things, machines that looked like soap bubbles but with rotors on top. Sandra had no idea what those could be, and so ignored them. She almost could have believed that the soap bubbles were also flying machines, except for the fact that they had no wings, nor anyplace for a wing to be attached.

Now, most of the planes in the junkyard had only been rusted skeletons, but a few of the machines stored inside a crumbling building were still intact, and one seemed repairable. Unfortunately, the yard was infested with some mutie form of millipede. With no other choice, Sandra had set fire to a forest to cause a stampede of animals through the yard. The millipedes attacked, eating everything that came their way, and in the bloody carnage, she and some eunuchs had been able to steal the Angel.

Over the next few years she had gone back twice more for spare parts, cloth and engines. But on the last raid, Sandra lost five eunuchs to the millipedes and still carried a nasty scar on her arm where one of the bugs had attached itself and started burrowing into her flesh before she'd doused it with shine and burned it off.

Someday, when she had a large enough army of sec

men, the woman planned to return to the junkyard, slaughter the bugs and build a wall around the yard and make it her private ville. But that was for the future. This day, she had to worry about the Demon.

Heading for the last tent, Sandra heard a pervading hooting. Inside one of the tents to her left was a row of iron cages with stickies inside, bowls placed underneath to catch the natural gluelike resin they oozed when tortured. A red-hot knife could get her more glue than boiling the bones of a hundred horses. And the bones of people produced very little glue, even if they were red-raw and fresh.

Entering the last tent, Sandra lowered her umbrella and savored the delicious drop in temperature. The roof of the predark tent somehow blocked most of the sun's heat, and a cooling breeze from the nearby river ruffled the edges of the cloth along the ground. Wonderful.

Using stiff fingers to fluff out her hair and help it dry faster, Sandra emotionlessly studied the Demon resting in the middle of the tent. A humming man was energetically polishing the wooden propeller while another worker checked the pressure on a tire with a patched hand-pump.

Trailing her fingers along the wings and tail, the woman slowly walked around the machine, marveling in its complexity, and simplicity. According to the old books she had found, this was called a biplane because of the two wings. Blasters were just machines, dead lumps of metal that killed. She snorted in contempt. A rock can chill a person. But planes flew! Something that wonderful desired a name. The first air wag she found was called the Angel, but all of the planes she had built were called Demons. Mostly because the damned things wouldn't work.

More than a dozen times, Sandra had launched an experimental plane, so lovingly duplicated from the Angel. But the craft always crashed, usually within only a few yards. One burst into flames from a leak on the rubber fuel lines. The wings buckled on the second because the wood had been too heavy. The cloth ripped off the body on another, making it veer into the rock rim of the crater. The propeller came off on a fifth, slicing a startled eunuch in two, and the next two simply failed to take flight. The engines roared, the propellers spun, but they simply rolled impotently across the ground like tumbleweeds.

But Sandra was grimly determined to build more of the air wags, and would keep experimenting until she learned the secrets of flight. Then an aerial army of her planes would expand across the Deathlands, stealing ammo and food and slaves for Thunder ville until it was the richest ville in the world!

"That is," she muttered, "if I ever get one of these to fly."

The eunuchs heard the remark, but said nothing and concentrated on their preflight tasks.

Obviously something was wrong with the design, and after a lot of tests, Sandra thought that she finally had the answer. The plane needed a less rigid body. Flexibility was the key. So she had stripped off all of the armor-plating, and left the stretched cloth of the body exposed. The weight of the air wag seemed to be a critical factor, which was one of the reasons why the Demon was only receiving a quarter tank of fuel, and had no weapons installed. Hopefully, that would do the trick. She was running out of options, and patience. She would rather die than abandon flying, but the Angel was in poor shape, and she dared not make major repairs to it until she knew exactly what the alterations would do.

This was the newest version of the Demon, a carefully built copy of the Angel, and to the naked eye the machines seemed identical. The cloth was strong, the wood frame solid and the wings perfectly curved. The predark nuke batteries never ran out of power, the oil had been filtered clean, and the fuel tank could hold enough shine for her to fly for eight hours. Eight hours, the length of daylight, that was how long she could fly. How the ancients found their way along the invisible highways in the sky the woman didn't know, but she needed light to spot landmarks to find her way home again; the Ohi River, Iron Hat mesa, the rad pit that resembled a star, the northern forest, the eastern ruins. Flying in the dark, she would easily get lost, and could fly smack into the side of a mesa, or try to land in the middle of the forest. Sometimes, she awoke from a nightmare of that happening.

Shaking her head to dispel the unpleasant memories, Sandra took hold of a guyline stretched between the two wings, stepped onto a recess in the fuselage and slid down into the snug cockpit. The dashboard was empty, the slots of instruments only gaping holes waiting to be filled. Aside from not wanting the meters and gauges damaged in a possible—All right, she admitted privately, likely crash—their absence also saved a little more weight. Besides, the woman had plenty of spares. Most of the instruments she'd modified from the ville wags, oil pressure, engine temp, gas level. Only the airspeed indicator was beyond her abilities to duplicate.

"Just one more reason to go back to the junkyard," she muttered, moving the joystick as if airborne. Out of the corners of her eyes, she noted the wing flaps correctly moving in harmony to the control. Good. The new bushing made of polished bone had really made a difference. That had been Digger's idea. Triple damn the man for wanting to recce Indy ville before her strike! Did it matter what their defenses were? When the Angel came screeching out of the sky, people screamed and fled.

"Here is the fuel, my lady!" Carter announced, stepping into the tent. The giant carried the ten-gallon can tucked under a thick arm as if it were a pillow.

"Give it here," she commanded, and took the heavy container from him. The gas tank was on top of the overhead wing, gravity helping it feed into the engine. However, that meant it could only be refilled from the cockpit. When she was done, Sandra screwed the lid tight on the fuel tank and heaved the empty container over the side. It landed with a crash near a table full of tools and her single roll of sticky gray tape.

"Let's go!" she ordered, standing in the cockpit, her arms resting on the top wing.

Rushing to obey, the two eunuchs untied the anchor ropes and spread wide the side of the tent. Meanwhile, Carter scouted under the Demon and yanked on a rope to remove the wedges of wood tucked beneath the wheels.

"Clear!" he shouted, raising the wedges high for her to see.

"Then start pushing!" Tregart directed, sitting again.

As the three men lifted the rear of the biplane and walked it carefully out of the tent, the woman set the choke and throttle, and locked them in place with a piece of gray tape.

On the airfield, the rest of the workers rushed to lend assistance, and soon they had the biplane aligned with a gap in the crater's southern rim.

Wetting a finger, Sandra tested the wind. "Two steps more to the left!" she directed.

The men gingerly lifted the rear of the ultralight biplane and shifted it slightly.

Now the wind blew directly onto the air wag, the wing flaps fluttering slightly from the pressure.

"Set the chocks!" she ordered, partially climbing out of the cockpit and lashing the joystick into position.

Carter disappeared beneath the plane, only to reappear a few ticks later. "Ready, my lady!" he announced, the rope tight in his fist.

In the distance, the door in the wall opened and Stone entered the crater. His hair was soaking wet, and his clothes looked clean and damp, as if the teen had washed wearing them. But the canvas bag over his shoulder was dry, and riding proudly at his hip was a badly frayed gunbelt and a well-oiled blaster. Spotting the crowd of people around the biplane, Stone stood straight, and started their way.

Setting the choke and throttle, the woman wet her lips before taking hold of the ignition switch.

"Get ready…contact!" Sandra cried, just as the old manual directed, and twisted the handle.

There was a painful whine as the propeller slowly rotated, then the engine sputtered and coughed a few times, faltered, then came back strong and built to a controlled roar as the propeller spun into a blur. With the wind whipping her loose hair around madly,

Sandra waited as the vibrating plane settled down and strained to be released. Blood of her fathers, was this time going to work?

"Set her loose!" she yelled, backing away from the Demon.

Using both hands, Carter pulled on the rope and the chocks came free. Incredibly the winged machine just sat there for a few ticks, and Sandra started to turn red in the face. Then the Demon finally started to roll forward.

"Come on you, beautiful bitch," the woman muttered, clenching her fists as the biplane moved across the flat ground. "Come on…that's it…yes…oh, yes…."

Accelerating constantly, the machine lifted slightly into the air, and the workers gasped at the sight. Stepping toward the biplane, Sandra was suddenly holding her breath as the Demon touched down again, only to lift once more.

An anguished cry rose from the men as a shift in the wind made the machine veer slightly off course. Sandra braced herself for the inevitable crash. Nuking hell, she had been so close this time!

Then the world seemed to go still as the cloth-and-wood machine leveled off and rolled smoothly up the sloped wooden ramp at the far end of the strip and sailed majestically into the air.

"Yes!" Sandra screamed, tears on her cheeks. "Look at her go!"

The workers erupted into wild cheers as the Demon stayed up past the ten-foot mark, the twenty, the thirty! From the milking tent, the frightened stickies started hooting madly at the unfamiliar noise. But then there came the crack of bullwhips, and the muties went quickly silent.

"My lady," Carter said, turning to her with shining eyes. "You have done it. The heavens are now yours to command, sky baron!"

The woman broke into a laugh at that. "Well, I do like the name sky baron," she admitted with a smile, but then it melted into a frown and she spit a virulent curse.

"Black dust!" Tregart screamed, starting after the biplane. "No. Stop it. Stop it, you feebs!"

Still rising higher than any previous Demon, the charging machine jerked slightly as it reached the end of the tethering line, and the old rope snapped. Now unfettered, it rose majestically upward and sailed over the jagged peaks of the crater rim.

"Shitfire!" Sandra snarled, drawing a blaster only to holster the weapon once more. Gone. It was gone. For a split second, the woman thought she might be asleep and having a nightmare, but as the air wag droned onward and began to vanish in the distance, Tregart knew this was no dream. Gone. And it could land anywhere. Anywhere at all. A shiver run down her spine at the thought that the sky might become a battleground instead of her private domain.

"Carter, get the Angel ready for an immediate flight!" she commanded, breaking into a run for the tents. "I've got to find that thing before somebody else does!"

"B-but, my lady, the Angel is having its engine serviced," Carter cried, grabbing hold of her arm. "It will take hours to get it back together! And by then it will be dark."

Almost beside herself, the woman stared at the man in unbridled rage and reached for her blaster. The suddenly pale eunuch let go, but stayed in front, blocking her way.

"You cannot fly at night, my lady," he said softly, splaying his arms. "Let us go, instead."

Sandra started to bark a laugh at the ridiculous concept of one of them flying a plane, but then realized that wasn't what the big eunuch meant. She hated to admit it, but the giant made sense.

"Karl, René!" Sandra barked, facing them. "Take two of my best horses and chase after the Demon! Find it and wait for me to arrive at first light."

As if embarrassed, Karl touched the disfigured side of his face. "But, how will you find us…" he started.

"Light a fire and toss green wood on it, feeb," the woman said impatiently. "I'll follow your smoke."

"Take lanterns, and longblasters," Carter added, crossing his arms. "And plenty of ammo."

Sandra frowned at that, annoyed she had not thought of it herself. "Longblasters and handblasters," she added to cover the slip. "If there's trouble, burn the air wag. But save the engine. Carter will bring a cart to haul the machine back."

The eunuchs bowed. "Yes, my lady," they chorused.

"Move, you idiots!" she screeched, pulling her blaster and firing a round into the air, making them jump. "The nuking plane gets farther away every second! Get moving and find the Demon, or I'll chill you in ways not even invented yet!"

Swallowing hard, the seminaked men turned to race across the airfield for the horse corral in the distance.

"Here," Sandra said, tossing over a set of keys to the chief eunuch. "Get them bolt-action longblasters, and a wheelgun from my tent."

Carter made the catch. "Very wise, my lady."

"Then get the Angel back together. And I want it ready before dawn, and carrying a full load of firebombs."

"Bombs?" He blinked in confusion, hugging the keys.

"If anybody other than my men find the air wag, I'll have to destroy it myself." And their ville, too, if necessary. Nobody controls the sky, but me!

Just then, a rumble of thunder from the dark clouds overhead heralded a strobing flash of sheet lightning.

Sniffing hard, she detected no trace of sulfur in the

wind and scowled in frustration. An acid rain would have solved all of their problems this night. Now the downpour would only hinder the search. Recovering the Demon was a task for her eunuchs. And nothing would save them if they failed.

Angrily, Sandra started for her tent, then changed direction for another. Carter stayed by her side, keeping his stride short to match her smaller steps.

"Shall I send the new boy to you?" he asked salaciously. "We will be too busy tonight to make him one of us."

Now there was an idea. But she had a better one.

"No, have Stone stand a post on the wall tonight. I'm going to handle the repairs on the Angel myself," Sandra said, unbuttoning a cuff to roll up a sleeve. "Then put all of our people on starting to make another Demon. No, four of them. Use all of the cloth and glue there is in stock."

His eyebrows went up. "All? Er, yes, my lady."

The clouds rumbled again, but this time Sandra looked back defiantly. "We know the secret now of how to make air wags," she said, doing up the other sleeve. "So there's no reason to delay building more warbirds, my army of sky raiders!"

Chapter Six

Just as the companions entered the exit tunnel of the redoubt, the noise of the opening door abruptly stopped.

Instantly, Ryan raised a clenched fist and the others came to a halt behind him, their weapons armed and ready. Listening hard, the one-eyed man couldn't hear anything unusual. The overhead fluorescent lights were humming softly, and there was a muffled shush from the air vents set along the wall. But that was all. Nothing more.

However, Ryan knew that there hadn't been enough time for the blast door to cycle open completely. So what was going on here? He knew that at the end of that zigzag passage was the yard-thick nukeproof door that could only be opened with the proper alphanumeric sequence tapped onto a keypad. The code to enter the redoubts was one of their greatest secrets, and none of the companions had ever revealed it, even under torture. Access to the redoubts meant life itself to them.

"Mebbe the machinery that works the blast door

is busted—" Krysty started, but was interrupted by the sound of a muffled gunshot.

"That was Jak's Magnum." J.B. frowned, turning in the direction of the stairwell.

"Or at least, it was a Magnum," Mildred said hesitantly just as another shot came. This one louder than the first.

"Okay, now that was Doc's LeMat!" Ryan confirmed, starting forward. "There's no mistaking that hogleg. Let's move!"

As the four companions charged across the garage, the sound of the opening blast door came again, slowly building in volume.

"Fireblasting hell, what is going on here?" Ryan demanded angrily, coming to a halt and glancing over a shoulder as the floor started to vibrate again from the cycling blast doors.

For a single long second, the companions stood undecided, torn between the two events.

"Fuck this. The rest of you go help Doc and Jak," Ryan ordered, holstering his SiG-Sauer and sliding the Steyr SSG-70 rifle off his shoulder. Quickly, he worked the bolt to chamber a 7.62 mm round. "I'm going to recce that door."

"Meet you back here in ten, lover," Krysty said, sprinting for the stairwell door.

"Stay sharp," J.B. warned, sliding the S&W M-4000 shotgun off his back and passing it to Mildred.

"Like a razor." Ryan grunted, facing the tunnel.

"Watch your ass. This could be a trick," Mildred cautioned, working the pump-action on the scatter-gun, then thumbing off the safety.

"If you see me running, just shoot anything behind," Ryan muttered, walking into the access tunnel.

At the first turn he lost sight of the others, but the man could still hear them running between the cars, followed by the slam of a door being thrown open. The next zigzag turn of the tunnel took even that away, and the man proceeded onward in silence, straining to hear anything in front.

Keeping his blind side covered, Ryan stayed near the left wall. The same as before, the noise of the blast door opening soon stopped, only to return once more after about a minute. Controlling his breathing, Ryan tried to concentrate on anything else moving in the passage. But aside from the overhead lights and ven-tilation system, the access tunnel was deathly quiet.

At the last turn, Ryan paused at the unexpected smell of greenery. It lingered in the air for a few moments, then was gone, carried away by the venti-lation system. Now suspicious, Ryan pulled a small plastic mirror from a pocket and carefully eased it around the corner for a look. At the far end of the tunnel he could clearly see the blast door, which seemed undamaged. On the wall alongside the massive portal was a small keypad for operating the exit. It looked normal. Searching for anything unusual, Ryan angled the mirror, but there was nothing else in sight.

Suddenly the predark machinery in the walls came alive and the nukeproof door slid out of the way. After a few seconds, a thin crack opened at one end, admitting a slice of bright moonlight. Then the portal ponderously ground to a halt and started to slide back into the recess of the jamb.

Pocketing the mirror, Ryan thoughtfully sucked his hollow tooth over that. There didn't seem to be anybody outside trying to get into the redoubt. There had been no movement or shadows in that crack of moonshine. But for some reason, the blast door was cycling open and shut, again and again. Mebbe there was a short circuit in the keypad? Yet the base was supposed nukeproof, so what could possibly have damaged it?

Since there didn't seem to be any danger from this direction, Ryan turned and started down the tunnel at a sprint to rejoin the others when a sharp whistle sounded from the garage.

Going flat against the wall, Ryan leveled the Steyr and prepared to fire as he gave two short whistles in reply. Then the man relaxed as two long whistles answered him back.

Resting the Steyr on a shoulder, Ryan nodded in

greeting as the rest of the companions appeared from around a corner.

"Anybody hurt?" Ryan asked, looking them over. Nobody was visibly bleeding or limping. Always a good sign.

"Indeed not, my dear Ryan." Doc's deep voice boomed. "Although we have discovered a most perplexing mystery."

"Prisoner in the brig," Jak said succinctly, jerking a thumb. "Couple of officers with him."

"They torture him?" Ryan asked, frowning.

"No sign of it," Mildred answered, adjusting the strap of her med kit. "I think they were just asking him questions. The prisoner was handcuffed to a chair, but he didn't seem to be harmed in any way."

"Unlike the galley," Doc muttered softly, suppressing a shudder.

"So what was the shooting about?" Ryan demanded.

"They blew off the lock to get inside," J.B. explained. "The electronic lock needed a pass card to make it open."

"Couldn't find, so shot," Jak corrected with a grimace. "Doc fired at a shadow."

"I could have sworn something was moving," the silver-haired man said, pursing his lips. "But when we went to look, there was nothing there."

"Must have just been a trick of the lights," Krysty suggested. "I could have sworn I saw something near the armory, but when I looked again, there was only some dust moving near an air vent."

Ryan looked questioningly at J.B., and the man shrugged.

"The ceiling lights were flickering at the end of the hall," J.B. said honestly.

Krysty looked past Ryan. "So what was with the door?"

"Come on, I'll show ya," he said, going back to the end of the tunnel.

As the companions turned the corner, the floor shook as the blast door started to cycle apart until the hair-thin span of silvery moonlight appeared, then it paused, closed once more.

"Well, I'll be a son of a—" Mildred bit off the word. "Great, the only door out of here is broken."

"Or is something trying to get in?" Krysty said, brushing back her bearskin coat to reveal her holstered blaster.

"I didn't see anyone," Ryan stated, heading for the keypad. "But there's only one way to know for sure."

Tapping in the access code, Ryan looked at the blast door, but nothing happened. He was starting to get concerned when the massive slab of laminated alloys finally began to slide across the opening. Keeping one hand on the keypad, Ryan half expected the door to stop again, but this time it kept going.

At first, the bright moonshine streamed in through the thin crack, but that soon became a flood of light as the blast door rumbled completely open. Prepared for anything, the companions raised their weapons and walked into a cool sweet wind that blew into the redoubt carrying the strong smell of green plants and fresh water. But some granite boulders and smashed masonry blocked their view of the world outside.

"Krysty, you better stay inside," Ryan said, "in case the door closes early."

The woman nodded and took a position near the keypad.

Spreading out in an arc so they wouldn't offer a bunched target to any hidden enemies, the rest of the companions moved stealthily past the boulders.

Below the swell of ground was a field of wild grass that reached to a meandering river of clear blue water. In the far distance, the companions could dimly see foggy mountains to the north, a dark forest to the west, and the familiar coloration of a sandy desert to the south.

"This all seems vaguely familiar," Mildred said, craning her neck. "Sort of like Ohio, or Indiana."

"Even if it was daylight, there would be no way of telling where we are with so much cloud cover," J.B. replied, squinting at the sky. The man touched the minisextant in his jacket pocket. With that J.B. could easily pinpoint their exact location anyplace on the planet, as long as he had an unobstructed view of the sun or stars.

"Not like clouds," Jak said, sniffing the air. "Bad storm coming."

"Acid rain?" Doc asked fearfully, raising a hand to shield his eyes from the bright moonlight shining through the banks of clouds overhead.

The albino teen shook his head. "Just rain."

Satisfied they were in no immediate danger from anything outside, Ryan returned to the entrance and looked inside the door's slot in the wall.

"Just as I thought, there's something in there," he said, running a hand along the interior. "Looks like a pressurized air tank, but its crushed smaller than a baron's honor." He gave an experimental tug. "It's jammed in there solid."

"Should damn well think so after a hundred years of being pounded by a ten-ton blast door." J.B. chuckled, taking a glance inside. "Damn, that does look like an air tank."

"Sounds like somebody was trying to jam the door open," Krysty suggested from inside the tunnel.

"Or were they using it to smash the canister?" Ryan said, furrowing his brow. "Only a feeb would think anything that small could stop this door."

"Bomb?" Jak asked, instinctively taking a step away.

"Could be," J.B. added, moving around in the

beams of moonlight and the fluorescent glow from the access tunnel. "Damn, I hate to use a flare for this." Reaching into his munitions bag, the Armorer extracted a plastic mirror, and carefully angled it to reflect some of the silvery light into the shadowy recess. "Ah, that's better. Okay, I can see a few touches of red paint on the canister, but no lettering…"

"Check the neck ring," Ryan suggested.

"Gotcha." J.B. shifted the mirror slightly and smiled in triumphant as a coded ID number came into view. Then the man went deathly pale. "Dark night, I know that ident code!" he breathed tensely. "That's CVX-Nine, military nerve gas!"

"Nerve gas!" Doc gasped.

"John, you must have read that wrong," Mildred scolded.

"The hell I did, Millie," J.B. retorted, tucking the mirror away. "And I sure as nuking hell didn't see any other of these things in the redoubt."

"Me, either," Ryan huffed, turning his back to the moon, and looking down the fluorescent lit tunnel of the redoubt.

Just then the blast door started to automatically close, and Krysty hurriedly tapped in the access code again. The titanic slab of metal paused, then receded.

"There's a prisoner in the jail, and somebody hides a canister full of nerve gas in the doorjamb," Ryan said. "That sure sounds like the redoubt was deliberately gassed. Just tuck the canister into the jamb as the door opens, and you'd have a good two minutes to get clear before the blast door cycled shut again to rupture the pressurized tank."

"Two minutes easy," J.B. agreed, pushing back his hat. "That would be plenty of time to get out."

"And the ventilation system would suck the gas straight into the redoubt," Mildred added with a disgusted expression.

"Who ever did this," Doc advised, "knew an inordinate amount of details about how the top-secret base operated."

"You got that right," Mildred agreed. "The killer must have been worried that the prisoner was going to talk."

"Triple-cold to ace a couple hundred people to get one," Jak muttered darkly.

"Which makes the fifty-bullet question," J.B. added. "Just who was that prisoner?"

"No way of telling now," Krysty answered. "There were no dogtags or wallets. No ID papers on the two officers in the cell with him."

"Were they carrying any insig?" Ryan asked pointedly.

She nodded. "Sure, one was a four-star general. The other a three-star."

Two generals? "Then we can be sure it wasn't some private found drunk on duty," Ryan said with a hard expression. "Big brass means big crimes. Spy type mebbe, or a traitor."

"Perhaps he was somebody working for Operation Chronos, or Overproject Whisper?" Mildred asked, glancing sideways.

Eloquently, Doc shrugged. "If he was, madam, I did not recognize him. But then again, in such a mummified condition, it would be hard to identify my own lovely wife, Emily."

"Looks like just another damn mystery to add to the list about the redoubts." J.B. sighed in resignation. "We'll probably never know what really happened here that day."

Ryan started to agree, but stopped. Some gut instinct told the Deathlands warrior that whatever had occurred here a century ago wasn't over yet. Gas in a doorway. Hadn't he heard about that trick before? Ryan narrowed his good eye as there slowly came to him a distant memory from when he was just a youth fighting in the Mutie Wars and...

Interrupting his thoughts, the blast door started to close again.

Quickly, Krysty tapped in the access code for a second time. "We've never done this before," she said with a worried expression. "Tried to keep the blast door open for this long, I mean. I sure hope this doesn't damage the machinery."

"There's probably a different code to hold the

passage open," Mildred rationalized. "But there's no way to guess what it is."

Jak stuck his head into the recess. "Getting this out be a triple-bitch," he drawled slowly. "Maybe implo gren?"

"Don't have any," J.B. answered, patting his munitions bag. "Just a few antipers grens, one thermite and a couple of homie pipebombs."

The teen clucked his tongue in disapproval. "Useless," he declared, red eyes squinting.

"Well, we can't leave it like this," Ryan pointed out. "Sooner or later, the door motors will burn out, and then we'll be trapped."

"Were there any suitable tools in the garage, John Barrymore?" Doc asked, easing down the hammer on his LeMat to holster it.

Adjusting his glasses, the wiry man smiled. "Bet your ass, there are. Come on, let's get moving."

Mildred stayed with Krysty to guard the open doorway as the men moved down the tunnel. They soon came back armed with an assortment of iron pipes, two crowbars, a sledgehammer and an acetylene welding torch. The tank pressure was very low, but J.B. used the torch for as long he could to warm the smashed canister until the acetylene ran out. Then Ryan quickly hammered a crowbar around the edge of the softened metal, while Jak pounded in another on the other side. Doc slipped the iron pipes over the end of the crowbars to increase the leverage, and the men worked in pairs, throwing their full weight to the task.

However, the century of compression by the blast door had done a good job, and it took the men more than an hour to force the flattened canister loose. Only to discover that behind the first one there was a second canister with different markings. CVX-Four nerve gas. It was an unnerving sight. Two different types of lethal chems had been used. Even if the soldiers in the redoubt had been warned in time, they wouldn't have stood a chance.

Chapter Seven

Bouncing from tree to tree, Jeffers staggered through the thick pine forest. The tree branches interlocked densely overhead, and virtually none of the moonlight seeped through, except for tiny silver beams that dabbled the carpeting of dropped pine needles on the ground.

The Ohi River was a good mile behind the baron, and Indera ville an unimaginable distance upriver from the point the wounded man had crawled out onto land. That bitch Sandra Tregart had nicked him twice with the blasters of her flying machine before he'd had to admit defeat. Jeffers had barely made it to the bank of the Ohi before she was on him again, and hot lead seemed to halo the man as he'd clumsily dived into the river. The cool waters had engulfed Jeffers, gently carried him downstream faster than the wounded man could possibly have run on land. Gulping air, Jeffers submerged for as long as possible. When forced to the surface by his laboring lungs, Sandra Tregart had been high in the sky over the river, obviously still searching for him. Jeffers had dived again and the next time she'd been much farther behind. A few times more, and he'd lost track of her completely.

After that, he'd allowed himself to float, giving his life to the currents. At a bend, he'd gratefully grabbed a large tree branch and locked an arm into its crook. Soon, the baron found himself jerking awake, the scenery along the banks radically different each time, until he was among the thick pine forest of the far south. Dimly, he'd wondered how long he had been in the river to have covered that much distance.

A flashing pain cut through his haze, and he grabbed a small wiggling thing that was feasting at the wound in his arm. Crushing its head, he cast it away as another attacked the bloody graze on his leg. Screaming insanely, the baron pulled a knife and slashed at the feeders in the river, kicking and thrashing until they suddenly were gone. Apparently they were carrion eaters and were unaccustomed to food that fought back. But the man knew that his blood would soon attract other river dwellers that no knife could stop, and he resolutely started fighting for shore.

The banks of the Ohi were high and slippery through the forest, the roots of the trees exposed below the waterline, but the shore proved impossible to reach. Jerking awake as he painfully banged off a large rock in the rushing water, Jeffers now remembered that the river turned into rapids somewhere and in his weakened condition that would mean death. Throwing all of his will into fighting close to shore once more, the man plunged his knife into the slippery clay as if it was the vitals of an enemy. Shaking off the tree branch, he dug his stiff fingers into the bank and slowly clawed his way out of the river.

As his head cleared the bank, he saw green grass and a pair of red eyes. Snarling in rage at the thing in the shadows, Jeffers was astonished when it bolted away in terror. Perhaps there was some deadly predator that lived in the river, and the creature had thought he was one of them. Or maybe he had simply frightened it away. The reasons didn't matter. Jeffers clawed and crawled for fresh footholds, as he pulled himself along with his good arm until he crested the edge and finally lay on solid ground.

Time unknown passed, and the moon ruled the sky when he awoke fiercely ravenous. But procuring food wasn't his main concern, safety was. Using the knife, he cut apart the sleeves of his dry shirt and bandaged the wounds on his arm and thigh, thankful that they seemed to be only superficial grazes, more painful than life-threatening. Rigging a sling for his left arm, the baron listened to the noises of the night as he reloaded his black-powder weapons almost entirely by touch. The weapons were undamaged by their immersion in the river, as was the lead and wadding, which was mostly dry. Some water had leaked into the leather pouch holding his powder, and he carefully removed the damp clump on top to reach the dry black powder underneath.

Reflected moonlight shone off the Ohi, and he was grateful for every little bit of it. During the process, something large rose from the river, and he froze motionless, trying not to breathe. The colossus drifted by the man sniffing the air, then was gone into the night.

Crawling away from the riverbank, Jeffers realized that he was lying on fallen needles from the nearby pine trees. The rich smell of the plants had to have masked the odor of his blood and saved the man. Quickly the baron stuffed his pockets with pine needles. But he couldn't risk such a thing happening twice, and redoubled his efforts to load the two blasters. When Jeffers was armed once more, he stiffly rose and shuffled deeper into the woods, trying to put as much distant between himself and the mutie in the river as possible before he collapsed again.

The rich smell of the forest filled his lungs, and Jeffers pawed at the black shapes of the trees until finding a branch low enough for him to reach. Hacking with his knife, he soon had a crude crutch and his progress became much faster as the weight was taken off his aching right leg.

Dimly, the baron could hear things flying in the darkness and recognized bats and owls. But thankfully no stingwings. In his present state, the man knew he would only have been a quick meal for them and no danger at all, even with his blasters.

The land rose and fell in rolling waves, as Jeffers moved onward through the night. He had no goal in mind, but knew that a wounded man sleeping unprotected would never awaken. Keep moving, keep going, ignore the pain in his leg, forget the yawning pit in his empty belly, motion meant life.

A sudden thrashing in the trees made him spin with a blaster leveled, but the noise stopped as there came a deep animal growl followed by a high-pitched shriek of something being torn apart alive. Even before the screams stopped, there came a horrible eating sound. Keeping a finger on the trigger of his weapon, Jeffers backed away from the feasting thing until he was a good distance from it, then turned and ran as best as he could. Had that been a griz? Mebbe a wolfling? Jeffers couldn't tell, and didn't really want to know. As long as the creature had found some thing other than him to eat for the night was quite enough, and the man felt no urge to satisfy his curiosity.

Eventually forced to stop, the sweating baron rested on a tree stump in a small clearing, and caught a new smell among the rich aroma of the mighty pines. Apples! He tried to reach any fruit on the branches, but couldn't find any. But crawling on the ground, he found several fruits and wolfed them down. A few had been found by insects, and he ate those, too. Food was food; he didn't question the source of the nourishment.

With his hunger and thirst both eased, the baron rested for a few more minutes then started to walk again, his strength renewed. The ground became hilly, the trees growing farther apart as rocks came through the rich soil. He was approaching the foothills of the Misty Mountains. Jeffers shook his head. No, those were to the north of Indera, and he had gone south. What mountains were in this direction? None that he knew of. He had to be out of known territory and into the deep wilds. Mutie territory.

Cresting a grassy knoll, Jeffers descended the steep side of the hillock in a combination of shuffling and falling. He was reaching the end of his reserves, and wisely decided to walk along the floor of the valley. The ground sloped slightly in one direction, which was the way he went to conserve his ebbing strength.

Oak, birch and a dozen other trees were mixed with the pines now, and the ground was covered with leaves as well as dropped needles. After a lifetime in the desert along the river, the thickly scented air was like a healer's tonic to the weary man, and he savored every breath. Then he stopped and sniffed more carefully, moving his head around to check the direction of the new aroma. Smoke. Wood smoke, with a touch of roasting meat. There was a campfire nearby!

Relief flooded over him, and he almost burst into laughter when he remembered that this was mutie country and quickly clamped his mouth shut. Was…was that an animal cooking on the fire, or another lost outlander like himself?

The words hit the baron like a blow to the gut. *Outlander.* Stranger. Jeffers had no home ville now, and he was no longer a baron. Just a wounded man with two blasters and a very limited supply of powder and shot.

But the smell of the meat was like a rope tied to his chest, and Jeffers had no choice but to head in that direction. Pausing to place a loaded blaster in both hands, the former baron hobbled toward the smell of cooking food, going slow and careful. Soon, he caught the reddish light of the fire and heard men laughing. But his jaw tightened at the sound. It was the hard laughter of a slaver whipping his property to death merely to test a new whip. Yes, he had heard such laughter before in his youth, and it was something Jeffers would never forget. The very sound made the old scars on his back itch and burn.

Or was his mind playing tricks on him? The man was so tired, and his thoughts were confused. Do a recce. Yes, that made sense. Just get a little closer and actually see what was happening before he decide to leave the delicious food behind in the cold, dark forest.

Easing past a bush, Jeffers stopped at a crude wall of pointed sticks rising from the soil. Past the primitive barrier, he could dimly see open ground, neatly raked into orderly rows. It was a farm! Could this be a ville?

Circling past the stick fence, Jeffers found a beaten path cutting through the forest and followed that. The smell of the cooking fire was strong now, as was the laughter of several men and the whimpering cry of a woman. He frowned and tightened the grip on his blasters. No, it was several women.

Holstering one of his weapons, the man placed aside his crutch and crawled forward in the darkness along the path until finding a wall made of cut logs. It was a ville! There was a large gate set behind another cluster of pointed sticks, and beyond that was a large hole in the wall, dancing firelight casting the trees in hellish lights. The sounds of men could be heard clearer now, and he caught some of the conversation, his frown deepening.

So that was it. A group of coldhearts had found the isolated ville and used some Molotovs made out of shine to burn a hole in the wall. The ville folk fought the invaders, and were now paying a terrible price for losing.

Starting to turn to leave, Jeffers paused and gave the situation a few minutes' thought. His decision came quickly.

The moon was starting to set behind the forest as the big baron hobbled out of the forest and into the gaping hole in the log wall. At the footsteps, a man drinking from a bottle turned sharply and gave a cry of surprise just as Jeffers triggered his blaster. The black-powder blaster tore off the coldheart's face, and the gurgling thing fell to the ground as Jeffers entered the ville.

Firing his blasters at anybody standing, Jeffers chilled four men holding longblasters. The loud shots rang out across the settlement startling everybody. With his pants down around his ankles, a coldheart looked up in wordless shock at the noise of blaster.

"What the nuking drek is that?" he demanded, just in time to see the leader of his gang slam against a stone well and flop the ground with the back of his head missing.

"Son of a bitch!" the coldheart cried, scrambling away from the girl he was about to rape. But as he tried to stand, he tumbled sideways as his chest exploded into bloody globbets. Naked and helpless on the bloody soil, the terrified girl tried to scream through her gag and only made mewling sounds.

Holstering both of his empty blasters, Jeffers grabbed a longblaster from a twitching coldheart and checked the ammo clip. Six shots. More than enough. But he grabbed another and worked the bolt to chamber a round just in case.

As more coldhearts rushed into the dirty street partially dressed, their eyes blurry from too much shine, Jeffers cut them down without pause or mercy. By now, people were screaming everywhere, which only added to the building chaos, and that was just fine by Jeffers. Chaos was his only armor.

In the center of the small ville was a stone house set prominently among the crude log cabins. Its front door slammed aside as a naked man came out with a wheelgun pressed to the head of a young woman. Her hands were bound, and her full breasts looked like ivory in the silvery moonlight. Standing behind her, the armed man looked around frantically, his eyes twitching from the effects of the addictive drug jolt.

A jolt head was the leader of the coldhearts? Jeffers sneered in disgust. Who the fuck was the baron of this ville that he couldn't stop these feebs from getting inside?

Then the two men found each other.

"Freeze, asshole! Don't come any closer or the slut gets it!" the naked man screamed, cocking back the hammer on the weapon. "Now drop that long-blaster and…"

Without hesitation, Jeffers shot the woman in the shoulder. As the nude man jerked backward, a bloody furrow along his ribs, his blaster fired, blowing off the top of the woman's head. As she fell to the side, the dying coldheart tried to swing his weapon toward Jeffers. So the baron fired again, blowing away most of the man's throat.

Blood arched from the impact, and the coldheart

dropped his blaster and tried to grab his neck to try to staunch the spray of red life from his ruptured veins. Coming closer, Jeffers pulled out his knife and slashed the trembling coldheart across the belly, making his intestines slither out onto the cold ground.

Silent words burbled red in the mouth of the chief coldheart, and Jeffers reversed his longblaster to ram the stock into the man's face, smashing teeth. Then Jeffers struck him again and again until the body fell, and the skull audibly cracked under the savage pummeling.

Stepping away from the corpse, Jeffers looked over the ville of death. The screaming had stopped, and now there was only the muted cries from the bound girl near the crackling campfire. Slowly, doors opened and frightened people shuffled into the night, stepping around the strewed bodies and weapons. Everybody seemed to be wounded in one way or another, arms were in slings, clothing bloody.

They had gone down fighting, Jeffers realized. Hands and clubs against blaster. Yes, these people would do just fine.

"Okay, I'm your new baron!" Jeffers shouted, raising the gore-streaked longblaster high. "Accept me, and I'll never let scum like this into the ville again! Say no, and I will leave, but I'm taking the blasters with me."

"As if we can trust an outlander!" a young man said, starting forward.

Lowering his longblaster, Jeffers worked the bolt and shot the man in the thigh. He fell, cursing and clutching his wounded leg.

"I don't see any other wounds on this man," Jeffers cried loudly. "Was this the sec man on guard duty when the coldhearts attacked?"

The faces of the ville folk changed from resentment to startled expressions at that pronouncement, and many now stared at the cringing sec man with open hatred.

"Yes, I can see that he was," Jeffers snarled, pulling out a handblaster to load a single chamber. "So he let them in without an alarm, and then said, what? That they jumped him while he was asleep, or taking a piss?"

"Taking a piss," an old man said, hobbling forward into the firelight. "How'd ya know all that if ya ain't wid them?"

Jeffers started to say that he used to be the baron of another ville, but cut his words short. Telling them he lost one ville, surely wouldn't make them want to accept him as their new baron.

"I've heard of yellow traitors doing the same trick to jack a ville," Jeffers lied. "Your old baron still alive?"

"They gave him six feet," said a woman with a bruised face, pointing toward the stone well.

Looking that way, Jeffers saw a mutilated body dangling from a rope tied to a stout tree limb, the bare feet of the corpse a good couple of yards off the hard-packed soil.

"Any family?" Jeffers demanded.

Heads shook no in reply.

"Good," Jeffers said, facing the others. "Then I'm in charge. Anybody object?" There was only silence. "Accepted then. Okay, I want two strong men to get the baron down. We'll bury him with the rest of our dead."

Baron Jeffers raised his voice. "The coldhearts get thrown to the pigs!"

"Don't have none," a man mumbled, holding a wad of crimson-stained cloth to the side of his head.

"Then we'll just throw 'em in the river," Jeffers said. "Probably only give a pig the shits, anyway."

A ripple of laughter went through the crowd, and their eyes brightened for just a tick with the dark humor.

Yeah, that's right. Come back to life, Jeffers thought grimly. There's lots to do, and I'm about to fall over.

As a couple of the men started for the hanging man, Jeffers raised a hand. "But first cut the girl free!" Jeffers barked, gesturing at the captive tied to the ground. "You there, old woman, patch her up, and give her all the shine she can hold. You know what to do?"

The wrinklie nodded in reply. It was an old hill remedy for such things. Blot out the memory of the gang rape with drink until the teenager wasn't sure it really happened.

Hobbling to the well, Jeffers sat on the stone rim

and started to reload his handblasters. He could see the roast dog on the fire and the smell was driving him insane with hunger.

"Every male with hair on his chest grab a blaster from the dead," Jeffers commanded, using the last of his powder and shot to charge the cylinders.

The locals paused, frightened, anxious, then slowly obeyed.

Closing the blasters, Jeffers tucked one away and kept the other in his good hand. It only contained two shots, but that would be enough for now.

"Those are now yours to keep!" the baron ordered. "An armed ville is a safe ville! This is my command, will you obey?"

The men stared at him in stunned awe, tightening their grips on the weapons, then one dropped to his knee and bowed in respect.

And so I find my sec chief. "What is your name?" Jeffers demanded.

The bearded man raised his face. "Dante," he said.

"That is a good name," Jeffers replied magnanimously, then added, "I was taught it means braveheart in the old tongue."

Dante blinked at that, no words coming.

"Now kneel before me, Dante," Jeffers said sternly, rising to his feet. "And swear on the blood in your heart that you will die before allowing an enemy to enter this ville, or harm a woman."

The old women and young girls snapped up their heads at that, their eyes wary and disbelieving.

"Yes, master," Dante said, bowing.

"You are now my sec chief," Jeffers stated brusquely. "And in the future, you will address me as my lord or baron. Not master."

"Of course…Baron," Dante said, cooing at the longblaster in his hands.

"As for the rest of you," Jeffers said, sitting again before his legs buckled. "Give Dante half of the ammo in the blasters, then take the boots off the cold-hearts, men need proper shoes to work in the field. Give the rest of the clothing to the children. All knives go to the women."

"The women?" One man started to laugh.

Stepping forward, Dante slapped the man across the face. "Obey your baron!" he snarled, working the bolt on the weapon.

"Yes, of course," the skinny man whimpered. "I meant no disrespect…"

"Let him be. There are more important things to do tonight," Jeffers said, looking over the crowd. He choose the three largest men. "You, you and you! I want a fire built, a big one just outside the hole in our wall. Then erect a nest of sharp sticks all pointing outward just inside the hole. Anything trying to jump the flames will impale itself, and be easy for us to chill."

"Like fish on a spear," a woman whispered, then covered her mouth in fear.

Jeffers laughed. "That's right. Only this time this spear is for keeping our skins whole, instead of our bellies full, eh, Mother?" He laughed.

"You heard the orders!" Dante said, walking among the crowd. "Strip those bastards! Cut down our old baron, and start gathering firewood!"

Just then an old man came up to the baron and offered him a wooden bowl full of hot wet cloths. "For your wounds, my lord," he explained.

Jeffers nodded and watched as the healer peeled off the old bandages and cleaned the wounds to apply clean cloth. The water stung a little, and he grunted at the contact.

"Sorry, my lord," the old man said, never stopping in his task. "But I have learned to add shine to boiled water and most wounds do not fester."

"You are good at your job, healer," Jeffers said in frank appraisal. "Now answer me this, are there any ruins nearby made of brick?"

"Brick?" the healer repeated thoughtfully, his hands busy. "Certainly. To the far south and east. But those in the south are death. Touch any stone there and soon your hair falls out, then you get a red smile and soon die."

A red smile? Ah, bleeding gums. That meant rad poisoning. A hot zone. "We'll take the bricks from the north. And start burning clay. I saw some in the riverbanks."

"Clay?" the healer asked frowning as if not sure he heard that correctly. "Why clay, my lord?"

"I have learned to burn clay into ash to make mortar for the bricks. Walls built with that don't fall in the acid rains." Jeffers grunted again as the last bandage was tightly tied. "Give me a month, and this ville…"

"Pinewood, my lord."

"And Pinewood ville will have a brick wall around outside those logs that nobody will ever breech!"

The old man raised an eyebrow. "You know of such tech, my lord?"

"Yes, and soon you will, too," the baron said.

The healer inspected his work. "These will do," he decided. "Now I'll get you some of the dog you've been eyeing for the past hour. A quick mind needs a full belly."

With a gesture, Jeffers hurried the old man along. Watching the other hurry about to obey his order, the baron felt a rush of satisfaction. He was safe once more, as protected as any man could be in this hellish world.

But first came weapons, then a wall, then food. If they worked hard, the ville might get in one, maybe two crops before the acid rains came. Break apart the soil and go down deep enough, and good farmland still existed in the Deathlands. But like everything else in the smashed world, it had to be obtained by brute force.

Carrying a wooden plank loaded with juicy hunks of sizzling meat, the healer placed it reverently alongside the new baron. His stomach rumbled at the sight, but Jeffers made himself eat slowly. He knew better than to ever show weakness in front of his people.

Chewing the hot flesh, the baron studied the rows of simple wooden huts, and the one stone building. They all should be stone to prevent coldhearts from attacking with fire arrows. He clearly had much to teach them. Including, how to knot ropes! There wasn't a fishing net drying in sight anywhere, and the Ohi River was only a short walk away. Foolishness.

Jeffers swallowed, then wiped his mouth on the back of his unbandaged hand. Fishing, farming, their bellies might be tight this month, but with any luck by winterfall the ville would be thriving under his guidance.

Eventually, Pinewood would be strong, then his people would be able to strike back at Sandra Tregart. It would be worth anything to squeeze out the bitch's life with his bare hands wrapped around her throat...

Wearing the shirt of a dead coldheart, a young blond woman walked by, her bare feet silent on the soft dirt. Her heavy breasts moved freely beneath the old fabric, and when Jeffers smiled, she blushed, but didn't look away.

Strong arms, wide hips, big breasts, she would

make a fine baron's wife, Jeffers decided, feeling a different kind of hunger. Someday Thunder ville would be made to pay for the crimes of its baron. Either by him, or his many sons.

Chapter Eight

Dawn was starting to lighten the eastern sky when Sandra Tregart strode from the tent pulling on her soft leather gloves.

"Move 'er out!" the woman commanded loudly.

Exhausted looking workers pulled back the flaps of the next tent and a team rolled the Angel into view.

This air wag was noticeably different from the Demon in numerous ways. It had two cockpits, one behind the other. There was a line of letters and numbers along the side of the fuselage, once painted on and now embroidered in colorful threads. The fuel tank was inside the machine, not exposed on the top wing, and there was a squat and ugly predark rapid-fire attached to the cowling directly behind the propellers. A greasy belt of .50-caliber brass cartridges extended from the side of the weapon to snake down inside the biplane.

Testing the wind with a finger, Sandra studied the sky carefully. There was a storm coming, and a big one, but it wouldn't hit today.

"Any word from our hunters?" the woman asked, walking alongside the air wag as the eunuchs set its nose into the wind. She knew that the Angel didn't need that to assist a takeoff, but the less others knew about the operation of the machine the better.

"No word yet, mistress," Carter said, fighting back a yawn. "And the lookouts say there is no sign of smoke in the sky."

"Damn," Sandra muttered, tying the scarf tighter around her neck. It was going to be a warm day, but in the air the temperature dropped fast, and the woman had felt like she was freezing to death on her first long ride. Suddenly she understood why the faded pictures of the predark pilots showed them in leather jackets, gloves and scarves. That hadn't been a uniform, but a basic necessity.

Checking the blaster at her hip, and the two small derringers hidden under her arms, the woman ran a mental checklist to make sure everything was covered. Oil, tires, spare air pump, food, but no water. Men could use a bottle to relieve themselves while flying through the air. But that wasn't possible for a woman, and so she had to deny herself any fluids for a good hour before a long flight.

"The fuel tank is topped off, my lady," Carter said, shivering slightly from the morning chill. The crater was warm in the day, but cold at night. "And the bombs are loaded."

"How many?" Sandra asked, checking for the butane lighter in her pocket.

"Ten fire bombs, two explosive. All the Angel can carry."

She nodded. "Good enough." Grabbing a guyline and stepping on the lower wing, the woman swung into the forward cockpit and strapped herself in tight. Nestled alongside the woman in the tiny compartment were a dozen mixed bombs, and on the dashboard was a crude map of the area sketched in white chalk. Major landmarks were etched in red to serve as guides to find the way back home if she lost sight of the Ohi River.

Turning the ignition key, Sandra got a reading on the battery, fuel, oil pressure and engine temp. All in the green.

"Have your people follow me for as long as they can," she said. "Then when they lose sight of the Angel, just keep going in the same direction. I will find them."

"Yes, mistress."

"If I'm not back by afternoon, send out a search party," Sandra ordered, placing the sunglasses onto her face. Lengths of ribbon dangled from the end of the earpieces and she tied the glasses tightly into position. Such things were considered useless trinkets these days, only she had discovered the hard way that the tinted glass was vital to seeing where you were going up in the air. This she had also learned from the photos of the old sky barons. The books had used another term—aviators—but she found it ugly and much preferred the commanding phrase of sky baron.

"I will lead the search personally," Carter said, standing tall.

Yes, she assumed as much. "Oh, and do nothing to Stone while I'm gone," Sandra said in a dangerous tone. "I haven't yet decided his fate."

The eunuch scowled, but nodded in acceptance.

"Clear the props!" she shouted, setting the choke and throttle.

The workers dashed away from the front of the biplane, and she hit the autostart. There was a revving noise and then the propellers started to move, slowly at first, then jerking into action, and the compact aluminum engine roared with power.

"Release the chocks!"

Carter pulled on the ropes removing the wedges of wood from under the wheels, and the Angel started forward in a rush of speed.

Taking the joystick in both gloved hands, the woman adjusted her trim and raised the flaps. The gauges on the dashboard fluctuated wildly as she gave the engine full power. With increased velocity, the Angel raced along the floor of the impact crater. The whole air wag was vibrating, the guylines started humming and the noise from the propellers abruptly changed pitch. Suddenly the ground was gone, dropping rapidly away as if she had gone over the edge of a cliff. An electric tingle surged through her stomach and she burst into joyful laughter. Yes! Flying! Not even sex could compare to the excitement of being airborne!

Swinging the Angel around in a wide gentle arc, Sandra kept the rising sun out of her eyes as she swooped low in the sky and skimmed across Thunder ville. The sec men on the wall gave crisp salutes, and the ville folk in the streets timidly waved, the smaller children hiding behind their mothers' skirts.

A sea of upturned faces watched her sail by overhead, and then she was past the wall once more and crossing the desert. Leveling the wings, Sandra circled back to the airfield and started along the same flight path of the runaway Demon.

From this new vantage point, she could see far over the horizon, and there was still no sign of smoke. The woman growled at that. It meant that either her eunuchs hadn't found the Demon, or else they were dead. Bad news either way.

Glancing behind, Sandra saw horses burst out of the wall of the crater and start to gallop across the dry ground, leaving a dusty contrail in their wake. She gave a tight smile at that, but then abruptly frowned as the wind shifted and began to force her upward toward the deadly clouds. Shoving the throttle to the stop, Sandra gave the ancient twelve-cylinder engine full power. Surging to top speed, she dropped the Angel until it was only flying above the ground at about a hundred feet. The sound of the props and motor echoed off the rocky sand below, sending a score of animals scurrying for cover.

Shifting her grip on the joystick, the woman laughed out loud at the sight. Let the whole world tremble in fear at her approach!

"Look to the heavens, fools!" Sandra shouted over the rushing wind. "Your master has returned!"

RYAN AWOKE WITH A START and instinctively reached for his blaster hanging from the back of a nearby chair. Sitting bolt upright on the bed, the man looked around the officer's quarters, wondering what had disturbed his sleep.

Just then, the bathroom door swung open and Krysty came out surrounded by a cloud of steam.

"Morning, lover." She smiled, toweling her arms dry. "It took a while, but the shower finally delivered hot water."

"Good," Ryan said, placing aside the weapon. "After last night, I could damn well use a shower."

Standing, the naked man stretched royally, and Krysty enjoyed watching the play of hard muscles under his heavily scarred skin. The man was an unstoppable chilling machine in combat, yet he was also the most gentle lover she had ever been with. His brutish looks hid the fact that Ryan was very well read for these days, and what he hadn't learned in the library of his father, Baron Cawdor of Front Royal, the man had been taught by the Trader or had picked up from Mildred and Doc over the years.

"Well, it had been quite a while since we last had some privacy," she said, with a twinkle in her emerald eyes. "But you made the wait worth it."

Giving a rare smile, the Deathlands warrior reached out to gently stroke Krysty's beautiful face, and she nuzzled his hand in return. In silence, the couple shared a private moment, saying things to each other for which there were no words.

It had been a very busy night. After closing the blast door, the companions conducted a detailed search of the entire redoubt, checking every room, every body, for anything useful. They found a wide assortment of knives, a fortune in utterly useless cash, countless dead digital wristwatches, a hundred radios without batteries, a dozen M-16 assault rifles in decent condition, but only twenty rounds of ammo for the rapid-fires. However, a couple of the airtight footlockers in the barracks yielded a wealth of underwear, including bras, good socks, new boots for J.B., a little soap, a score of MRE food packs, and amazingly four boxes of assorted ammo and two precious grens.

It was a windfall of munitions, and the companions celebrated with self-heat cans of soup and MRE. The Mylar envelopes yielding something Mildred called lasagna this time, instead of the almost constant fare of military-grade beef stew and biscuits. It was a welcome change.

Concluding dinner, the companions hit the showers, and found they had quite a long wait as the pipes had a hundred year of accumulated sludge to flush out before the redoubt finally produced clean, hot water. Wearing towels and blasters, the people next used the washing machines in the laundry, and during the dry cycles Mildred gave everybody a haircut, except Krysty who only rarely cut her animated Titian tresses. It was an almost unbearable process.

Fed, clean and warm for the first time in weeks, the companions had taken over the officers' quarters. With a bit of effort, they'd assembled six clean beds, and separated into groups: J.B. spending the night with Mildred, and Krysty with Ryan, while Doc and Jak set up bachelor quarters in the commanding officer's private suite. The two men had unearthed some extremely well-aged Scotch from a locked drawer in a private liquor cabinet, an open wall safe that had been hidden behind an oil painting of the White House yielding a cornucopia of pornography suitable as trade goods, and the men spent a pleasant night arguing swords versus knives, and discussing the attributes of predark models. The other members of the companions enjoyed a more intimate evening behind locked doors. However, nobody mentioned the emptiness they all felt from the lack of young Dean Cawdor in their midst.

In the timeless depths of the redoubt, there were no alarm clocks to sound revelry, no sunrise at dawn to banish sleep, and the weary travelers slept their full, safe and secure in the armored bunker. If anything moved through the shadows of the redoubt, avoiding the bright lights of the fluorescent strips, they didn't hear a sound behind their barricaded doors.

"Yes, it has been a very long time," Ryan agreed as he moved closer. Krysty gave a small sigh and lowered her towel, the one-eyed man sliding a muscular arm around her trim waist. There came a loud knock on the door.

"It can't be breakfast, because it's my turn to cook today," Ryan said, playfully patting the woman on her shapely rump, her red hair flaring in response.

"Now don't start something you can't finish, lover," Krysty purred, completely dropping her towel.

Smiling, Ryan paused at the sight and pulled her close when the knock came again.

"Sorry to disturb you folks," Mildred said from the other side. "But Doc found an airplane."

"In the redoubt?" Ryan asked incredulously.

"No. Outside. In the sky. Somebody is flying an airplane."

Their special moment broken, Krysty and Ryan shared a glance, then separated and grabbed their clothes, dressing quickly. The magic of the night already fading into just another memory.

Rushing down the corridors, the three took the elevator to the garage level, then headed into the access tunnel. At the end of the zigzag passageway, they found the exit portal wide open, the rest of the companions standing in brilliant sunshine as they scanned the clear blue sky.

"I thought it was a stingwing at first," Doc said in greeting. "And started to duck back inside, but then I realized the truth."

Adjusting the patch over the ruin of his left eye, Ryan didn't blame the man for wanting to avoid a stingwing. They were the terror of the Deathlands. Flying almost too fast to see, their needle-sharp beaks would stab a man and drink his gushing fountain of blood. They were easy to chill, but a triple-bitch to shoot.

"You sure it was a plane?" Ryan demanded, rubbing his smoothly shaved chin.

Scratching the side of his nose with his ebony cane, Doc grimaced. "I should think so. No bird alive could have done that loop."

"A what?"

"A loop de loop," Doc answered, making a circle in the air with a finger. "Like that."

"An Emmelman maneuver," Mildred muttered.

"That's got to be a plane, all right. And one with either a very experienced pilot, or a foolish newbie who doesn't know any better."

"Why foolish?" Krysty asked, her red hair seeming to blaze like molten copper in the noontime sun.

"It is a very dangerous maneuver, to fly upside down like that. Fun, but dangerous. And as they say, there are old pilots, and there are bold pilots," Mildred said, reciting from memory. "But there are no old, bold pilots."

Lowering his binocs, Jak cackled. "Good one." He grinned. "Will remember!"

"Well, I don't see anything now," J.B. said, reaching into his munitions bag. Shifting the new grens, the Armorer pulled out a brass Navy telescope and extended the antique to its full length. He had found the relic a few years back in the window of a pawn shop located in a deserted city. It didn't have the range of military binocs, but it was a lot lighter and compacted down to the size of a soup can.

"Anything on the horizon?" Ryan asked, shading his eye from the sun with a raised hand.

"Nothing yet," J.B. replied slowly, swinging the telescope around. "Seems to be clear… Hey."

The companions waited, squinting skyward for any sign of danger.

"Nuke me," J.B. stated in awe. "It is a bastard plane!"

"Impossible." Mildred snorted, stepping closer.

"No way in this hell of a world that a jet fighter could get airborne. Just to make the fuel…"

"I said a plane, not a mil jet," J.B. replied curtly, lowering the telescope. "Here, see for yourself. You know these things better than us."

Because I'm from the past when air travel was a simple matter of buying a ticket and hoping there was good movie on your flight across the world. Mildred swept the sky where J.B. indicated and soon found the moving speck. She wasn't sure what it was at first, then it banked into c turn and she got a good glimpse of the four wings.

"It's a biplane," Mildred said at last. "I've seen them on television and in the movies."

She worked the length of the Navy telescope trying to get better focus. But then it was gone, hidden behind a rocky mesa. "It's a biplane, probably an old crop duster from some farmer's barn. Not much more than cloth and wood."

"And fly?" Jak asked, brushing back a cascade of white hair. "Bull."

"You remember the paper plane," she replied, passing the telescope to Ryan.

Jak scowled. Yeah, he did. It was in a redoubt where they had found nothing but tons of what Mildred called office supplies. Paper clips, pencils, files, envelopes and other items. Utterly useless. No food, ammo, or even decent blankets. What a shithole. But that night over the evening campfire, Mildred had performed a miracle and folded a piece of stiff paper into a sort of little arrow and sailed it across the room. Young Dean had been delighted, while the rest of them immediately turned their talk to war planes, and what they could do if they found any. Mil wags… No, that was the wrong word for them. Warbirds—yeah, that was it—were too complex to survive skydark. They took crews of dozens of techs to keep them operational, fancy electronics, special fuels. They finally decided that it simply couldn't be done. Air travel, such as it had been, was impossible.

Except that now, somebody was doing it.

"If this holocaustian Icarus should learn the secret of making more of such biplanes…" Doc said thoughtfully, his voice trailing off.

"Air wars," Ryan added grimly. "And the world would soon have a new emperor. A baron of all barons. A sky baron."

"Millie, I know how to make black powder—" J.B. started.

She cut him off. "No good, dear," the physician stated firmly. "Even in my day, planes were difficult to shoot down. And even if we had working Stinger missiles with heat-seeking warheads, they wouldn't be able to track a cloth airplane. Just not designed for the job."

"Take lotta lead," Jak said.

"To put enough holes in it? Damn straight. During which the pilot would be dropping bombs on you."

Bombs from the sky. The teenager shuddered. Sky bombs. It was a curseword that few people used these days, a hundred years after skydark.

"We could leave," Krysty stated, looking toward the opening to the redoubt. The interior of the base was clean and warm, so completely different from the harsh world outside, it seemed foolish for them to ever leave. But she knew the fallacy of that thinking. There weren't enough supplies to keep them alive.

"No, lover, it's not smart to leave an enemy running free behind you." Ryan growled, collapsed the telescope and put it away. "A plane like this could easily destroy Front Royal, Zero City, or even Haven. Nobody could stop it from smashing apart every friendly ville in America. How do you stop bombs falling from the air?"

"The villagers would panic, the sec men revolt, and then outlanders would start to attack everybody," J.B. said knowingly, swinging his Uzi in front as if for protection. "Dark night, it would be a feeding frenzy for the stickies and howlers!"

"Be the Mutie Wars all over again," Krysty said through clenched teeth. Then she softly added, "Only this time, we may not win."

"Yep," Jak agreed, staring hatefully at the clouds. "Gotta ace."

"But my dear Ryan, we do not know that this pilot is in fact our enemy," Doc pointed out.

"Or a friend, either," Ryan agreed. Walking around a pile of predark rubble, he looked at the empty sky stretching into the distance. The dark storm clouds were already starting to build. Soon they would blot out the sun and cast the world into shadows once more.

"So I think we better find out," Ryan declared.

Chapter Nine

Since there was no sense trying to walk after a plane, the companions decided to try to get a few of the wags in the garage working. As expected, the civilian vehicles were all dead. But most of the mil wags were in usable shape. Starting with a Hummer, Ryan repaired the tubeless tires, while Jak installed a spare nuke battery from storage, and Doc filled the fuel tank, along with a couple of extra cans.

The fuel pumps had been dry, but there were several cans of condensed fuel in the locked supply closet. The companions had no idea what the stuff was, not even Mildred. It burned like gasoline, but didn't evaporate when poured into a puddle on the floor. It would, however, power a gasoline or diesel engine and seemed to last forever. Coldhearts chilled for even a small can of the stuff, and barons would pay any price imaginable to obtain it for their war wags. More than once the companions had bought the freedom of a friend in chains with the juice, and once use it to firebomb an entire ville to permanently stop a hated enemy.

Meanwhile, Mildred and Krysty raided the redoubt for whatever trade goods could be found, the pocketknives, rolls of toilet paper, some spare tools, pencils, boots, empty brass for reloading and several of the M-16 assault rifles. Filling a couple of footlockers with the items, the women each thought they saw something moving in the shadows, but every time they went to investigate there was nothing there.

"It's all these mummified corpses lying around creeping us out," Mildred said with a strained laugh.

"Mebbe," Krysty said hesitantly, but she withdrew her revolver and kept it in her hand from that point onward.

Off by himself, J.B. was draining brake fluid from the civilian wags and mixing it with some chems from the janitor's closet to make smoke bombs. He had done this before, and the charges worked great. But this time, he just wasn't sure how effective the smoke would be against somebody looking down from above. But lacking air-to-ground missiles, it was their best defense.

A second Hummer was brought back to life, and then Ryan tried to get one of the motorcycles parked along the wall to turn over. Of the dozen bikes in the garage, only five hadn't seized up solid over the decades, and he could only get two of them to run without constant tinkering.

"Good enough," Ryan declared, fine-tuning the

carburetor on a big silver Harley-Davidson. The powerful engine lowered its throaty roar to a smooth purr under his guidance.

When satisfied, Ryan started doing the same thing to a BMW motorcycle. It was a good bike for combat. Instead of a drive chain like the Harley, the Beamer used a transmission like a wag, so it was incredibly silent. However, its gas mileage wasn't very good, and this particular bike was covered with fancy electronic equipment, none of which worked. So he ripped it all off, knowing that every ounce removed meant fuel saved.

"Here. Found this," Jak said, passing over a spray can, another sticking out of the pocket of his leather jacket.

Snapping off the plastic tap, Ryan gave a nod in thanks and started painting over the shiny chrome trim of the bikes. Stealth was important in tracking, as well as speed. Two Hummers and two bikes would be more than enough for this recce, and a hell of a lot more than they usually had. Nine times out of ten, walking was the way of the day. But this redoubt was well-stocked with wags, and they would happily make use of transport that came their way. Wisely, Ryan had passed on the APC as the engine of the armored personnel carrier would have required days of work, and while the half-track was in fine shape and could go practically almost anywhere, it was slow and heavy. Armor was good for a ville wall, but over the years the companions had found that maneuverability and speed served them better.

In short order, the companions were ready, and the Hummers piled with supplies and trade goods. As J.B. made some final checks on the wags, Ryan and Krysty went to the blast door and the man stepped outside while she closed the portal. After a few moments, the massive door rumbled open again and Ryan walked back inside.

"Okay, the external keypad works," he said with some satisfaction. "Just had to make sure we weren't locking ourselves outside permanently."

"Better safe than sorry, lover," Krysty said with a smile as they walked back along the tunnel.

He grunted. "Carve that on my tombstone, lover."

In the garage, the two found the rest of the companions ready to go. J.B. was behind the wheel of the black Hummer, with Doc riding shotgun, and Mildred in the camou-colored Hummer with Jak in the passenger seat.

"Keypad work?" J.B. asked, shifting the cigar stub in his mouth from one side to the other.

"No prob," Ryan said, climbing on the Harley and kicking the machine alive. The engine roared with power, then settled to a steady rumble.

"So let's roll," Krysty shouted, twisting the ignition of the BMW. Only the wisps of exhaust from the tailpipes and the flickering gauges on the curved dashboard showed the luxury motorcycle was in operation.

"'Half a league, half a league,'" Doc said in a singsong tone that meant he was quoting somebody.

"Just don't finish that, okay?" Mildred asked, throwing the camou-colored Hummer into gear. "I always hated the ending of that poem."

Arching a silver eyebrow, the scholar didn't reply, but merely worked the bolt on the M-16 assault rifle cradled in his arms. As a defensive weapon it was ideal. The rapid-fire made less noise than his LeMat, fired faster and considerably farther. But more importantly, many people would back off from others armed with rapid-fires, when they might try to jack folks merely armed with wheelguns. Doc and Jak had split the few rounds of ammo, so each had fifteen rounds in their clips. After that, it was handblasters and grens.

"Move 'em out!" J.B. called, starting forward in the point position.

Staying close behind the black Hummer, Ryan and Krysty took the rocking chair and Mildred covered the rear.

As the convoy disappeared around the first corner of the antirad tunnel, something moved in the shadows of the grease pit and slowly started dragging itself after them.

Reaching the blast door, Ryan pulled alongside the keypad and tapped in the access code. As the portal slide aside, J.B. drove out slowly, maneuvering around the rubble until there was enough space for the others.

Impatiently, the convoy waited for the door to close again, and then proceeded over the mounds of smashed masonry to finally reach the grassy side of the hillock.

Thunder rumbled overhead and lightning flashed in harmony on the horizon. Glancing at the turbulent sky, J.B. saw a break in the clouds and slammed on the brakes. Quickly, he pulled out the minisextant and focused it on the sun. J.B. barely got the sextant aligned when the clouds rolled in to fill the brief opening, and the land was cast into orange light once more.

"You called it, Millie," he said, tucking the device under his shirt. "This is Southern Indiana, that's the Ohi River."

"Any airbases nearby?" Ryan asked, twisting the throttle on the handlebars to rev the engine. The Harley was riding rough, and he suspected water contamination in the fuel tank. Damn, he should have checked that.

"Nothing on the map," Doc replied, folding the colorful sheet of plastic into a small, easier-to-hold wad. "But then, this is merely a travel guide for tourists."

Switching on the radio, Mildred played with the controls for a while, then turned it off again. There was only static and crackling from the radioactive material in the upper atmosphere. Even in the relatively clean areas that had only been lightly nuked, radios were only good for line-of-sight communications. Once you went past the seven-mile mark and dropped below the curve of the Earth, the transponders were useless.

"Smoke!" Jak shouted, pointing out the window. "Two o'clock!"

Ryan snapped his head in that direction and saw the white plume rising from behind a sand dune on the distant horizon. The smoke was still rising so it had to be from a new fire.

"Think it's our pilot cooking dinner?" Krysty asked, her whole body faintly shaking from the restrained BMW engine.

"Or being cooked as dinner," J.B. retorted when the plume thickened and a bright orange fireball expanded into view.

The companions waited expectantly, but there was no accompanying sound to the roiling blast.

"Too far away," Jak told them, squinting. "Four, mebbe five miles."

"Our mysterious plane may be no more," Doc said, leaning out of the Hummer window. "Should we continue?"

"Hell, yes," Ryan growled, gunning the Harley and leaping into the lead. "Until we see the wreckage, I'm going to assume it's still around. That blast could have simply been the plane bombing something."

"Biplane," Mildred corrected automatically. "Yeah, makes sense. Either way, we need to know."

"It is better to learn for certain that something believed to be disproved is wrong," Doc intoned, "than to believe in the lie of an incorrect fact."

J.B. just stared at the fellow, but Mildred burst into laughter. "And as soon as I figure out what the hell that means," she said with a chuckle, "I'll have a snappy comeback."

"Indeed, madam. And so shall I."

Following the river, the companions drove Hummers and motorcycles over the rough ground, trying to keep on a northern route in the general direction of the explosion.

Skirting dangerously near the edge of the riverbank, Ryan scowled at the rushing water below. It was deep and fast. Not an easy thing to cross. Unless they found a way, this was going to be a wasted trip.

After about a mile, Ryan and Krysty took point, the nimble motorcycles able to traverse the irregular terrain easier than the lumbering Hummers. Soon, they were driving through a field of weeds, the ground littered with the bits of pieces of a predark city. A smashed stone gargoyle peered out from a bush, the top of a telephone pole jutted from a mound of bricks and decay and a rusted mailbox lay embedded in the hard-packed dirt.

Finding himself trapped in an arch of rusted metal debris, Ryan stopped his bike to walk it back out. Braking to a halt on the crest of windswept mound, Krysty waited for him to rejoin her before continuing.

As the Hummers rolled into view again, Krysty noticed that there seemed to be some sort of a brick road under the weeds she was parked in, patches of the broken street still visible here and there among the waving plants. Hoping the road might lead to a bridge, she tried following its course with her eyes, but it seemed to sweep inland to the east. Useless.

Then Krysty sharply inhaled at the sight of the brick road ending at a large shiny patch of what looked like ice. But she knew better, and her heart started pounding hard. It was a lake of glass. The telltale mark of where a small nuke had gone off. The big ones left deserts that stretched for hundreds of miles. The really big ones leveled mountains.

"Ryan, check your rad counter!" Krysty snapped urgently, looking to the right.

"Already did," Ryan replied, pulling alongside. The predark device on his denim shirt showed they were nowhere near the danger zone yet. "We're safe enough here. But I wouldn't go any closer."

Starting forward once more, the two rolled through the field of weeds, the nameless city only a cracked suggestion under the layers of windblown sand and stubby cactus. Here and there small pieces of predark buildings jutted, and at one point the corner of a building stood several feet high. The jagged cinderblock wall formed a natural windbreak, and there was a burned spot on the ground to show where the ruins had recently been used as a campsite by somebody.

"Looks like the place burned down, rather than got nuked," Krysty said, her hair streaming in the wind. "Probably from the heat flash of the nuke that made the glass lake."

Ryan started to agree, when a motion behind the busted wall caught his attention.

"Ambush," he cried, pulling his blaster and throwing the Harley into motion.

As the bikes lurched away, two stickies darted out of hiding, hooting in delight at the sight of the norms. But as the shambling mockeries started forward, Ryan and Krysty simply kept going and soon left the muties far behind.

Coming into view through the tall weeds, J.B. cursed at the sight of the stickies and savagely twisted the steering wheel. The Hummer swerved hard, and just missed colliding with the stickies as they rushed, hooting at the wag. Sounding the horn as a warning, he glanced in the rearview mirror and saw the camou-colored Hummer try to arc around the two muties. But another stood from a depression in the ground and spread its arms wide as it embraced the wag. The working suckers lining its flesh made wet smacking noises as they dripped a thick gelatinous ooze. Mildred cursed at that. If the mutie touched the Hummer, the only way to get it off would be with fire.

"Ram it!" Jak snarled, leveling the M-16.

Grimly, Mildred hit the gas. Jak fired, and the round hit the stickie just under the left eye, making a neat round hole. As the creature fell to the ground, the Hummer rolled over the mutie and was in the clear.

In the rearview mirror, Mildred saw more stickies rise from hidden positions among the ruins and realized the place was infested. This was no trap for careless outlanders, but their home. A nest of stickies!

Leaving the creatures behind, Mildred and Jak soon joined the others on top of a small hill overlooking the river. More smashed buildings stood there, but more importantly, a sagging railroad trestle crossed the rushing water.

"No way we're getting across that," J.B. said, chewing his cigar stub. "Maybe the bikes could, but not these Hummers."

"Well, there's nothing else in sight," Krysty said, craning her neck. "Mebbe if we went one at a time?"

"No way," J.B. stated. "Can't be done. All that's holding the bridge together is rust and bird shit."

From downriver, the angry hooting from the ruins got a little louder.

"Our moist friends are disappointed over us not

staying for dinner," Doc said, tightening his grip on the rapid-fire. "Time for a decision, my friends."

Kicking down the stand, Ryan parked his bike and walked to the edge of the trestle. Carefully, he studied the water below, then tossed in a stone to check for depth. Yes, it might just work.

"Whatever you're doing, hurry it up, lover!" Krysty said, pulling her S&W wheelgun.

Just then, a stickie rose into view and began to run their way. Closing an eye, the redhead aimed and waited for the mutie to come within range.

"Okay, get ready!" Ryan said, reaching into a pocket. Pulling out a gren, he yanked the pin free, dropped the handle and tossed the bomb onto the weakened trestle.

"Down!" he cried, ducking low.

Eight seconds later the gren detonated and the entire middle span of the bridge was violently blown apart, the fireball almost spanning the river. Shrapnel flew everywhere and, with a tremendous groan, the whole structure came loose from its moorings and tumbled into the river.

"Get moving!" Ryan cried, scrambling back onto the Harley and gunning the engine.

Taking the lead, the Deathlands warrior rolled to the edge of the riverbank, then spread his legs to help support the two-wheeler as he eased it over the side and down into the water. The wreckage from the destroyed trestle was still moving as it settled into the mud, and he nosed the Harley onto some wooden railroad ties to start working his way to the other side along the loose piles of bricks and steel girders.

A few seconds later, Krysty and the Hummers were in the shallows and following his example. The BMW bike rolled along the shifting materials with ease, Krysty darting expertly from pile to pile until she reached dry ground.

The Hummers didn't fare as well, the ancient timbers cracking under their weight. Both mil wags dropped into the river, the churning water almost reaching the windows. But the machines were designed for this, and the exhaust stacks on their hoods stayed well clear of the cold Ohi. Switching to four-wheel drive, J.B. fought his wag up a slope of settling bricks and went sailing over the top to land in the shallows with a tremendous splash. But the tough Hummer dug its wide tires into the black mud and battled onto the shore to join Ryan and Krysty waiting for them.

"Hey, great plan," J.B. said sarcastically. "I never would have considered blowing up the bridge."

"Never thought it was smart," Ryan replied from his bike. "Only that it would work."

"Not yet it hasn't!" Krysty cursed. "Millie and Jak are stuck!"

The brown-and-green-patterned Hummer was in

the middle of the destroyed trestle, its engine revving loudly, gears clashing as Mildred tried to rock the vehicle back and forth. The undercarriage was obviously caught on something.

Tumbling over the embankment like blood-crazed lemmings, the stickies fell into the rushing water and started hooting as they clambered over the moving rubble. One of them jumped onto a timber, only to have the wooden beam flip over and smash it underwater. A red stain began to spread downriver from that point, but the other muties ignored their fallen brother to continue pursuit of the tasty twolegs.

"Fireblast!" Ryan spit, starting to pull his blaster, then holstering it again. There were too many stickies, and he had a better idea. Climbing off the Harley, he went to the front of the black Hummer and disengaged the towline.

"Cover me!" Ryan ordered, hopping off the bank.

The man sank to his ankles in the soft black silt on the bottom of the shallows, and pulled his combat boots free with loud slurping sounds. The braided steel towline trailed loosely behind the man, Krysty feeding it along with her bare hands as Doc started firing the M-16 at the stickies, placing his shots with extreme care to try not to hit the other Hummer.

Crawling onto a rock, Ryan jumped to a steel girder and started sliding closer to the trapped wag. When the beam began to move from his weight, Ryan grabbed on to a stanchion and took the ride until the girder started to dip into the water.

Leaping forward with all of his strength, Ryan landed sprawling on the sinking pile of bricks under the trapped Hummer. From this position, he could see the cluster of twisted iron rod from inside the support columns of the bridge holding the wag prisoner. If the Hummer had been a civilian wag, it would have been pierced in a dozen spots, but the armored belly of the mil wag was undamaged. Just trapped like an impaled rat on a roasting stick.

There came the ripping sound of an M-16 on full-auto as Ryan struggled to his feet and attached the towline to the steel ring on the front of the Hummer just below its winch. He tugged on the braided steel to make sure it was firmly secured, and a stickie appeared on the roof of the wag, hooting insanely and waving its arms.

Drawing and firing in a single motion, Ryan blew out its throat, and the mutie sank to its knees, dark red blood gushing from the hideous wound.

"In!" Jak ordered, throwing open the side door.

Moving fast, Ryan dived inside just as the towline began to straighten across the watery destruction.

"Hold on!" Mildred shouted as the Hummer jerked forward.

But the wag only moved a few feet before stopping again.

A stickie appeared at the window and Jak blew off its face with his Colt Magnum. Squeezing into the rear compartment, Ryan threw open the back window and started blowing hot lead into the inhuman horde wading through the rubble. Then he missed a mutie as the Hummer jounced forward once more, only to slide back a few feet to its original position.

"Time leave!" Jak snarled, emptying the Colt and thumbing in fresh rounds. The opposite shore was only twenty feet away and looked as distant as the moon.

A stickie rose from the water alongside Mildred, and the physician put a single round from her Czech ZKR revolver directly into its heart. With a terrible human moan, the mutant crumbled back into the river and disappeared.

"One more fucking time!" she snarled, and gunned the big engine to the red line.

Throwing the Hummer into reverse, Mildred slammed into a stickie, the body plastering along the chassis of the wag. When she could go no farther, Mildred waved at J.B. on the shore and threw the transmission into forward.

Metal screeched and something bent under the Hummer as it slammed forward only to jerk to a halt and start to tilt sideways, heading for the river. Holding on for dear life, Ryan and Jak fired steadily out the windows now, the telltale boom of Doc's LeMat mixing with the sharp crack of Krysty's revolver.

Slamming into reverse once more, Mildred heard the towline twang like a cord on a guitar from the tension, and felt her belly turn cold at the thought of it coming free to whip backward through the windshield like a scythe. Then something loudly snapped under the Hummer. The machine dropped a foot, all four tires dug into the loose bricks, sending them spraying out backward like a shotgun blast, and the war wag surged forward, free at last!

Covered with dead muties, the camou-colored Hummer jounced and bucked through the submerged debris and barely managed to lurch onto the shoreline. As Mildred braked the machine to a frantic halt on solid ground, Krysty dashed to disengage the hook, and then J.B. hit the winch controls, reeling back the steel cable with a whizzing sound.

More stickies were shambling from the river now, as Krysty ran back to the BMW and hopped onto the bike. She took the lead as the Hummer drove away from the river. In the back of the wag, Ryan scowled as the Harley was surrounded by stickies, then the wag went around a sandy hillock and it was gone from sight.

"No going back now, I suppose." Mildred sighed, flexing her sore hands.

"Not that way, anyhow," Ryan agreed, leaning back in his seat and carefully reloading.

"Mebbe all fly home, eh?" Jak said half jokingly, rummaging in his pockets for more shells.

Stopping a good distance from the river, the companions got out and used a few of the trading knives to hack the dead stickies off the chassis of the black Hummer. When they were down to just fingers and toes, J.B. poured a little condensed fuel on the oozing gobbets and burned them off. The smell was horrendous.

Finished with their grisly task, the companions climbed back into their vehicles and drove off, each of them trying to think about what a stickie's deadly hands could do to human flesh if they got a good hold.

At first the driving through the grasslands was easy and the three vehicles made good speed. But after about an hour, the companions were forced to slow down as loose sand began covering the ground in larger and larger patches. Soon, the grass and weeds were gone and they found themselves rolling through a proper desert.

Rising over the horizon came a mesa, the steep column of gray stone giving the barren vista an alien feel.

"You sure we are going in the correct direction?" Doc asked, the blue swallow design on his handkerchief appearing to flutter as his words moved the cloth.

Blinking the sweat from his eyes, J.B. glanced at the open compass on the seat between them. "Ten degrees off true north," he said, switching his attention back to driving. "That was the mark for the explosion.

"Then lay on, MacDuff," Doc said, wiping his

hands dry on his frilly shirt before cradling the assault rifle again. It was down to only five rounds now, but was still an impressive piece of hardware.

J.B. shot him a look. "That another poem?" he asked.

Beaming in delight, Doc said, "No, indeed! It is from a Scottish tale of murder and sex, madness and revenge."

With both hands on the wheel, J.B. shrugged. "Sounds good. Tell me some."

"With pleasure, John Barrymore! In fact, your own name has a theatrical connection to the story, that I shall elucidate shortly. It all begins on a dark and stormy night…"

In the black Hummer, Mildred snorted a laugh. "Poor John." She chuckled. "I can see Doc waving his arms about, so he must be reciting something. Probably the entire damn 'Iliad.'"

"Any good?" Jak asked, hugging the rapid-fire tight in his arms to try to keep out the dust.

Shifting gears to climb a dune, Mildred started to speak, then paused and thought better of it. "Why, no," she lied smoothly. "Boring as hell."

Not stupid, the teen accepted the rebuff and returned to looking out the dirty window at the endless terrain of windblown sand.

As the cool air from the river was left behind, the heat of the sun started slowly building in spite of the heavy cloud cover. Distant thunder rumbled menacingly as the wind increased and the loose sand formed little dust eddies. Wiping their stinging eyes, J.B. and Mildred tried closing the windows and switching on the air conditioners. However, the old units only rattled and delivered warm air. With no choice, J.B. and Mildred cracked the windows again, and everybody tied handkerchiefs around their mouths and noses to keep out the swirling dust particles.

Shrugging out of her bearskin coat, Krysty did the same, then also loosened her shirt and rolled up her sleeves to try to keep cool.

The BMW's engine had been running slightly warm since the redoubt, and the slower she went, the more the motorcycle struggled to maintain speed and keep up with the Hummers. The fuel was dropping at an almost noticeable rate, and the engine temp climbed dangerously high every time she paused to rest her arm, or wipe the sweat from her forehead.

All around the three vehicles, the whispering dunes rose and fell like waves at sea, the rare cluster of cactus or large rock only serving to heighten the feeling of emptiness.

Braking to a stop, Krysty raised a closed fist and the Hummers came to a halt. Turning her head, the woman sniffed and caught it again. Wood smoke. And something else.

"This way!" she shouted through her makeshift mask, and sent the Beamer rolling forward.

Going around a particularly tall sand dune, Krysty slowed as the she weaved through smaller dunes. Then she saw it. The burned wreckage of a smashed biplane partially embedded in the side of a sand dune. Braking to a halt, the woman waited until the two Hummers arrived and parked slightly apart from each other. For a few minutes the companions stayed with their vehicles and studied the area. There had obviously been some sort of a battle here, but it was impossible to tell what had happened.

"Ain't this the damnedest thing," J.B. muttered from behind his cigar stub.

Slowly climbing out of the camou-colored Hummer, Ryan had to agree with his friend. The sand was churned with dozens of overlapping footprints, and a few large brown stains that could only have been spilled blood. But there were no bodies in sight, aside from four chestnut stallions. The horses were lying motionless on the ground with feathered arrows deep in their throats. Flies buzzed around the wounds and crawled thickly over their matted hide. The four animals were wearing saddles, the saddlebags still firmly lashed closed. Yet in spite of that, the sand was dotted with clothing and personal items: a couple of canteens, a leather pouch, a shoe and a blaster. A small campfire was glowing a few yards away from the burning plane, the dying embers still red-hot.

Retrieving the weapon, Ryan dusted it off and

checked the cylinder. The revolver was still loaded. Shitfire, he thought, whatever happened here had to have been so fast that the horse riders never even got off a shot. He frowned at that realization. Only who would leave a working blaster behind?

While J.B. started going through the saddlebags, Mildred went to the smoldering remains of the biplane. Using a tire iron from the Hummer, she prodded the ashes and turned over a few pieces of the fuselage, inspecting the wreckage carefully.

"Bad news, I'm afraid," she said, straightening. "This biplane isn't predark. It was made by hand."

"Is that possible?" Ryan demanded.

Resting the tire iron on a shoulder, she shrugged. "Sure. The Wright brothers did a lot more with a lot less than is available these days. And some of these instruments even have car manufacturer logos on them. Nobody from before the Nuke War would have done that."

"Damn!"

"There's more," Mildred added, brushing back a length of her beaded hair. "This plane was fire-bombed after it crashed."

"After? Mebbe the fuel tank just blew when it hit," Krysty said, still on her bike. She had the engine off to let it cool, but was keeping a hand on the throttle. Her hair was moving against the dry breeze, and Krysty was starting to get a bad feeling about this place.

Using the tire iron, Mildred tapped the dented aluminum canister lying amid the blackened wood-frame skeleton. "Fuel tank is still intact," she stated as a fact. "This probably crashed when it ran out of gas."

"Something else started the fire," Ryan said thoughtfully, tucking the new blaster into his belt.

Going to the front of the wreck, Mildred tapped the engine block. "See those pieces of scattered glass? My guess is this was hit with a Molotov."

"Nonsense! That does not make any sense, madam," Doc rumbled, gesturing at the campfire. "Why would somebody standing on the ground next to a blazing fire throw a Molotov when they could have simply set the plane ablaze with a burning stick…" The man paused, and bit a lip. "Oh, yes, I see. They would not have. Thus this was attacked by somebody not on the ground. A second plane."

"Exactly. It must have been that manned plane we saw earlier," Mildred said, pocking among the charred remains. "This was a drone. See? The controls were lashed into place. Some of the rawhide straps are in place."

"No pilot?" Jak said suspiciously. The teen was leaning against the hood of the black Hummer, his face set in a scowl. There wasn't a single thing about this that he liked. The tracks on the ground were all wrong, and those arrows…!

"There was no pilot when it took off, yes," she

replied, scratching her head. "If the wind is right, there's no problem about that."

Licking a finger, Mildred tested the direction of the desert breeze and walked past the dead horses to look across the sandy landscape. But she saw nothing along the flight path of the biplane except empty desert. How far had this thing gone by itself?

Crouching near the campfire, Krysty lifted a green stick from the ashes. "Then explain this," she said. "Somebody built a big fire, then tossed in green wood."

"That made a good smoke signal," Ryan said, pushing back his fedora. "So they must have wanted to be located."

"To let their baron know they found the plane?" Krysty asked. Then she frowned deeply. "Only the baron returns to blow them all to hell."

"Perhaps these men came to steal the plane," Doc started to say, then cut himself off. "No, if that was true, they would not have lit a signal fire."

"Which means, the baron betrayed them."

"Or that it was too dangerous to land," Ryan said very slowly. "And so the baron destroyed the crashed plane in the only way possible." Going to one of the dead horses, Ryan pulled an arrow out of its neck. The workmanship was excellent, and while the shaft was wood, the tip was carved bone.

"Sounds like your typical baron, all right," Mildred said with a bitter sigh. "He burned the plane to keep it out of the hands of another baron, and left his people behind to die."

"Which means the sec men couldn't tell anything under torture," Krysty said in brutal logic. "Or else he would have firebombed them, too."

Ryan gave a slow nod. Which meant that if they aced this sky baron, that would be the end of flying machines and skybombs. Or were they reading all of this wrong, and something else entirely had happened here?

"Well, there's only food and water in the saddle-bags," J.B. said, dusting off his hands as he stood. "None of it eaten, so the riders couldn't have come from very far away. Less than a day's ride distance, at the very most."

"That would only be a few hours in the Hummers," Doc said, moving around the crash site.

"If that."

Carefully going to a clean area, Ryan hunched low and scanned the ground. The jumble of footprints was already starting to fill in from the windblown dust and sand.

Kneeling alongside the man, Jak ran his fingertips across the muddled prints, his ruby-red eyes narrowed in concentration.

Saying nothing to disturb the teen, Ryan watched him carefully. Although Ryan had been hunting all of his life, to him the marks were an indecipherable mess.

"Four sec man," Jak said at last, lifting his head.

"Big man, good boots. Jumped by nine other men. All norms, barefoot."

Barefoot? "Savages," Doc mumbled, fingering the trigger of his LeMat.

"Or worse," J.B. added, working the bolt on his Uzi machine pistol. The rapid-fire was wrapped in an oily cloth to keep the sand out of its works, which gave the weapon an odd bulky appearance, as if it was a swaddling child.

"Looks like that smoke signal attracted more than just the sky baron," Mildred said, taking a swig from her canteen.

"What did they do with the bodies?" Ryan asked pointedly.

Setting his jaw, Jak scowled. "Not dead," he stated. "Took alive."

"All of them?" Krysty asked incredulously.

The teen nodded.

Sliding the Steyr SSG-70 longblaster off his back, Ryan worked the bolt, chambering a round. If it was torture, then only one or two of the sec men would have been needed. No need to haul all of them alive to the dungeon of some ville. And it couldn't have been slavers, because they would have taken the dropped blaster. That alone was worth more than the four men, their gear and horses combined. The sec men had been jacked by barefoot savages who had captured them alive, left behind a year's supply of horse meat and didn't want the blasters.

"Nuking hell," Ryan swore. "Gotta be cannies!"

That was when the top of a sand dune flowed aside to reveal several half-naked men armed with bows, and arrows suddenly rained down upon the companions from every direction.

Chapter Ten

"Get along, Moses," the old man said, leaning forward in the wag to shake the reins. "Come on now, boy, you can do it."

Obediently, the lead mule threw itself forward against the harness, and the others followed suit. With loud creaks, the rear tire was triumphantly pulled out of the rut it had been trapped in, and once more the rickety cart started rolling along the dried riverbed.

Setting his battered hat to a better angle against the sun, the ancient driver settled onto the splintery plank that served as a seat, and tried to get comfortable.

Forming a ragged line, there were five other carts similar to the wrinklie's. Loose sheets of canvas were draped over the cargo in the back of each of the flatbeds, the contents rattling and clanking at every pothole and gully. Turning was a difficult job, but the driver really didn't care. This was a one-way trip. Once they reached Indera ville, their troubles would be over. Baron Jeffers was a good man and never went back on his word.

"Unlike so many other barons," the wrinklie muttered to himself, shaking the reins again. "Steady there, Moses! Good boy, that's it."

Loudly braying in reply, the mule twitched a shoulder to dislodge a buzzing fly and kept going. The five other beasts dumbly followed his lead.

In the second cart, a young man controlled the reins and a middle-aged woman sat alongside with a loaded crossbow in her lap. In the third, that mix was reversed, and in the last cart two burly women sat side by side. Their faces were grim and hard, their expressions only softening when they glanced at each other.

The riverbed was relatively flat, but studded gullies from the hard summer rains. Bare rocky hills rose sharply on either side of the passage, casting whole sections of the riverbed into shadow. But the old caravan leader had been ready for that. Each wag in the caravan had a pair of torches set alongside the driver, the wads of cloth and rope soaked in sticky tar that had been cooked out of chunks of predark asphalt. The torches would reek like a burning outhouse, but the flames would be bright as a lantern and no amount of rain or wind could put them out.

Barking dogs raced freely on the riverbed, darting under the carts and dodging the slowly rolling tires. The fur of the muscular animals was patchy with scars, their ears chewed and tails broken. Each had been given a name, but they all responded to the universal call "dog."

Playfully nipping and chasing each other as they escorted the lumbering caravan, the dogs stayed well clear of the harnessed mules. When first introduced back at the old ville, the leader of the pack had bitten the hind leg of a complacent old mule to establish authority. The ancient pack animal didn't change its dull expression as it violently kicked backward and drove a sharp hoof into the dog, shattering its rib cage and crushing its heart. The dog went tumbling from the deadly blow to lie on the dusty ground heaving for air while the other dogs circled it, yipping in confusion until it expired. Since that, no dog in the pack had been stupid enough to ever bother the mules again.

The old driver jerked up his head at the sound of a distant mountain cat snarling over a fresh chill, and he laid a gnarled hand on the crossbow on the seat next to him.

Some of the people in the caravan had blasters, but they were crude weapons, iron pipes reinforced with hot steel wire bound tight around the length until it cooled and contracted, tightening and strengthening the barrel. Nothing fancy like some big ville sec man's pride, these were heavy longblasters that could also serve as a club. The black powder weapons were muzzle-loaders, and packed with anything that would fit, sharp, rocks, bent nails, broken glass. There were small holes on top with bits of fuse sticking out, pieces of string rolled in black powder, but they worked most of the time.

At short range, the crude weapons laid down a hellstorm of debris and could blow a man out of his saddle. They were even more effective against the vultures and stingwings that sailed the desert sky. But against stickies and howlers they were useless. The muties took little damage from the garbage scatterguns, and the thundering booms only attracted more of the nuke-blasted monsters. The caravan drivers had learned fast to save the blasters for people, and to only use crossbows on the muties.

Under the canvas sheets covering the carts were wooden barrels, steel drums, copper tubing and other assorted paraphernalia of their craft.

Shine. Although, one crazy old wrinklie used to call it moonshine. The members of the caravan weren't blood-kin, but close enough. They were brewmasters, and made the cleanest, tastiest shine in the territory. Nobody went blind drinking their brew, and it burned just as smooth in a lantern as it did fueling an engine. Made nuking good Molotovs, too.

Couple of seasons ago, word had reached the mountaineers that Baron Jeffers wanted brewmasters in his ville on the Ohi. Having lost a host of friends and kin to the wolves that winterfall, the mountaineers thought walls and sec men sounded mighty fine.

So they built some carts, gathered tools and started the long journey from their craggy peaks down into the burning desert.

Discovering a small green lizard on the ground, one of the dogs started circling the reptile, snarling. The lead mule shied away from the commotion, taking the rest along with him, and the elderly driver nearly lost control of the cart.

"Whoa, Moses!" he said in a soothing tone, tightening the rein. "Easy, big fella. Easy there."

Slowly remembering that the man fed and whipped them, the harnessed mules grudgingly obeyed, and settled back into their endless drudgery of hauling the heavy carts.

Hissing defiantly, the lizard scuttled forward to attack the barking dog, and another hound leaped upon its back to sink sharp teeth into the mottled green hide. Trying to escape, the lizard thrashed around, squealing, a pair of iridescent wings unfolding from its ridged back. Shaking its head, the dog snapped the spine of the little mutie, and the lizard shuddered before going still. Gleefully, the dog ripped off a mouthful of flesh and ran away, allowing the others to converge and finish the meal. The tiny reptile didn't go very far among the large dogs, and the famished animals began to race around again, forever on the prowl for anything else to fill the yawning pit of their taut bellies.

Chuckling in amusement at the show, the old driver reached into his tattered vest and pulled out a silver flask. Thumbing off the cap, he took a short swig of the tepid water. Shine had a lot of uses, but curing your thirst wasn't one of them.

Snapping the plastic cap back on, the wrinklie tucked the flask away, then paused to look around. Eh? Now what in world was that odd buzzing sound? Looking upward, the man frowned at the sight of something moving in the sky.

Was…was that a stingwing?

WITH THE WIND BLOWING in her face, Sandra Tregart was soaring through the sky with an electric tingle in her belly. Black dust, flying was better than anything! She would never come down if that were possible.

High above her biplane, thunder peeled in the fiery orange clouds and a downdraft hit her plane, carrying the reek of ozone and chems. Pulling the scarf tighter across her mouth and nose for protection, Sandra leveled out the Angel and fed more fuel to the hungry engine. She was about halfway back to Thunder ville by now. All she had to do was to follow the dry river to the mesa, then head for the Ohi and she was home.

Cutting through the excitement of flying was a stab of remorse over leaving her eunuchs in the clutches of those savages in the desert. She had wasted time destroying the Demon first, and then when she circled back to chill the cannies, everybody was gone. Sandra had randomly dropped two of her dynamite bombs on the dunes, but aside from creating spectacular geysers of sand there had been no noticeable results. Her men were gone, and there was nothing she could do about that. Not even get the satisfaction of revenge. Wild anger boiled up inside the woman, and she suddenly screamed curses at the world until her throat became sore.

Finally running out of breath, Sandra tried to push the matter from her mind, when she noticed something moving along the riverbed below. Dipping a wing, she swooped lower for a better view.

Ah! It was a convoy of some kind, four large carts being pulled by teams of mules. Leveling the biplane, Sandra scowled at the idea of more outlanders invading her valley. Or worse! They could be mercies hired by another baron to attack her ville. Baron Marengold, or perhaps even the fat fool of a woman Baron d'Vulea. Clutching the joystick with both hands, Sandra gave a throaty chuckle. Well, she could easily handle the two of them at the same time once she refueled. That was always the limiting factor. There was just not enough shine to fuel all of the missions she wanted to fly.

Fingering the trigger on the joystick, Sandra debated easing some tension by strafing the little carts with blasterfire and chilling the mules. That would leave the people in the middle of mutie country with no way out but walking, which was the equivalent of a death sentence. It would be kinder to let them buy the farm here and now. Slowly, the woman began to ferociously grin. Unfortunately for them, she wasn't feeling very generous that afternoon.

Lowering the wing flaps, Sandra dropped her speed and began to swing around for a second pass when she caught a glimpse of something under the canvas of the second wagon the looked like red metal snakes. The woman gasped as she realized the truth, and then narrowed her eyes in raw greed. Copper tubing. There was copper tubing in that cart! That was the one item she needed to be able to make a second still. That would mean twice as much flying time! The very thought filled her with a wild giddiness, but that was swiftly replaced by a cold resolution. She had to have that tubing!

However, a glance at her fuel gauge told the brutal truth that Sandra was already at the point of no return. If she turned back right now, Sandra could get very close to the crater, and her sec men would be able to escort her and the biplane safely inside. But only if she didn't tarry, or delay.

Impulsively, she looked again. Black dust, they had so much tubing! Maybe enough for a third still, possibly even four! That would mean unlimited fuel, and all the flying she could ever want. Unlimited air time for the Angle and all its sister Demons.

Shoving the joystick all the way forward, Sandra almost flooded the engine as she angled into a steep dive, building speed until the guylines supporting her wings began to hum from the wind pressure. All. She wanted it all!

As the Angel dropped screaming from the sky, most of the people in the carts shrieked in terror and covered their faces. Only a couple of the drivers raised crossbows and started launching arrows her way. The feathered darts arched into the sky, most falling behind to miss her completely. The Angel was too fast! But then one accidentally went through a wing, leaving a ragged hole in the silky cloth. Recoiling from the sight, Sandra held her breath, wondering if the puncture would rip open wide, tearing off the wing and sending her tumbling down to a fiery death. But the predark material held. The Angel was okay. It was just a flesh wound, nothing mortal. Both she and the biplane would live.

Lining up the spinning blur of the propeller, Sandra reached out to flip the safety on the big machine gun. She only had a hundred rounds of ammo in the belt in an effort to save weight and fly longer. Now Sandra regretted that economy, and cursed the fact she didn't have a full nine yards of lead in the big predark blaster. There had been thousands of rounds in the junkyard where she found the biplane, but time had weakened the powder in the brass cartridges to the point where only a handful would work, and none of them had enough force to operate the feeder mechanism of the rapid-fire. Her eunuchs had painstakingly reloaded each cartridge by hand with the finest black powder until she fully armed. However, this measly hundred was all Sandra had with her this day. It would have to be enough.

Sweeping across the caravan, Sandra stroked the trigger and the entire plane recoiled as the .50-caliber machine gun spit out gouts of flame between the spinning propellers. She had seen it before on the ground, but while in flight the sight was incredible. A complex mechanism under the cowl allowed the hot lead to pass between the spinning wooden blades without touching them. It was unbelievable, and as far as Sandra was concerned, the tech bordered on magic.

The heavy-duty combat rounds slammed along the caravan, ripping the canvas and punching through the contents to hit the ground below. Men and women screamed, mules reared in blind panic, and the last wag exploded into flames. Yes!

Now blasters sounded from the people, and Sandra slipped sideways along an airstream to slide out of range and let them waste precious ammo. After a few moments, the booming stopped and she circled back to speed past the carts once more, now concentrating on the harnessed mules standing in neatly arranged

Get FREE BOOKS and a FREE GIFT when you play the...

LAS VEGAS
GAME

Just scratch off the gold box with a coin. Then check below to see the gifts you get!

YES! I have scratched off the gold box. Please send me my **2 FREE BOOKS** and **gift for which I qualify**. I understand that I am under no obligation to purchase any books as explained on the back of this card.

▶ DETACH AND MAIL CARD TODAY! ▶

366 ADL EF6L   **166 ADL EF5A**
(GE-LV-07)

FIRST NAME   LAST NAME

ADDRESS

APT.#   CITY

STATE/PROV.   ZIP/POSTAL CODE

| 7 | 7 | 7 | Worth TWO FREE BOOKS plus a BONUS Mystery Gift! |

Worth TWO FREE BOOKS!

TRY AGAIN!

Offer limited to one per household and not valid to current Gold Eagle® subscribers. All orders subject to approval. Please allow 4 to 6 weeks for delivery.

double lines. The animals simply collapsed as the hot lead from the Angel stitched across them in crimson fury. Then a second cart exploded into flames, and Sandra pulled back on the joystick to climb high once more before the people below could get off a single shot in reply.

By now, chaos filled the riverbed. A couple of men were on fire, and ran around flapping their arms like headless chickens. A few of the others were trying to throw sand on the two burning carts, having no effect whatsoever on the blaze. Even as Sandra watched, the second wag erupted, sending out a fiery rain. Soon the entire caravan was ablaze, people, carts, mules and dogs. Thrilled, Sandra laughed insanely over the throbbing engine. So it was a shine convoy, eh? Even better! Normally nobody sane would dare to attack a shine wag. One wrong shot and all of the precious cargo would be destroyed. At the very worst, the drivers could hold their own shine hostage with a torch. But the outlanders had simply not considered that somebody would only want the copper tubing, and what better way to get it than to remove the owners by detonating the shine. Blind norad, it was all so easy from up here. So childishly simple!

"I am a god!" Sandra Tregart screamed over the rumbling thunder, as the people below burned and screamed and died.

DODGING THE INCOMING arrows, Ryan fired the Steyr from the hip. The soft-nose 7.62 mm round smacked a cannie in the chest, spinning him, blood going everywhere.

As an arrow slammed into the ground between his legs, J.B. cut loose with the Uzi sending out a hellstorm of hot lead. Then thunder boomed as Doc unleashed the LeMat. The .445 miniball slammed into another cannie, lifting the skinny man off his feet and sending him flying backward over the dune and out of sight.

Triggering his Colt Python, Jak jerked as an arrow hit the collar of his leather jacket. But the slim wooden shaft shattered as it ripped open the leather, exposing the hidden steel blades sewn into the lining. Shifting his aim, Jak returned fire, and a cannie fell minus most of his throat.

Then Krysty screamed in mortal agony as an arrow passed dangerously close to her face and went through her flexing red hair. As several of the animated tendrils fell away, the woman dropped her revolver and collapsed to the ground violently shaking from the waves of unimaginable pain coursing through her entire body.

Drawing the SiG-Sauer, Ryan kept shooting and stepped protectively in front of the shaking woman. The Uzi raking the top of the sand dune, J.B. moved to cover her back, and Doc filled the protective triangle, his LeMat blowing flame and thunder with devastating results.

Acing a cannie notching a fresh arrow into his crossbow, Jak holstered his Colt and pulled out a gren. Arming the charge, the albino teen lobbed it high and it landed right on target just as two more cannies came into view. The newcomers barely had a chance to react when the gren detonated and crest of the dune vanished in deafening report of chemical flame.

As a gritty cloud of sand began to drift to the ground, the companions quickly reloaded and looked around for any more trouble coming their way. But the area seemed to be clear. The tattoo-covered bodies of the fallen cannies lay scattered in various stages of dismemberment. The wags were undamaged, and Ryan was relieved to see that nobody was bleeding badly, but…

"Where the hell is Mildred?" he demanded, feeling his stomach muscles tighten in apprehension.

Caught in the act of slapping a fresh clip into the Uzi, J.B. paused and jerked his head around, then turned, quickly looking for the woman. She was nowhere in sight.

"Millie!" J.B. bellowed at the top of his lungs as the wind blew off his hat. He paid no attention. *"Millie!"*

But there was no answer, the only sounds were the whispering rustle of the shifting sands and the dying crackling of the burning plane.

"Shitfire, this was a suck play!" Ryan realized,

feeling rage boil up inside. "Just a fucking diversion to keep us busy!"

"While they grabbed her," J.B. whispered in shock. The man went pale at the knowledge that the cannies had taken the woman alive. Again. Memories of their last encounter with cannies were so fresh in their minds.

Just then, a sharp whistle cut the air and the companions spun, their weapons at the ready.

"This way!" Jak stated. "They got, but she fighting."

"By the Three Kennedys, if these hellish visigoths dare to harm that sweet lady again—" Doc began.

"Can that crap," Ryan barked, cutting him off. There were enough raw emotions running wild at this point. They had to stay sharp if they wanted to ever see Mildred again.

A startled Doc gave the man a stern look, then nodded in comprehension. Yes, of course. This was a time for the head, not the heart.

"J.B. and Doc, take the Hummers!" Ryan ordered, removing the spent clip from inside the Steyr and ramming home a full one. He worked the bolt to break the seal and chamber a round. "I'll go with Jak. Krysty can… Krysty!"

Wiping her blaster clean, the woman waved that she was okay. Ryan didn't believe that for a moment, but knew she could handle the pain. Having her hair cut was like a person losing a finger. His hand went impulsively to the patch on his face. Almost as bad as losing an eye.

"Krysty, take the bike and cover our six," Ryan urged in a gentler tone. "Can you do that?"

"No prob, l-lover," Krysty said, forcing herself to stand straight. "Let's go get her."

"Enough talk, let's move, people!" J.B. shouted, a touch of panic marring his voice. Scrambling for the black Hummer, the man jumped inside, slammed the door shut and cracked the engine hard until it roared to life, thick smoke pulsing from the exhaust stack on top of the hood.

Still feeling nauseous from the aftereffects of the mutilation, Krysty ignored her pounding temples and clumsily climbed onto the Beamer. She needed two tries to finally get the big engine purring.

Seeing her rattled condition, Doc wanted to offer assistance, but knew better and got into the camou-colored Hummer. The woman had been through a lot worse and survived. Krysty would be fine. He started the engine. And God help the first cannie she ever got her hands on.

"Hey, J.B.!" Ryan called.

Hunched over the steering wheel, the man looked out the open window of the Hummer. "Yeah?"

"Stay sharp, and we'll find her," Ryan said solemnly.

"Bet your ass we will," J.B. snapped, slamming the Hummer into gear and starting to roll forward.

Walking around the dune, Ryan found Jak yards away, moving fast as if trying to keep ahead of the windblown dust filling in the tracks. Wisely, Ryan kept clear of the albino teen and let the hunter do his work. Jak watched the ground, and Ryan watched Jak. Overlapping fields of operation, was what the Trader used to call the tactic. When everybody had somebody's back, then nobody died but the enemy. Stupe coldhearts would just rush into a fight, but trained sec men would move in groups. Five trained people could slaughter thirty disorganized individuals every nuking time.

Slowly and steadily, Jak moved across the shifting sands, his face tight as he tried to follow the confusing trail. Going around a large boulder, the teen reappeared from the other side, frowned and went back to try another path. He started along a different trail, then stopped and picked up some more beads. Mildred had to be pulling them to drop along the way. That was triple-smart, and it helped a lot. But Jak would still have to be careful that the cannies didn't discover what she was doing and have somebody rip out a handful to take off and lay a false trail to nowhere. A storm was coming and the wind was increasing. If he lost the woman now, she was gone forever.

"Sons of bitches mixed up their trail pretty good," J.B. cursed impatiently.

"These bastards hunt norms," Krysty said, riding alongside the Hummer. "They're not stupe."

"They were today," J.B. retorted, tightening his hand on the wheel until his knuckles turned white. "Just like they were the last time they took Millie."

Flinching slightly as the desert breeze riffled her hair, Krysty started to reply when she saw something move near the top of a nearby sand dune. In a rush of adrenaline, she clawed for her blaster, but then realized it was some sort of plant up there. No, those were fronds, the feathery top of bamboo!

Jak was nowhere in sight, but she could see Ryan running in the direction of the bamboo. Revving the Beamer, Krysty raced ahead to join them. Nearing the dune, the loose sand suddenly became much firmer, and the woman spotted dead grass mixed here and there in a patchy carpeting. Soon green grass was pushing through the sand and flowering bushes dotted the land as small grooves of bamboo trees thrust upward to form a natural windbreak.

Slowing the purring bike, Krysty maneuvered through the burgeoning plants, trying to keep a watch on Ryan. She lost him for a second, then Ryan reappeared from break in the swaying bamboo and waved her onward. Easing the motorcycle through the gap in the clacking wall of bamboo, Krysty wasn't surprised to discover a small oasis.

Safe from the ravages of the desert sand, green grass

and flowering bushes spread across the hidden patch of land surrounded by the thick bamboo grove. A large pool of clear water filled the center of the oasis, buzzing bees moving in a dark cloud around a large hive set among the rusted chassis of a predark van. Braking to a halt at the edge of the pool, Krysty could see fish swimming in the water below the lily pads. Gaia! It was as if a small part of the predark world had survived in the very heart of the Deathlands.

Staring intently at the greenery, Jak was moving through the weeds and rushes growing along a bubbling spring that fed the shimmering pool. With his longblaster and handblaster held at the ready, Ryan stayed behind the teen, clearly watching the bushes for any signs of suspicious movements.

From behind, Krysty heard the Hummers arrive and then cut their engines. A moment later J.B. and Doc walked through the small passage in the bamboo having wisely decided not to announce their arrival by nosily forcing the wags through the grove.

Then J.B. stopped dead and thrust a hand into a thorny bush to pull out Mildred's med kit. Having trouble breathing, the man closed his eyes for a moment, then snapped them open and slid the strap of the canvas bag over a shoulder.

"She's here," he stated in a strained whisper, both hands clenching the plastic grip of the Uzi machine pistol.

"Here!" Jak called, touching a crimson stain on a flowering bush. "Fresh split."

As the others started closer, Ryan noticed a ripple of motion in the pool and only caught a brief glimpse of an armed figure before he shot from the hip, the silenced SiG-Sauer coughing gently. Grunting from the impact of the 9 mm round, the naked man rising from the water fired his crossbow, the arrow flashing across the oasis past Doc to slam in the bamboo grove, causing a series of clatters and clacks.

Ruthlessly, Ryan fired again and the cannic dropped the crossbow to splash into the water. Groaning into a sigh, the man stumbled and fell over sideways into weeds along the shoreline. Slowly, a red stain began to spread across the clear water of the pool.

Alert for treachery, the companions gathered around the corpse. Lying sideways in the mud, the man's slack mouth was hanging open, exposing the rows of teeth filed to sharp points. Leanly muscled, his entire body was heavily tattooed in wild designs of swirls, his only clothing a woven belt around his waist supporting a rubbery tube and a sheathed knife.

Spitting out his cigar stub, J.B. aimed his shotgun at the dead man, only to lower the barrel.

"An aquatic assassin," Doc said with a frown. "Do you suppose he was left behind to try to ambush us?"

"Not likely," Ryan replied, pulling the rubber tube from the dead man's belt. There were teeth marks at one end, but not the other.

"This is for staying submerged," Ryan said, scanning the pool.

Below the lily pads and darting fish there was a dark shape that could be an underwater cave. Instantly, Ryan understood the brilliance of the trap. Lots of predators waited for their prey at waterholes. The cannies had merely taken it one step further, and were hiding inside the damn water. When outlanders camped along the lake, the cannies could simply come out at night to gather the sleeping harvest of meat.

"We go swimming," Jak said, sliding off his leather jacket. The garment hit the grass with a muffled clatter.

Dropping the med kit, J.B. slung the shotgun and checked the clip in the Uzi before tucking the rapid-fire into his belt to keep it from flailing around.

As Krysty waded into the shallows, Ryan started to shrug off his lined jacket, then paused to glance at Doc. The man was scowling at the lake, one fist clenched on the grip of his LeMat. Shitfire, he hadn't thought about that. A black-powder wep, the LeMat didn't use shells. Dip the blaster into water and the powder would flow out the sides of the cylinder like black pudding. There were other blasters in the

Hummers, but the time traveler was attached to the Civil War handcannon as if it was blood kin.

"Doc, you stay here and guard the wags," Ryan ordered, transferring a gren from his jacket to the pocket of his pants. "Stay sharp! We may come running."

Slowly nodding, Doc pulled out the monstrous hogleg and clicked back the curved hammer. "None shall pass," the man rumbled in his deep voice.

Taking a huge breath, Krysty submerged and started swimming for the bottom of the pool. The fish weren't frightened by her intrusion, which seemed to imply this sort of thing happened often.

Tucking his glasses into a pocket, J.B. went next, with a knife in his teeth and hate in his eyes.

After tying off his mane of white hair, Jak dived in with hardly a splash, his powerful arms propelling him downward with amazing speed. Filling his lungs, Ryan followed with equal ease.

Standing alone on the shoreline, Doc pulled the long steel blade from inside his ebony cane and took a position where he could watch both the pool and the Hummers outside the bamboo.

The man had already decided to give them an hour, then he would go in after them anyway. There were other blasters in the wags; the M-16 used bullets that were totally water resistant. The LeMat was a precious link to his past, a physical reminder of a peaceful world that still existed, and a loving wife waiting for him somewhere in time. But his friends were equally important, and where they went, so would Theophilus Algernon Tanner.

But for the moment, Doc would wait, and watch, praying to God for their safe deliverance.

Chapter Eleven

Wiggling and kicking furiously, Mildred tried to get loose from her captors, but the two cannies holding her only tightened their grips and gave a guttural laugh. This infuriated the woman, and she struggled even harder, but with the same lack of results.

A strip of cloth was tied around her eyes, and scratchy ropes bound her wrists and ankles. With surprising ease, the men were carrying her like a suitcase, her back constantly bumping into the ground. First sand, and now rock.

Mildred had nearly died when they went under water, and ever since they emerged, the wind and sand were gone, the air oddly cool and echoes came the distance. Obviously they were underground in some sort of a cave, or cavern. In cold logic, the physician knew that wasn't good. John would never stop searching for her, but while Ryan and Jak were both superb trackers, she doubted if even they could find her now. That water entrance trick was sheer genius. Grimly, Mildred had to accept the fact that she was alone in this, unlike last time, and would need to free herself. Somehow.

The ground dipped slightly as the cannies hauled her through some sort of a doorway. In passing, Mildred got a gentle bump on the head, and realized this was her chance. Instantly the woman grunted as loud as she could and went completely limp.

The two cannies tightened their grips in response, then slowed their walking and shook her. It took everything Mildred had to stay slack, letting her head loll sideways, tongue extended. She was blindfolded, but they could see, so she had to make it good. Only had one chance at this.

Come on, boys, Mildred chided mentally. You only want live food. If I die on the way to the table, you're both in dutch with the boss.

With a jarring thump, she landed on the hard ground and gave no response. Mildred heard the two men mumbling angrily in an unknown language. One offered a suggestion that the other shot down. Then he countered with an idea of his own that the first cannie didn't seemed too pleased with. This went on for a few moments, then clearly some sort of decision was reached. The cannie holding her wrists knelt and started feeling her head to search for a wound among her beaded locks, while the one holding her bound ankles started pinching her calf.

Which meant that he had only one hand holding her ropes.

Moving fast, Mildred snapped her head around and buried her teeth into the cannie's hand. He screamed and began slapping her face with his free hand. Mildred swung her bound wrists to find his leg, slid up his hairy thighs and grabbed his genitals to bury her fingernails deep into the soft tissues, then twisted and yanked with every ounce of strength she possessed.

The man shrieked in response. Shouting angrily, the other cannie released her ankles. Moving fast, Mildred brought up her knees and kicked out with both of her boots, heels first. There was a solid connection, the crack of bone and the man screamed in pain.

Releasing the first cannie, Mildred rolled away from the wounded men and clawed the blindfold off her face. She blinked for a few moments to clear her sight, then bitterly cursed as she realized that there was nothing wrong with her. The cavern was pitch-black.

Then, she heard lots of naked feet padding on the rock floor of the cave, and Mildred knew that rein-forcements were arriving. Shit! Bound and blind as she was, there was nothing else for Mildred to try but one last desperate ploy. To attack and try to make them mad enough to kill her fast, instead of the slow torture of being cut apart alive for their hellish meals. Today a leg, tomorrow, an arm, or a breast...

Screaming obscenities, Mildred threw herself

forward and lashed out with her two fists clenched tight. But she encountered only air in her effort, then something hard clunked against the back of her head and she abruptly lost consciousness.

RISING FROM the cool water, the companions slowly walked up the sloping concrete, dipping their weapons to make the water run out of the barrels. They had expected an underground cavern, but this was some sort of a huge predark tunnel. About a dozen yards wide, the floor was a mix of sand and rocks blending into the curved brick walls that topped with a ceiling alive with a softly glowing green moss.

Quickly, Ryan checked the rad counter on his shirt collar, but it read in the neutral. Yeah, that was expected. He had seen such fungus before. It wasn't a mutie plant, just some kind of natural moss that Mildred said worked on photo-something or other, he forgot the word. That didn't matter. The plant gave off a weak light and could be found almost everywhere under the Deathlands.

One heartbeat later, Jak appeared, his .357 Magnum in one hand and knife in the other. The teen looked like a drowned rat with his snowy hair plastered flat to his head, but his red eyes burned with cold hatred. They had all seen what cannies did to their food before finally eating it, and their experience in Louisiana was fresh in their minds. Sometimes the victims were still alive when the slicing commenced, their screams primitive music for the cannies as they feasted upon the flesh.

Krysty pointed at the sand along the shore, and Ryan grunted in reply. It was churned up with barefoot prints, boot prints and red blood.

Just then, an echoing scream came out of the dimly lit tunnel ahead of them, every blaster snapping up and ready.

"That was Millie," J.B. whispered, then screamed, "Millie, we're coming!" He triggered a blast of the shotgun, the flame lighting the tunnel for yards to show an intersection only a short distance away.

"Idiot!" Jak snapped. "All cannies come now!"

"Let 'em!" J.B. snarled, thumbing a fresh cartridge into the S&W M-4000 to replace the one just spent. "I'll take 'em all on!"

Without speaking, Ryan grabbed his friend by the arm and gave a crushing squeeze. Arching an eyebrow, J.B. turned angrily. Then he met Ryan's gaze and let out a breath.

"Sorry," he muttered. "I'm losing it here."

"J.B. It's horrible that Mildred has to go through this again," Krysty said, starting forward. "We understand. Now let's find our friend."

They heard running footsteps, and Ryan raised the SiG-Sauer as the dark figure came into view. But he withheld firing until he saw it wasn't Mildred. He triggered a 9 mm Parabellum round into the face of the cannie. The half-naked man jerked his head as the back of his skull blew out to hit the brick wall in a grisly froth of blood, bones and blood.

The body was still slowly crumpling to the ground when the companions swept past to the intersection.

As the cannie had come from the left, they looked to the right and, sure enough, there was another cannie waiting in hiding there. Armed with a spear, the man seemed startled that he had looked in his direction first, and that was the last thing he ever did before Jak sent him into the blackness of eternity.

Retrieving his knife, the teen saw that the passage behind the corpse was bricked solid. This was just a side passage used to ambush potential invaders.

Then Krysty inhaled sharply and pointed her blaster at a freshly severed human arm hanging from the wall.

"Gaia, is this their food locker?" Krysty demanded in disgust.

"No," Ryan corrected, working the bolt on his rifle. "It's the wall to their ville."

"Good. If these cannies were strong, they would hide this and lure folks in deeper," J.B. agreed in a tight voice.

"But they put this drek here to frighten off would-be rescuers," Ryan continued, starting deeper into the tunnel. "Which means there aren't a lot of them. They're weak, and need tricks for protection."

"Good," Jak snorted, testing the balance of the leaf-bladed throwing knife in his palm.

Starting toward the other tunnel, Ryan stopped to dig a circle in the sand with the heel of his combat boot, then slashed across the sign with the steel-tipped toe. Hopefully, they wouldn't need a marker to get out of the tunnels, but he had fought cannies before in Texas, and their warren had been a maze of passages that was almost impossible to exit.

The brick tunnel extended in a slow curve, only to stop as it opened into a large cave. The place was huge, the ceiling and opposite walls completely out of sight.

"This is concrete," J.B. said, touching the floor. "Mebbe some kind of a predark water reservoir."

"Good place to live in the middle of the desert," Ryan muttered.

Waving a hand, Jak gave a sharp whistle and started across the predark material, bent low as if he were sniffing the trail like a hunting dog. The others stayed close, their sodden clothing making soft squishing noises, their weapons sweeping for viable targets.

Going to the heart of the darkness, Jak slowed at an opening in a concrete wall. As the teen slipped past, a drop of water fell from the blackness above to wetly impact the floor. Ryan and the others were right behind Jak. As they stepped into another tunnel illuminated by green moss, Jak eased the trembling body of a cannie guard to the floor and withdrew his bloody knife from the back of the man's neck.

This tunnel was short and ended in another huge cavern.

"Struggle here," Jak said, sweeping back his damp hair.

"Was it Millie?" J.B. asked, his whole life in the question.

Jak nodded. "Alive, kicking," he replied.

"This way," Ryan stated, studying the floor. Apparently, this deep in their home, the cannies weren't even trying to hide their trail. And why should they? This was safe territory.

Just not this day, the Deathlands warrior added grimly.

The green-tinted darkness flared for a moment as the SiG-Sauer coughed once more, and a body dropped to the ground. Stepping over the trembling corpse, Ryan scowled at the sight of nets stretching between erected posts, dividing the huge cavern into smaller areas. Taking the first turn, Ryan soon saw it was a maze of turns. Fireblast! He had expected this.

Moving through the warren of nets, the companions marked their passage as best as possible until reaching another intersection.

Squinting hard against the dim light, Jak checked the ground but couldn't find any sign of recent travel. He started to report that when a scream split the cavern, followed by callous laughter and the high-pitched wail of a man in mortal agony.

"Not Mildred," Jak said bluntly as he stood. "But he might know where prisoners kept."

"Let's go," the Armorer said calmly, breaking into a run.

Their boots made hard slapping sounds on the predark concrete, but nobody arrived to investigate as they pelted along the roped-off corridors.

Reddish light flared in the distance, and the companions braced themselves as they got close. The layers of netting blocked only pieces of the hellish scene, and none of the screaming. Keyed up for battle, this only spurred them on faster and soon the group dashed around the last net.

The area was a kitchen, with big stone tables lined with battered predark chairs made of rusty chrome and plastic fabric. A dank hole in the corner reeked of human waste, and on the opposite wall was a large man howling in pain, his arms and legs spread out on netting and tied securely in place. A group of laughing cannie women were running the tips of steel knives along his body, slowly cutting off the remains of his tattered clothing and leaving countless tiny cuts in his skin, rivulets of fresh blood trickling into bowls on the floor. Even as the man's crimson-soaked shirt came off, he hawked and spit in the eye of the old woman. But the cannie only laughed harder and reached for his pants.

In a lightning-fast move, Jak flipped his hand and a cannie dropped her knife, gurgling horribly from the throwing blade buried into the back of her throat. As the others turned, Ryan fired twice and two more fell away, life spewing from their punctured hearts.

But the rest separated fast, and an older cannie snarled something in an unknown language. Instantly another reached into a pouch hanging low at her side and threw a hand of the contents upward. As if a switch had been thrown, the green light from the moss winked out, leaving the area in near total darkness.

Moving fast, the companions rushed away from the spot where they had just been so the cannies couldn't find them. J.B. sent a burst from the Uzi into the darkness, the strobing muzzle-flash briefly illuminating the kitchen. A cannie cried out and fell, her sagging breasts pumping out blood from the line of holes across her tattoo-covered skin.

Now, shouts began to sound in the distance, and Ryan knew the hammer had fallen. The alarm was being sounded, and soon every cannie would be rallying to defend their ghoulish ville.

He felt the briefest urge to cut and run, but chilled it with a thought.

"Place your shots!" Ryan commanded, firing twice. "We're not leaving without her!"

Spinning, Krysty fired and cut down a cannie who had been trying to sneak close from behind.

The man clutched his belly and staggered away, mortally wounded, but not aced yet. Krysty forced herself to not finish him off. They were going to need every round. And the very last was reserved for herself.

"Flare!" Jak snapped, firing into the darkness. There was no answering cry of pain, and a few seconds later there came the sound of a ricochet off hard stone.

"Don't have any," J.B. said from nearby. "No, wait, I do!"

There was a rustle of cloth, a scraping sound, and light returned to the cavern in blue intensity. J.B. was holding what looked like a road flare, only the top was a dancing blue flame of unusual strength.

Caught in the light, a young female cannie snarled a war cry and charged, waving knives in both hands. With the pointed teeth and flashing blades, her charge should have paralyzed any person with fear, but Ryan stood his ground and cut the teenage girl down.

"Spear..." the man on the net gasped, his eyes darting to the right.

Her hair flexing madly, Krysty suddenly stepped to the left as a spear came out of the darkness. The shaft went by, just missing her, and Jak ducked under it. They both fired in response, but with no result. Then J.B. triggered a burst from the Uzi and a blood-curdling scream answered.

"Baron…Tregart…?" the prisoner whispered hoarsely.

"We're not from your baron," Ryan snapped, too busy to lie as he fanned the netting with blasterfire. He could only hope the wild shots didn't ace Mildred. "We're after a black woman, short, mil fatigues, beaded hair."

"I…know where…"

Fully aware that the man could be lying just to try to save his own skin, Ryan took the chance and slashed out with the panga to cut away the netting.

Coming free, the big man fell to the floor, landing on top of a dead cannie. Then he rose to his knees with her knife in his hand and proceeded to stab her again and again in the chest.

"Yeah, you like that, slut!" he yelled insanely, fresh blood welling from his own minor wounds at the action. "You want more! Huh? I got ya more, bitch! Now you sing for me! Sing for me!"

Stepping close, Ryan slapped the man across the face, the impact sounding louder than the crack of a longblaster.

"Cut the shit," Ryan snapped. "Take us to our friend, or we'll leave you here alone. Got me?"

As Krysty and J.B. took out another charging group of cannies armed with spears, the big man stared at Ryan in wild fury, then slowly nodded and stumbled to his feet.

"This way," he said, heading across the kitchen to step over another chilled cannie to go out the only opening in the wall-nets.

As the companions followed after the former prisoner, J.B. passed Ryan a half-used flare and started another. Ryan moved to the point position, and J.B. took the rear. They had fought in darkness before and knew the basic tactics. Spread out your lights, don't give the enemy a group target, and keep moving at all costs!

Elsewhere, cannies were shouting orders in their unknown language, and a metal gong began to ring slow and steady.

In the passageway, the nameless man paused, then turned to the left, then quickly to the right again. Ryan had to move fast to keep abreast, but only went a few yards before the former prisoner darted into a side passage. The room inside was lined with dark cloth, rendering it nigh invisible in the dim green light from the ceiling moss. The posts were covered with rusty chains and shackles. There were two prisoners here, and one was Mildred.

Placing aside the flare, Ryan went to work on the lock. J.B. entered the room and gave a wordless cry of delight at the sight of Mildred.

"Kill her," Mildred said in a hoarse voice, looking to her side. "Please…"

"Gaia," Krysty whispered.

Even Jak inhaled sharply at the sight. The other prisoner was a stark-naked woman hanging from her arms, but both of her legs were gone, the horrible stumps scarred with burns obviously made to prevent death from blood loss.

The mindless person in the chains looked at the companions without comprehension, the sad eyes pools of madness, a string of drool dripping from her slack mouth.

"Hush, now, it's all over," Krysty said softly, aiming the hot barrel of her wheelgun to the prisoner's temple. "You are free now."

The woman began to whine in dim understanding and for a split second the madness lifted. "Thank you," the woman said, moving her torn lips, bit no words came.

Without looking away, Krysty stroked the trigger and gave the woman the only freedom that was possible.

"Done," Ryan said, as the last shackle dropped to the ground.

Lurching away from the post, Mildred half fell into J.B.'s arms and the couple embraced for a long moment before finally parting.

"God, I'm happy to see you all!" the physician said with a weary smile. "Now give me a motherfucking blaster! I've had it with cannies."

"Got your six, Millie," J.B. stated, giving her the shotgun. "Four up the pipe, and six on the strap."

"Not nearly enough," Mildred stormed, working the pump-action alleysweeper. "But it'll have to do." Then she registered the newcomer.

"And who the hell is this?" the woman demanded, swinging the scattergun his way.

"Karl," the man replied, standing nervously near the opening in the net that served as a doorway. "Second sec boss for Lady Tregart of Thunder ville. Please, we must leave before—"

A howl cut the cavern, sounding vaguely canine, but with something more added.

"Not dog," Jak stated flatly, furrowing his brow.

"Something mutie," Karl answered, starting to leave. But then his knees buckled and the bloody man slid weakly to the floor.

Passing Krysty the sputtering flare, Ryan grabbed the man by the arm, draped it over his shoulder and stood, carrying most of the weight. Karl reeked of blood and sweat, but there was something else. Machine grease and shine. Was this one of the sec men sent to find the lost drone?

"Start walking," Ryan ordered, moving forward. He'd ask later, if there was a later. This was not the place for a discussion.

Karl weakly grunted in acknowledgment, and did his best to keep pace as Ryan took the middle position in the group.

With Krysty in the lead now, the companions started

for the exit, ruthlessly chilling anything they saw moving. Something vaguely animal-like charged at the group from the other side of a net, and J.B. riddled it with blasterfire. In the concrete cave, a cannie dropped from the ceiling and managed to land among them before Mildred blew off its head with the shotgun.

Reaching the brick-lined tunnel, the companions raced along the sandy floor using Ryan's marks, while J.B. lit a fuse and dropped a homie pipe bomb in their wake. A few moments later, the bomb went off, and a chorus of screams announced that the deadly shrapnel charge of nails had caught several of the cannies. Then the tunnel violently shook, and bricks started raining from the ceiling. As the vibrations steadily increased, the ceiling moss began to fall still attached to chunks of brick and concrete.

Moving fast, the companions raced through the end of the collapsing tunnel and rushed into the water. But at the first contact, Karl gave a shudder and went limp. Muttering a curse, Ryan holstered his piece and slung the big man over a shoulder. Then he pinched Karl's nose and mouth shut before diving into the pool and swimming for the glow of sunlight ahead.

He only hoped Doc was still there, and that they weren't heading straight into another group of cannies.

Chapter Twelve

With a large coil of blackened copper tubing slung over a shoulder, Sandra Tregart started to walk along the dried riverbed toward the Angel when a low ghostly moan sounded over the rustling windblown sand of the desert.

Spinning, Sandra drew a blaster and thumbed back the hammer. Black dust! She had stayed too long and the smell of fresh blood had attracted the attention of some howlers. The muties were on the way right now!

Dropping the precious tubing, Sandra raced for the biplane and jumped into the cockpit, throwing the blaster to the floor. At least her tanks were full again from the few containers of shine that hadn't been burned in the wreckage. But her hands trembled as she swiftly operated the controls and started the propellers sluggishly spinning. *Come on....*

As the 12-cylinder engine fully engaged, the Angel started rolling along the hard ground, and Sandra caught a glimpse of something moving on the raised bank. It was a howler! The head of the mutie was split in two, or maybe there were two heads, along with multiple limbs that writhed bonelessly. It was an accepted fact that howlers ate everything that came their way. They were the scavengers of the Deathlands, and as far as she knew nobody had ever succeeded in chilling one.

As the Angel started to roll forward, the howler moaned louder at the sight and started for the aircraft in renewed speed.

Revving the engine to full power, Sandra held her breath as the biplane went straight past the onrushing howler, its multiple limbs lashing out for the wing. Thankfully, the ropy tentacles missed.

The woman yanked back on the joystick and fought to get the Sky wag airborne. As the wheels left the ground, Sandra let out the breath she had been holding and fell back into the seat.

Climbing high, the woman felt oddly at ease when her growing proximity to the toxic death clouds began to burn her skin and the engine started to falter. She dropped a hundred or so feet until the Angel was running smoothly once more, and then settled to start looking for landmarks to find her way home. The clouds she could understand. Rad and chems were a normal part of life. But she never wanted to see another howler, and made a private vow not to land in the desert again. Ever. Under any circumstances.

Suddenly the woman felt embarrassed and decided

she needed to do something, anything, to take away the bitter taste of defeat. Checking the gauges, Sandra saw that she had enough fuel to do a pass over that nest of stickies down the Ohi River and blow apart that rickety old bridge they used to cross over. Yeah, that sounded triple-smart.

Putting her back to the sun, Sandra settled in for the long flight. And mebbe on the way back she'd strafe the howlers just for good measure! But the thought sent a shiver down her spine.

Then again, mebbe not.

BOLTING UPRIGHT, Karl awoke screaming, his hands clawing at the air.

"Easy now, easy," Mildred said softly, wiping his face with a damp cloth. "You're free now. Out of the caves."

His chest heaving, Karl looked around frantically. He was in the back of a wag, surrounded by boxes and canvas bags. The sand dunes were moving past the windows, and he could feel the vibrations of the engines through the metal floor. Another wag moved alongside the one he was in, the other painted as black as midnight, and a busty redhead was riding some kind of a two-wheel machine. Karl had never seen anything like that before.

Checking his wrists, the man saw bloody cloths there, and realized that they were bandages. He really was free, and alive. Incredible!

"Did…" His voice cracked and a coughing fit took the man.

Taking the top off a canteen, Mildred passed it over and the man took a long draft. His eyes went wide at the taste, and he slowed, savoring it, a small trickle of the excess brew flowing down his chin.

"Blast me to hell," Karl said, finally lowering the canteen. "Clean water. Like that mountaintop snow we once melted. Got no taste of iron, or nothing. Haven't had that for years."

"There's more if you want," J.B. said from the passenger seat of the moving Hummer, thumbing fresh rounds into an empty clip for the Uzi. "Food, too, if you think you can stomach any."

The very idea of eating made his stomach rebel, and Karl vehemently shook his head.

Sitting behind the steering wheel, Ryan gave no reaction to the expected response.

"You got me free?" Karl asked, gingerly touching the strips of white cloth binding his chest. They were damp with something that smelled like shine. What was the purpose of that?

"Yeah," Ryan said, steering around a bunch of cactus plants. "Seemed the thing to do."

"Did Baron Tregart send you?" Karl asked slowly. "You folks mercies?"

Ryan only grunted in reply. Doc and Jak were in the black Hummer just to the side, with Krysty covering the point in the BMW motorcycle. It seemed to Ryan that she was checking the dashboard a lot, but gave no other sign that there was anything wrong with the two-wheeler.

"What ville are you from?" Mildred asked, capping the canteen.

"Thunder ville," Karl replied with a touch of pride. "Got us the best damn baron in the world! Why she…"

Suddenly alert to the look of concentration in their faces, Karl cut off his talking.

"Where you folks from?" he asked.

"Doesn't matter. Just around," J.B. replied, tucking the clip into his munitions bag and starting to fill another. "So what can this baron do?"

"Nothing special," Karl muttered, then glanced out the rear window. He caught a fleeting glimpse of the green oasis and swaying groove of bamboo trees before they were gone.

"Where are you—we going?" Karl asked nervously.

"Away from here," Ryan replied. "The cannies must have a back door and they're going to be looking for some payback." Then he added, "Know any way across the Ohi River?"

"The Ohi?" Karl asked, titling his head. "Not for war wags this big. What's on the other side? Your ville?"

"Something like that," Mildred answered, and told how they got across in the first place.

The man was impressed. "Blew a bridge to make

a bridge?" Karl laughed, then stopped and touched his chest. "Triple-smart. Well, if you're trapped on this side anyway, take me back to Thunder ville. Lady Tregart will pay a lot to get me back."

"Takes care of her own, eh?" Ryan asked.

"We are her children," the man said in an odd tone. "We would die for her."

"Well, we got no objection to making some extra jack," J.B. lied smoothly, glancing in the rearview mirror to lock eyes with Mildred. She gave a silent nod.

"Sounds like a deal," Ryan affirmed. "So how do we get there?"

Karl gave him directions, then settled against the soft canvas bags, allowing himself to relax while listening to the sound of the predark engine. His mission had been to find the Demon so that it could be destroyed. That had been done. Now he should return to Thunder ville, but the man wasn't sure how happy Lady Tregart would be about him arriving with a heavily armed group of outlanders. True, they had saved his life. But even warring barons saved each other's sec men from cannies if it was possible. And he had shown them where their friend was hidden. Had he already paid his debt, or did he owe them more service? Just how much was his life worth?

Starting to drift asleep, the exhausted man awoke with a start as the war wag rolled off the shifting sands and dropped a few feet onto a dried riverbed.

"Already?" Karl asked, stiffly sitting upright. "That can't be. Took us all day on horseback to get here."

"You've been gone for an hour," Mildred said, rubbing some sort of cream on her chaffed wrists. "And these Hummers, er, these wags go a hell of a lot faster than a horse."

"Guess so," Karl murmured uneasily. "We got wags, but nothing like these."

"Not even the baron?" J.B. asked, forcing himself to look out the window.

"It's almost like we're flying," Ryan said from the front seat, shifting to a higher gear.

Karl started to reply, when J.B. worked the bolt on his Uzi. For a split second, Karl thought the man was going to ace him, but then saw that he was staring at something they had just passed on the raised bank. When Karl looked, there was nothing in sight.

"Dark night," J.B. whispered, adjusting his wire-rimmed glasses. "What the nuking hell was that?"

"Didn't get a recce," Ryan said, checking the mirror. "Was it a stickie? Or have the cannies found us?"

The Armorer gave a shudder. "I have no idea," he muttered.

"Hey, look there!" Mildred said, pointing straight ahead.

Smoke was rising from over the horizon, and as the motorcycle and two Hummers raced closer the companions could see some dark objects on the ground.

"Somebody got jacked," Ryan said gruffly as they drove by at 60 mph.

"I recognize that equipment," Mildred said slowly as the wreckage receded behind them. "Those were homemade distillation units."

J.B. frowned. "A shine convoy?" he asked. "Who would bomb that? You'd lose all the juice!"

"Copper tubing," Karl said, his voice faltering. "They must have been hauling tubing. She wanted more, and so just aced them and took it." The man scowled. But the outlanders were not the enemies of Thunder ville. How could they be? Shine merchants were traders, not coldhearts.

"Your baron did this?" Ryan asked pointedly.

Dumbly, Karl nodded, his thoughts swirling.

"The one with the biplane?" J.B. asked, pushing.

Startled, the man stared at the Armorer. "How do you know that word?" Karl demanded.

Before anybody could answer, the black Hummer sounded its horn in warning, and Krysty slowed the Beamer to drive alongside Ryan in the camou-colored Hummer.

"Get sharp, lover!" the redhead said, gesturing forward with her chin. "From this distance I don't think they're norms!"

Checking the SiG-Sauer at his side, Ryan agreed. There was a group of humanoids walking down the middle of the riverbed a short ways ahead of them.

Or at least, they were the right height for norms, but aside from that Ryan really couldn't make out any details. It was the damnedest thing, the things seemed to be smoking, or surrounded by some kind of mist that traveled along with them, which made no nuking sense at all.

"Those are howlers!" Karl cried, leaning out the side window. "Turn around! Run for your lives! Don't let them get close!"

And this from a man who had spit in the eye of a cannie cutting him up for dinner? Ryan wondered.

"Incoming!" Ryan shouted, and hit the horn a fast three times.

As Krysty pulled out her blaster and peeled away, Jak accelerated the other Hummer and Doc leaned out the window to level his LeMat. The black-powder weapon roared like thunder, but a howler only staggered from the .445 miniball, then lashed out with its collection of tentacles.

Veering wildly, Jak slammed the Hummer into the embankment to get away. But there came a crunch of metal, and incredibly the detachable roof came off to fall behind, still in the grasp of the misty howler.

Immediately, J.B. cut loose, but the 9 mm rounds of the rapid-fire had even less effect on the writhing howlers.

Crouching on the Beamer, Krysty weaved through the middle of the howlers, her bike popping up on its rear wheel for a moment as a howler grabbed her saddlebags. Machine and mutie battled for only a split second until the straps burst. As the bags went flying, Krysty streaked away.

"Our turn," Ryan muttered, shifting gear.

"Floor it!" Mildred barked, pulling out her revolver. Then she reached into one of the trading sacks and thrust something at Karl. "Here! Cover the other side!"

Looking down, Karl was astonished to see that he was now holding a blaster. The outlanders had armed him in their midst? Clumsily pulling back the hammer, Karl clutched the big-bore weapon in both hands and watched as the impossible things rushed their way. He would wait until the very last second before shooting, to not waste a single precious charge of ammo.

But then the man felt his stomach lurch at the sight of them, and shut his eyes tight before frantically pulling the trigger nonstop. Chill 'em! Gotta chill 'em all!

J.B. dropped the Uzi to the floor and swung up the shotgun, racking the slide to blow 12-gauge hellfire at the howlers.

Banking sharply, Ryan sent the Hummer into a skid and went sideways past the howlers, just missing ramming one. As the other muties rushed closer, he braked and shifted gears, suddenly going backward and straight past them. Furious over the trick, the howlers lunged after the escaping prey, but it was too late. Ryan pressed the gas pedal all the way down to the floorboards, and the big Hummer rocketed backward along the riverbed, rapidly building speed.

As the howlers receded into the distance, Ryan applied some brake, and swung the Hummer around to point forward once more. Changing gears, he started driving again, and soon caught up with the other companions. With their pale hair streaming in the wind, Doc and Jak appeared extremely unhappy about losing their roof, and Krysty was hunched low over the handlebars of the BMW as if the howlers were still in hot pursuit. The entire rear fender of the Beamer was gone, the spinning tire now completely exposed.

Keeping a safe distance, Ryan pulled alongside the woman, and Krysty gave him a nod to let Ryan know she was okay.

"That was close," J.B. exhaled, pushing fresh rounds into the scattergun. "What did you call those again?"

"Howlers," Karl said, slumping into his seat, the blaster cradled in both hands. "Very bad."

"Howlers? They weren't quite like howlers we've encountered before!" J.B. told him.

"Good thing we're in wags, 'cause they move faster than most norms can run."

Suddenly, Ryan craned his neck to look around the inside of the Hummer. "Fireblast, now what?" he demanded angrily, easing on the gas. "What's making that buzzing sound? Did the wag take damage?"

Buzz? Karl became alert at that, but said nothing.

Sounding the horn, Ryan braked to a stop and got out to inspect the Hummer. Swinging around, the others returned to park nearby.

"Trouble?" Jak asked, one arm hanging out of the wag with the Colt in his fist.

"Not sure yet," Ryan said, pulling the SiG-Sauer to crouch and warily check under the vehicle.

Easing to a halt between the two wags, Krysty killed her bike, pushed down the kickstand and gratefully slid off the machine.

"Good thing we stopped," the redhead said, hurriedly opening her canteen and liberally pouring the water all over her clothing. "I'm almost out of juice."

"Already?" Ryan asked, raising his head.

"Fuel line got torn open when that thing…"

"Howler," Karl supplied.

Capping the empty canteen, she nodded. "Right. When the howler that didn't quite seem like a howler ripped off my fender. Been leaking gas for the last mile. I'm soaked to the skin."

"Better change your clothes, just in case you need to use a blaster," Ryan warned. There was no smell from the condensed fuel, but even with the water diluting it, the slightest spark could turn the woman into a human torch.

"Change into what?" Krysty asked, gesturing at the rear of the bike where her backpack used to be attached.

"Think I have some stuff you can fit into," Mildred said, climbing out of the Hummer. Opening the back, she pulled out a duffel bag and started removing clothing. "Shirt might be a little tight, but the pants should be okay."

"I'll fix that fuel line," J.B. said, swinging open the door and stepping down. "Jak, keep a watch for any more howlers."

"Got your back," the teen said, already facing in that direction.

"Do you need a hand, John Barrymore?" Doc queried, rising from the other Hummer.

Getting a tool kit from the Hummer, J.B. snorted in reply. "You better start lashing down everything," he said, "or else you'll start losing supplies at every bump."

"Quiet!" Ryan ordered, pulling his blaster. "There it is again."

Now everybody started looking around as the strange buzzing sound returned once more.

"Keep an eye on the sky," Mildred suggested as something flew out from behind a mesa to streak directly along the riverbed.

"Son of a bitch!" J.B. swore. "That's it! What I saw before!"

"A plane," Ryan stated, taking a step in that direction before stopping himself. They had just been in its shadow a heartbeat ago, and already the Sky wag seemed far out of blaster range. Nuking hell, just how fast did the thing go?

Gathering together, the companions watched as the biplane streaked above the riverbed, following its every curve. Just then a group of howlers appeared from around a bend, and the little plane dived toward them.

A few seconds later, a powerful explosion ripped the ground apart and the muties were engulfed in a fiery detonation. As the inhuman bodies fell sprawling to the riverbed, the biplane circled around only to swoop low and strafe the howlers with what sounded like large-caliber rapid-fire.

"That your baron?" Ryan asked, holstering his piece.

"Yes!" Karl cried joyously. Running forward, he waved his empty blaster at the biplane. "Lady Tregart! Down here! My lady, I'm down here!"

Abruptly changing direction, the two-winger headed directly for the shouting man. Then the riverbed began to kick up little geysers of dust in a neat double-row coming straight for the startled Karl. With a cry, the man fell over, red blood spraying out from his wounds.

"You fucking feeb, she thinks you were attacking her!" Ryan yelled, moving away from the Hummers. "Everybody run for cover!"

The companions frantically scattered as the twin row of bullet holes stitched across the dried mud to hit the vehicles. The rounds ricocheted off the

armored chassis of the black Hummer, but tore apart
the inside of the coverless Hummer. With a whoosh,
the spare can of fuel ignited and the wag erupted into
a fireball, throwing out a halo of burning debris.

As the flaming wreckage rained down around the
companions, they pulled out blasters and started
shooting. But if their barrage of hot lead had any
effect upon the Sky wag, it wasn't readily apparent
as the little plane climbed higher into the sky and
vanished from sight.

Chapter Thirteen

Lowering her blaster, Mildred cracked the cylinder and started to reload. "By God, a biplane," she said in astonishment. "I still can't believe it."

"What kind is it, Millie?" J.B. asked, swinging the Uzi machine pistol around behind his back. Pulling out his Navy longeyes, the man scanned the sky.

"'Kind?'" she repeated, frowning, pocketing the spent brass. "Hell, I don't know, John. Those things disappeared long before my time."

"Great."

"Now, there was a cartoon strip with one and they called it a Sopwith Camel," Mildred added hesitantly. "But I honestly don't know if that was a joke or its real name. And I recall something about farms using them to dust crops."

"Dust the crops?" Jak asked.

"To kill the bugs eating the plants," she explained. "Dust meant kill in those days." Then again, Mildred realized, that was what the crop dusters had been doing. Dust always seemed to mean kill, even in the old Western movies. How odd.

"Anything else?" Ryan asked, working the bolt on his Steyr SSG-70 rifle.

Mildred shrugged. "I'm sorry, when I flew in planes, they were jetliners, bigger than ten war wags, and crossed the whole continent in a few hours." She pointed skyward. "That little thing would have rattled around loose in the cargo hold on a 747 jumbo jet."

A groan sounded from Karl, lying on the broken ground.

"He alive?" Jak asked, sounding incredulous.

"Mildred, go see what you can do," Ryan directed, slinging the longblaster.

While the rest of the companions continued arming, Mildred grabbed her med kit from the black Hummer and rushed over to the fallen man.

"Fireblast!" Ryan snapped, pulling out the SiG-Sauer and checking the clip. Two rounds remaining inside. Rummaging in a pocket, he found some loose shells and started pressing them into the clip.

The burning Hummer exploded once more, spraying out hot shrapnel.

"Ain't no jolt dream," Jak said darkly, holstering his Colt Python.

"Indeed, not," Doc agreed, using his teeth to work the pull string on a bag of powder before tucking it away.

Kneeling by the groaning Karl, Mildred saw that

the man was cradling his left arm. Gently, she pried away his fingers and inspected the wound.

"Oh, this is nothing serious," she said with a smile, using her best bedside manner. "See? The lead went clear through. No arteries are hit, and the bone is intact. You were lucky."

Karl grunted.

"This could have been a lot worse," Mildred continued, opening her bag to pull out some bandages and a bottle of shine. "Now, this will hurt."

"Life is pain," Karl muttered in a flat voice, his face going strangely immobile.

As Mildred washed and cleaned the wound, she studied his blank expression. Yes, she had unfortunately seen that look before on slaves who were constantly whipped by their taskmasters. The poor bastards had learned to disconnect their minds and think about something else while they were being brutalized. It was the hard face of animal survival.

"Why did the one-eyed man..."

"Ryan," she supplied, wrapping the wound with a clean bandage.

"Yes, Ryan. Why did he ask you about the Angel?" Karl asked hesitantly. "Are you a healer, or a whitecoat?"

"A little of each." Mildred smiled, draping the sling over his neck.

"You know old tech?" he asked, sounding surprised.

"I know some," Mildred replied, helping the man stand. His legs were wobbly, and she could see that his brief rest in the Hummer had been nowhere near enough. Karl needed food, and sleep, in that order. And pretty damn quick.

Rubbing his wounded arm, Karl stared at the woman. "You're an Old One?" he asked, a tremor of fear marking his voice.

"No, I just learned some stuff," Mildred lied as she helped him walk back to the Hummer.

Ryan walked once around the black Hummer, pleased to see that it was merely badly dented in spots, but otherwise not seriously damaged. A window was cracked and the right-side rear door refused to open, but that was about it. Good. If they shifted some of the supplies out of the rear section, the one wag would be able to carry everybody.

"How's the bike?" Ryan shouted, turning.

Krysty stood from behind the Beamer. "Not a scratch," she told him, dusting off her hands. "Although the fuel tank is now completely drained." She pointed to a muddy puddle on the ground that shimmered with rainbow colors.

"Dark night, I never did get a chance to fix that before," J.B. said, heading for the motorcycle. "Jak, grab a can of fuel!"

"Aces," the teen replied in agreement, going to the rear of the Hummer and pulling out a sloshing canister.

Warily, Ryan walked closer to the burning wag and shook his head. All of that fuel and trade goods gone. They could probably scav something when the flames died out, but that would take hours. He glanced at the sky. It would be night soon, and Ryan wanted to be moving long before it got dark just in case there were any more of those odd howlers around.

Tightening the cap on the fuel tank, Jak gave a thumbs-up.

"Okay, let's give it a try," J.B. said, sitting on the Beamer. He twisted the ignition switch and the engine came alive with a gentle purr.

"Thanks for the fix, but somebody else can use that thing," Krysty said, crossing her arms. "I'll ride in the wag this time."

"Why, dear lady?" Doc asked, leaning on his ebony stick.

"The bike engine runs hot, and I don't want to risk touching that hot exhaust with my damp clothing."

"No prob. Mine now," Jak declared with a grin, running a pale hand along the sleek two-wheeler.

"Fine by me." Krysty smiled, then her red hair fanned out in every direction and she felt her heartbeat quicken. Inhaling sharply, the woman felt her every nerve tingle for a moment, and then the sensation of danger was gone, vanished like a dream at dawn.

"Something?" Jak asked frowning.

"Mebbe," she said softly, resting a hand on her blaster. "You know about my powers, they come and go."

A soft buzz came to them on the desert breeze, only to disappear then return in a moment louder and stronger.

"By the Three Kennedys!" Doc cursed, starting to draw his sword, and then slamming it back again. "That accursed biplane has returned!"

"Everybody into the Hummer!" Ryan shouted, shrugging the Steyr into his hands. He worked the bolt and scanned the sky. "We can't fight her on open ground!"

Grabbing his hat, J.B. pelted for the black Hummer, with Krysty close behind. Tying his long hair into a ponytail and stuffing it under the collar of his leather jacket, Jak climbed onto the Beamer and started the motor.

"Move it or lose it, son," Mildred said, sliding a shoulder under the armpit of the wounded man to hurry him along.

"But I am her loyal sec man," Karl finished lamely. "Lady Tregart would not harm me!"

"I know what you are," Mildred said in a whisper. "And your lady has already tried to ace you once."

Going pale, Karl had no answer to that, and meekly followed her lead into the rear of the

Hummer. As he slumped into a seat, Mildred handed him the weapon he'd dropped.

"You're with us, or with her," she ordered brusquely. "Now make your choice!"

Breathing hard, the man stared at the blaster and ammo in his hands, clearly unable to decide what to do.

Moving fast, Doc started throwing out boxes of supplies from the rear of the Hummer to make additional room, then climbed in through the opening and closed the hatch. Sliding behind the steering wheel, Ryan was gunning the engine alive, Krysty was in the passenger seat, her S&W Model 640 in one hand and the M-16 assault rifle in the other. The rapid-fire was down to its last few rounds, with no replacement ammo, but the longblaster had a much greater range than her short-barreled handblaster.

"The Veri pistol!" J.B. shouted suddenly from the rear seat. "If the flares still work, those can easily ace the bitch!"

"Great! Where is it?" Ryan demanded over a shoulder.

As the buzzing got steadily louder, J.B. frantically looked at bags in the rear of the Hummer, boxes scattered on the ground and the burning wreckage of the other wag.

"Damned if I know!" The Armorer cursed in frustration.

"Fireblast!"

Casting a worried look at the sky, Jak revved the bike and impatiently waited for the others to get moving. What was taking so damn long?

"Ryan, what arc wc waiting for?" Doc demanded from the cargo compartment. "Speed is our armor!"

"Not yet," the one-eyed man muttered, working the clutch and gearshift. Then a shadow moved across the windshield.

Without another word, Ryan slammed the gas pedal to the floor and took off in a spray of dust. A sharp whistle built and a few seconds later something impacted the ground where they had just been parked to violently explode. The shock wave slapped the Hummer hard, almost forcing Ryan into the embankment. It took all of his strength to regain control and get back into the middle of the riverbed.

"Molotov my ass, that was TNT!" J.B. stormed, watching the brownish cloud of dust thin out to reveal a gaping crater in the soil yards across. "If one of those babies hit us, we're vapped!"

Leaning out the window, Krysty fired a single round from the M-16 at the sky. The little plane circled, the soft buzz coming and going on the warm breeze.

Yanking the steering wheel back and forth, Ryan sent the Hummer zigzagging down the riverbed. After a few moments he hit the gas and raced straight for a while, before braking hard and swinging randomly left and right again. Speed was their only armor; Doc sure had that one right.

Suddenly, Jak zipped past the Hummer on the motorcycle, then swung past in front of the wag and dropped behind it.

"Can we outrun her?" Doc demanded, worrying the silver handle of his stick. The LeMat was a deadly weapon, but its range was pitifully insufficient against an enemy who flew. There was nothing he could do to help in the current crisis.

Mildred frowned. "No way in hell," she stated flatly.

Lowering the side window, J.B. sent a short burst skyward. The hot brass arched from the flickering ejector port and hit the ceiling of the Hummer to ricochet to the floor with almost musical ringing sounds.

"Any smoke grens?" Krysty asked, triggering the M-16 until the bolt snapped back, showing it was empty. Dropping it to the floor, she raised her revolver in both hands and tried again.

"In the other wag," J.B. said, squinting and firing another burst.

Responding to the adrenaline of battle, Karl started to load his borrowed blaster, but then lowered the weapon. Even to save his own life he couldn't do it. The man couldn't shoot at his lady. Mebbe she didn't know he was among the outlanders. Or maybe she was trying to save him from torture. But his life was hers, and he couldn't fight back.

Tears flowed down his cheeks as Karl dropped the revolver and slumped in the seat, uncaring of how the battle ended.

Slapping in a fresh clip, J.B. stared at the sec man as if he were insane, but Mildred understood the conflict of emotions he had to be suffering. Eunuchs often fixated on their masters, and Karl had been beaten down for so long he couldn't strike back any more than a whipped dog. Tregart had truly taken away his manhood, and Mildred felt a true hatred for the lady baron.

A whistle sounded once more, and Ryan raced for the embankment. Jak got out of the way and leaped ahead. Just before ramming the soil, he veered straight across the riverbed for the opposite side. The whistle grew loud and terminated in a thundering blast just ahead of the Hummer, a rain of debris and shrapnel falling to pepper the wag.

Savagely turning the wheel, Ryan skirted the blast crater, barely missing slipping inside by inches. Damn, the bitch was good with those bombs! Unfortunately, until they reached open ground, the Hummer and bike were trapped like bullets in the barrel of a blaster, with nowhere to go but straight ahead. Easy meat for this Tregart and her skybombs.

"Krysty!" Doc shouted urgently, extending an arm and snapping his fingers for attention. "The Steyr!

Ryan's longblaster! Give it to Mildred so that she may clip the wings of this diabolic Icarus!"

Looking sideways, Krysty blinked, but Mildred got the idea.

"After Ryan, I'm the best shot," the physician said, hefting her Czech ZKR wheelgun. "But these short-barrels are useless against a plane. Only that rifle has the range to hit the Angel!"

"Take it!" Ryan shouted, driving with both hands.

Reaching out, Krysty undid the strap and pulled the Steyr free. As she passed it to Mildred, a sharp whistle came from directly behind the racing Hummer, and a fireball blossomed in their wake, the halo of debris striking the rear of the armored wag sounding like winter hail.

"Just stones and dirt," J.B. said grimly. "But if that plas had been packed with nails…" He decided not to finish the thought.

Wrapping the strap around her forearm to help steady her aim, Mildred clicked off the safety and worked the bolt on the SSG-70 sniper rifle. Looking through the telescopic sight, she altered the focus and tried to ignore her sweating palms.

"Mebbe she's out," Krysty said, biting a lip. "How many bombs does she carry on board that thing?"

There was no answer from the man in the back seat.

"Karl!" she demanded loudly. "How many bombs?"

"A dozen," he whispered, as if the information had been torn out of his living guts. "Sometimes more."

Krysty frowned at that. Then Tregart had plenty left. Damn!

"I'm ready," Mildred said in artificial calm, tying off her riot of beaded plaits with a handkerchief.

"Just a few more ticks," Ryan breathed through grit teeth, sending the Hummer all over the riverbed.

The black wag and Jak wove a tapestry of misdirection along the ground, constantly changing their speeds and directions.

The Angel passed by overhead, but didn't drop anything this time, clearly unable to zero in on a target. Slowly, Ryan was starting to get a feel for this new enemy. The biplane seemed to have a lot of good points—he had never seen anything move so fast—but it wasn't very maneuverable. It could only attack in straight lines and gentle curves. That gave the wag and bike a telling advantage. But was it enough?

Reaching a smooth stretch of dirt, Ryan eased up on the gas and held a steady course. The riverbed looked rough up ahead, so this might be their last chance.

"Do it," Ryan ordered tensely.

From above the buzzing began to get louder, and then suddenly swelled in volume as J.B. slammed open the Hummer's roof panel. Spreading her legs wide for a better stance, Mildred stood and raised the longblaster to try to find the tiny speck moving in the orange sky. The roiling clouds behind the biplane made it difficult for her to get a clear sighting, then the handkerchief came loose and her beaded hair whipped madly around her face.

Suddenly there were multiple flashes of fire from the shadowy plane, and Mildred knew the pilot was firing that big blaster again. Good.

Shifting her aim to slightly behind the sputtering bright flowers, Mildred held her breath and quickly squeezed off all five shots, working the bolt as fast as she could.

There seemed to be no reaction. No puff of smoke, no explosion of flame. As she started to calmly reload the weapon, the Angel abruptly swung aside and headed out into the desert. Chambering a round, Mildred waited expectantly, but the Sky wag kept going this time until it dwindled into a speck from the sheer distance.

Dropping back into her seat, the physician exhaled and released the longblaster as J.B. closed the roof.

"Well, she's gone," Mildred said, freeing her arm from the canvas strap. "But she can come back at any time."

"Do any damage?" Krysty asked.

"I don't think so," Mildred replied honestly. "Maybe I scared her off."

"Highly unlikely, madam," Doc said in a somber tone. "Old pilots and bold pilots, remember?"

"You think she was just being cautious?"

"Yes."

"We'll know soon enough," Ryan added as the Hummer started shaking over the rough terrain. If the wag had hit this only a few minutes ago, they would all have bought the farm today. Timing, everything was timing.

"Gotta find someplace with cover," Ryan said, slowing their speed to ease the bouncing. "Any forests around here?"

Mildred nudged the man next to her with an elbow.

"Forests?" Karl said in a slur, as if drunk. Then he pointed to the north. "Yeah, sure. There's some heavy green that way. A half day's ride on horseback."

Ryan mentally translated that into about eighty miles. Say, less than two hours in the wag.

"North it is," he decided. Slowing the Hummer to a crawl, he started working the wag up the sloped side of the embankment.

Coming to a halt, Jak pulled out his blaster and nervously waited for the Hummer to reach the crest and send down the towline. This peaceful-looking riverbed was really not someplace that he wanted to be left alone in for any length of time.

CLAMPING A HAND on her bleeding leg, Sandra tried to hold the joystick steady. She couldn't believe they had hit her with a longblaster! It was incredible! There she had been diving in for the chill, when something burst through the fuselage and her leg suddenly felt as if it had been smashed with a white-hot club.

Pulling off her scarf, the woman tied a tourniquet around the wound, the pressure making it hurt even worse. Black dust, those outlanders were going to pay for this! Along with that traitorous little bastard, Karl. She had trusted the eunuch with her life, and he turned on her at the first opportunity! The stinking yellowguts better start running now, because if she ever got her hands on him not even the dogs would eat his carcass once she was done.

Studying the world below, Sandra tried to locate one of the landmarks on her chalk map, but nothing seemed familiar. Suddenly, her skin began to itch and she glanced upward to see the roiling chem clouds dangerously close. Nuking hell!

As thunder boomed, shaking the Angel with its strident peal, Sandra eased the biplane into a level flight, and began to carefully descend. The winds were tricky this high up, she had to stay alert for downdrafts that could flip the Angel over or simply tear it apart like a child plucking the wings off a fly.

Slowly, the pins-and-needles sensations went away. Sighing in relief, the woman gently rubbed a hand on her aching leg. She had to stay awake. But there was a growing cold in her belly, and she knew that wasn't good. She had lost a lot of blood, and needed to land as fast as possible.

With a shout, Sandra started awake as the Angel clipped a wheel off the rocky ridge surrounding the crater. Home! She had made it home!

Dropping fast, too fast! She fought the plane back up and tried to level it out. Bouncing the wheels off the smooth ground, Sandra clutched the joystick in both hands and struggled to fight through the growing fog in her mind. Sleepy, she was so sleepy…

No! She had to stay awake! Biting her lower lip until drawing blood, Sandra used the pain to keep herself conscious long enough to turn the biplane into the wind, drop the flaps and kill the engine.

In the distance, a group of sec men came running from the tents. Carter was in the front, armed with a longblaster. The rest of the workers were carrying plastic buckets full of sand in case the Angel burst into flames.

As the machine coasted along the ground, Sandra slumped over in the wicker seat and finally allowed herself to fall into a warm velvety blankness that seemed to have no bottom.

Chapter Fourteen

Maintaining his grip on the steering wheel, and a death watch on the sky, Ryan didn't relax until they were driving underneath the thick canopy of the northern forest.

If Lady Tregart wanted them now, she would have to send in sec men on horseback, and that was simply not going to happen. According to Karl, the ville was just recovering from a famine, and the sec men were down to about twenty. Mebbe thirty in total, twenty walking the wall around Thunder ville and a dozen in the armed camp around Lady Tregart's workshops and the Angel. Now that sounded like a major hardsite. For all intents and purposes, those were two different villes.

Night had fallen, so Ryan and Jak were using the headlights to drive through the dense forest. Everybody knew that would reveal their position from above, but according to Mildred's best guess, Tregart probably couldn't fly at night. She needed landmarks to find her way to a target and back again. Apparently, nobody at Thunder ville had ever heard of a compass. That was bad news for Lady Tregart, good news for the companions.

Going around a clump of bushes and then over a fallen log, Ryan noticed a silvery light ahead through the foliage. Slowing, Ryan could see the overhead coverage stopped at the edge of a wide grassy field. Coming to a halt, Ryan set the brake and exited the wag, longblaster in hand. Krysty, J.B. and Mildred were right behind, with Doc grunting as he unfolded himself from the cramped cargo compartment. Slumped over against the closed window, Karl was asleep, occasionally twitching from something disturbing in his troubled dreams.

A few seconds later Jak parked alongside the black Hummer and killed his headlights. The nuke batteries would supply power almost forever, but the lamps had a limited life and needed to be conserved whenever possible.

Walking almost to the edge of the woods, the companions studied the wide-open vista of flatland spreading in front of them to the horizon. Illuminated by the moon the friends saw a field of dried grass. A few trees were scattered here and there, and there was a small pond with what looked like a salt lick nearby, but not much else.

"Looks safe," Jak declared.

Krysty rested a hand on Ryan's neck and gently

massaged the knotted muscles. "We'll make camp here," she decided bluntly. "We can always drive back into the deep woods for cover if necessary."

"We got any MREs?" Ryan asked, his stomach loudly rumbling.

"For a couple of meals, sure."

"Any heats?" Jak asked eagerly.

Mildred shook her head. "Nope. It's just stew and spaghetti tonight."

"Had worse," the teen said with a shrug.

Going back to the wag, Ryan killed the headlights but not the amber parking lights, to offer some illumination. With Krysty standing guard, Mildred gently woke Karl, as Doc and Jak dug out the MRE food packs from the rear compartment. J.B. had unearthed the remaining fuel cans and topped off the bike before pouring the last of the condensed fuel into the tank of the Hummer.

Checking the dashboard, Ryan frowned at the gauge. "Less than half a tank," he reported. "That's not good."

"We lost a lot of juice when the other Hummer got bombed," J.B. said, straightening his fedora. "Going to be a long walk back to the—" he cast a glance at Karl "—place where we first got it," J.B. finished lamely.

"Any sign of that Veri pistol?" Ryan asked hopefully, studying the interior of the vehicle.

"Not so far."

"Let's check everything."

"Sounds good."

The two men went to work, but after several minutes of opening bags and boxes, looking under the seats and inside sleeping bags, it was soon painfully clear that the flare gun wasn't present. Their best weapon against the Angel had been destroyed with the other Hummer.

Hunger finally drove the two men to join the others. The Trader had always said that empty bellies made empty heads. They would think better on a full stomach.

There was a chill to the evening air, so the companions had spread their bedrolls on the ground and formed a circle in front of the Hummer to savor the heat radiating from the grille. Everybody had jackets except for Karl, so the sec man used the new knife he had been given to cut a slit in a blanket to make himself a crude poncho, tying a spare piece of rope around his waist to cinch it shut.

The MREs were passed around, and Karl stared in wonder at the Mylar envelopes as the others took their choice, leaving him the last pack. Hesitantly, he took the pack and held it unsure of what to do next. He had eaten canned goods before, but nothing like this.

"So, what do we do?" he started. "Mix them all together, or…"

"That's your share," Krysty said. "We each get our own."

With half of his scarred face frowning, Karl stared

at the envelope in frustration. There were symbols on the material—letters, he thought they were called—but what the markings meant he had no idea.

Using the plastic knife included, Ryan began to spread the gray Army cheese over the salted crackers, then noticed the sec man's obvious confusion. Fireblast, the man couldn't read.

"That one's coffee," Ryan said, pointing to the little brown envelope. "Just add hot water. That one is sugar. Powdered milk. That one is chewing gum. Sweet stuff for after the meal, it's good for your teeth. The little thing is cheese and crackers, the box is dessert, usually some kind of nut cake. The big envelope is the main course. You got spaghetti. That little tube has more cheese to sprinkle on top."

"Here, allow me," Doc said, pulling out a knife.

Karl watched in fascination as the old man sliced open the big shiny pouch. An unknown aroma rose from inside, and the sec man angled the package, about to try to see inside using the amber lights of the Hummer. Finally successful, he recoiled in horror at the sight of what looked like dead white worms in congealed blood, along with several unidentifiable soggy globes. Gagging slightly, Karl could not hide his utter revulsion at the sight. This was food?

"Trade ya," Jak said, passing over his already-opened pack.

Hesitantly, Karl exchanged.

As Jak dug into the spaghetti and meatballs, Karl warily sniffed the contents of the replacement bag. But this time he smelled meat. Lifting the silver pouch, he saw that it was full of chunks of cooked beef, mixed with some veggies in a thick brown gravy. Eagerly, he dug into his beef stew with gusto.

"Food fit for a baron!" Karl laughed around a mouthful. "Black dust, do you eat like this every day?"

"More often than not," Ryan admitted truthfully, finishing the last cracker and starting on his own envelope of stew.

For a while, there was only the sound of people eating and the ticking of the cooling engine.

"So, were you the pilot of that crashed plane?" Ryan asked very casually. "Krysty, pass the salt? Thanks."

"No, I was with three other sec men sent after the Demon on horseback," Karl said, his mouth full. "It wasn't supposed to leave the airfield, but something went wrong and it flew away on the wind."

Airfield? There was a word Mildred hadn't heard in a long time. "Airfield?" she said out loud.

Swallowing his mouthful, Karl turned the good side of his face toward her. "That's the word Lady Tregart uses," he said. "Big place inside a blast crater. The ridge that goes around is so high, we're always surprised when the Angel flies over."

"Why doesn't she just wheel it outside then?" Ryan asked casually, not looking at the man.

The man shrugged. "Can't. There's only a door in the gate for passage. And that's just big enough for a man on horseback."

"No other gate?" Jak asked, frowning.

"No. Just the one. Could I have some of that salt, too?"

Ryan passed it over.

"Thanks."

"And you were supposed to bring the Demon back through that?" Doc asked curiously.

"No, destroy it," Karl said, running a finger around the inside of the envelope to get every last drop of gravy. "But we were ordered to save the engine. Lady Tregart can build more Demons, those are easy, but not the engine."

The companions exchanged pointed looks.

Regretfully, Karl laid the clean Mylar pouch aside. "How do you make the coffee again?"

Unfolding a plastic cup, J.B. showed the sec man how to mix the French roast crystals into some cold water from a canteen. As the mixture began to softly bubble, Karl felt his eyes go wide at the smell of fresh coffee. The water was heating itself without a fire?

"Magic?" Karl asked, his voice quavering slightly.

"Tech," Krysty replied, tucking the hard slab of military fruitcake into a pocket for later. "So, what was special about the engine?"

The sec man shrugged, risking a sip of the hot brew. "Dunno. It was big, twelve cylinders, but light as wood. It was just as shiny as steel, but she called it all-low, or something like that."

"Aluminum," Ryan pronounced slowly.

"Yeah, that was the word," Karl said, cradling the plastic cup and breathing in the heady fumes. Coffee was for barons, not sec men. He had only smelled the stuff before while standing guard behind Lady Tregart's chair at dinner. It tasted good!

"So only the one engine left, eh?" J.B. said in a joking manner.

"Nah, she's got six," Karl answered, taking another sip. "And Carter said she knows a place where there's hundreds more."

The companions all stopped eating and drinking at that remark, but Karl didn't notice and went on. "The prob was something to do with the wings," he said. "All of the other warbirds crashed after a few man-lengths. But this one flew and flew and flew!" A small part of him felt it was wrong to discuss such things with outlanders, but they had saved his life twice and he felt honor-bound to answer their questions. It wasn't as if they were asking him anything important, like how to get into the ville, or where the spare blasters were hidden.

"I guess Lady Tregart solved that wing trouble," J.B. muttered, stirring some powdered milk into his cup of coffee. The predark creamer instantly curdled, and the annoyed man cast it away into the bushes.

"Which means she can make more," Ryan intoned in reply. "At least six to start with, and after that, who knows how many?"

"Hundreds," Karl said absentmindedly, scratching at his bandaged arm with the bottom of the cup. He was starting to itch all over from the cuts given to him by the cannies. The healer called Mildred had washed the wounds with something that smelled like shine, and said there was danger of them going bad. But Karl had seen norms die screaming with swelling limbs from the tox on a cannie blade. It was a triple-bad way to get chilled. Not the worst, but almost.

"Does she have any other Angels?" Krysty asked pointedly.

"Nope, just the one," the sec man said, then suddenly went stiff and thrust his hand forward.

Dropping his coffee, Jak dodged out of the way as the knife went straight past his head and slammed into a tree. Pulling his blaster, the teenager thumbed back the hammer then noticed the rest of the companions looking behind him. Turning, Jak saw that the knife was sticking through the twitching body of a fat spider, a greenish fluid dripping from its needle-sharp mandibles.

"That's a Dakota," Karl said in explanation. "One bite an' you go perm craz."

"Sounds like a neurotoxin," Mildred muttered,

looking at the dead insect. The punctured body was dripping a clear ichor that she would expect to see in any large insect. Thankfully, it wasn't that weird urine-yellow blood from the artificial bio-weps that had been set loose in the final days of skydark. But they were incredibly difficult to kill, which wasn't surprising since they were genetically designed biological weapons.

With a calloused thumb, Jak eased down the hammer. "Thanks," he said, holstering the piece.

Going over to the tree, the albino teen pulled out the blade. Wiping it clean on the grass, he ran the flame of his butane lighter along the steel for a few seconds just to be sure, then flipped it back.

The knife went tumbling straight for the ground between Karl's boots, but the sec man caught it by the handle and slipped the weapon back under his poncho.

Grunting in amusement, Jak nodded at the fellow blademan and sat again. His coffee gone, the youth pulled out a needle and thread to start repairs on the rip in the collar of his battered leather jacket. The visibility seemed poor under the amber lights, but the albino proceeded with the task easily, his red eyes wide and untroubled.

"Well, even the one Angel is going to make other barons surrender," Krysty said, taking a shot in the dark. When was there a ville not at war with another one?

"We ain't at war with nobody," Karl said, puzzled,

hugging himself for warmth under the blanket. "Lady Tregart just wants to protect our ville by acing the barons planning to jack us. Then we take some trib as punishment, that's all."

Unwrapping a bar of compressed fruitcake, Ryan started chewing on the resilient dessert. Okay, he got the basic idea. Sec men on horseback raided the ruins of the villes she attacked from the air, and took as tribute everything of value. After only a couple of raids like that, Thunder ville would have enough blasters and horses to attack anybody they wished. This Lady Tregart wasn't stockpiling supplies, she was building an army. And with even the one Angel paving the way from above, who could stop her? Mebbe she could not damage a predark tank with her skybombs, but to anything else in the Deathlands, Lady Tregart and the Angel would be death incarnate.

"Skybombs," Krysty muttered, her hair curling protectively around her face.

Gnawing off another chunk of the military snack, Ryan agreed. Hellfire, just the sight of a plane would make most villes surrender. Tales of the Nuke War were burned into the memory of everybody sucking air. Repeated by mothers, and sec men and gaudy sluts in bars. Skybombs had changed the shape of the planet. One big nuke had made the capital of America into Washington Hole, a circular bay that still glowed green at night.

"Got any idea about range, Millie?" J.B. asked, sliding off his glasses and polishing the lenses on a soft clean cloth he kept for just that purpose.

"A couple of hundred miles at the most," she replied slowly. "Depending on payload and weather."

"Weather?" Jak asked, putting a wealth of inquiry into the word.

"Plane's go slower in damp air. It's thicker and harder to get through. Dry desert air is the best for flying."

"You know such tech?" Karl asked surprised. "I heard Lady Tregart say that very thing once, and…" He started to reach for his back, then went silent.

"And she had you whipped to keep quiet," Krysty said softly. "Didn't she? And this is the woman you say merely wants to protect the ville and not jack other barons?"

"Sounds like a coldheart to me," Ryan said bluntly.

Could it be true? Was his mistress a coldheart? Karl looked at the ground, his mind swirling with conflicting emotions. Yesterday the world had made sense. This day, he wasn't sure of anything anymore.

"I don't know what to believe anymore," the sec man mumbled, hugging the blanket tighter.

"Oh, believe anything you want," Mildred stated. "But unless something is done, this Tregart will soon be the first emperor of America."

"How far away is your ville?" Ryan asked, chewing steadily.

"In your wag?" Karl asked, fighting back a yawn. "Less than a day."

Seeing the exhaustion in the man, Mildred scowled. "Okay, enough chitchat," the physician stated forcibly, in the same whipcrack tone she'd formerly used to make hospital interns jump. "Karl, go lay down on the rear seat of the Hummer and get some sleep. I'll check on you in a few hours."

Trained to take orders from a woman, the man obediently stood and shuffled off to collapse inside the predark wag. Soon there came a rhythmic snoring.

"We can talk openly now," Mildred said, pulling out her target pistol and removing the bullets as a prelude to a thorough cleaning.

"Smart move, babe," J.B. said with a smile.

"Yes, a wise precaution, madam," Doc complimented with a gesture. "And I must ask, is there something wrong with the fellow? In spite of his harrowing misadventures today, there seems to be an odd quality about the man, although I cannot clearly tell you what it is that troubles me so. Most perplexing. Is he ill, by any chance?"

"Eunuch," Ryan said, pulling out his own blasters for some needed maintenance.

Inhaling sharply, Doc narrowed his eyes. "Indeed," he mumbled in displeasure. "So this Tregart is another one of those kinds of barons, eh? Neutering young boys to create guards overly protective of her."

He grimaced. "By God, that is a foul practice! I had hoped we would never see it again after that mad woman at Castle Rock."

"Just another reason to chill the bitch," Ryan said pragmatically. "And if she is the only person who knows the secret of building a plane that could fly, then…"

Angrily, Ryan cut himself off. "No, damn it, chilling her won't end the matter. Remember Silas?"

The faces of the other companions showed that they recalled the incident clearly. After the insane whitecoat had been dealt with, his assistant had taken over and proved to be an even tougher adversary, more vicious, and more aggressive. It was a hard fact for the Deathlands warriors to accept, but sometimes chilling folks only made a problem worse.

"So putting Tregart into the ground is just half the job," Krysty said, her hair swirling around her face like lazy smoke. "We also have to make sure that all of her records are destroyed so that nobody else can build more planes."

"At least not from her ville," Mildred added, then frowned. "No, not from any place. This world is just not ready for air travel yet. I mean, if we were to reintroduce running water to the villes, a few barons would only use it to drown people in public executions!"

"Got that in the crosshairs," Jak said, biting off the end of the thread and inspecting his work. Slipping into the leather jacket, he shrugged and a knife dropped out of a sleeve into his waiting palm. Satisfied, Jak tucked it away again.

"Any more coffee?" the teen asked.

Reaching into his backpack, J.B. pulled out an open MRE pack. "Sure. No more cream, though."

"S'okay."

"Taking out Tregart and burning down her workshops…" Ryan said very slowly, hunching his powerful shoulders. "Sounds like nightcreep work."

"I'm afraid so, lover," Krysty sighed, reaching out to touch the man.

"Don't like being an assassin," Ryan added. "But there's no other choice. We've seen what one Angel can do. Now, think of a dozen, a hundred!"

"Put us right back into the Stone Age," Mildred said grimly, wiping the last of the desert sand from her weapon. "Maybe for good. And what passes for civilization these days is already hanging on by its fingernails!"

"If what Karl said on the ride out here is true, then Tregart has herself a private fortress tucked inside an old blast crater," J.B. said with a frown. "No way we're busting in to level the place."

"What about hot-air balloons?" Krysty asked, brushing back her hair. "We could drift in over the wall and drop down inside, silent as ghosts."

Rubbing the scar on his face, Ryan gave that some thought. They had used hot-air balloons to escape from villes before, but never to get into one. And balloons were easy to build, just cloth and rope and wicker for the basket. Unfortunately, they flew at the mercy of the wind. Against that biplane, a balloon would be only a crip asking for chop.

"Too slow," Ryan answered. "We'd only get chilled trying."

"Use rockets blow down gate," Jak stated with conviction, as if settling the matter.

"None in the, ah, place," J.B. answered, unwilling to even say the word "redoubt" with the outlander so close by. "And by the time we made enough to do the job, she'd have another warbird flying. Maybe three or four."

"One enough," the teen muttered honestly.

"Can't we make rockets?" Mildred asked. "We know the formula for gunpowder. Along with several other explosive compounds."

"Yeah, me, too, but that would take weeks to make," J.B. pointed out. "If we could find all of the ingredients. Gun cotton is easy to make, there are plenty of sheets…back home. But the cooking would take months. Even if we got enough sunshine."

"To make the nitric acid?" Mildred guessed.

He nodded.

"Not enough fuel for Molotovs." Jak spit, rubbing the scarred back of one hand. "Not for a whole ville."

"Madam, would it be possible for us to make a plane?" Doc inquired. "Perhaps to engage the Lady Tregart in aerial combat?"

"Oh, don't be foolish. That would take years," Mildred replied with a snort. "If ever. We don't have the right kind of wood or cloth or…. Now, the motor is no problem. Plenty of those we could use at the—" she glanced at the Hummer "—place. But we'd have to hand-carve the propeller, and that would be nigh impossible."

"Take off boat?" Jak asked.

"Wrong pitch," Mildred said, frowning. "And too small."

"And the one at the crash site in the desert was burned in two," Krysty said.

"Damnation, we are quite well equipped with predark technology and weapons," Doc said, frowning, holstering his blaster. "And still we are stymied. What chance does anybody else have against this baron of the air?"

"An air baron," Mildred muttered. "Like in the German Luftwaffe? Not bad, old-timer. Tregart and Hitler would have gotten along just fine."

"Who, Mildred?" Ryan asked.

Mildred bit a lip, trying to translate the entire rise and fall of the Third Reich to people who barely understood the concept of politics, or nations.

"The Lord Kaa of my time," she replied simply.

"Ace him?" Jak asked, sipping his coffee.

"Damn straight, we did," she declared with an unexpected surge of pride. "And we'll also send this lunatic into the ground."

"Pity we don't have any of that nerve gas," Krysty said in unaccustomed brutality. "There aren't supposed to be any civies at the airfield, so we could simply roll in a canister and watch 'em drop."

Mildred started to bridle at the suggestion, then sighed and went back to loading her blaster. It was a new world with new morals. The ethics of her time were as dead as Medieval chivalry.

"Indeed, dear lady, your loquacious observation is most astute," Doc stated unhappily. "We would need an army to accomplish the task."

An army? Ryan picked up his head at that. Now there was a razor idea. But would it work?

"How about crossbows?" Mildred asked. "Those will reach the biplane when it's diving in for the chill. We can make them from the spring leaves of the civilian cars."

"If hit warbird," Jak said slowly, "only make hole in cloth."

"Not if the arrow was on fire," Krysty corrected. "Shine fire would go out, but this grease from the garage level of…home should do the trick."

"Fire arrows," J.B. muttered, pushing back his fedora to scratch his head. "Yeah, might do the trick."

"How long to make crossbows?" Doc asked, leaning forward.

The other man shrugged. "A couple of days. But we'd need the resources at the other place. And that means getting over the Ohi, which we don't know how to do, and then getting back over it again."

"We don't have days. Tregart will have more planes flying soon, and then it's all over. She'll spread her air war across the Deathlands like a plague, smashing apart dams and bridges and walls, looting the world for her ville to survive."

"Worse, chill friends," Jak muttered, tossing away the last few drops of cold coffee. "Not gonna let happen."

"Indeed, we will not," Doc whispered softly, his eyes unfocused to see a private world. "My Emily would not like for us to do that."

"We could jack the crossbows from her ville sec men—" Krysty started. "No, that won't work. At the first sign of trouble, Tregart would come flying out and shoot us to drek."

"Yes, she probably would do just that," Ryan said.

"You've been awful quiet, lover," Krysty said. "Everything okay?"

"Been working on a battle plan," Ryan said, pulling out his panga and starting to draw in the dirt. "Now tell me if you think I've gone crazy, or if this blaster is packing a full mag…"

WITH AN INARTICULATE cry, Sandra Tregart sat upright in bed, the soft blankets falling away from her bare breasts.

"My lady?" Brian asked, rising from a chair across the tent.

It took a few moments for the fog of sleep to leave her mind before Sandra realized that this was her tent on the airfield. So, she had managed to survive the landing, after all. Excellent.

The cool evening breeze felt good on her bare skin, so she made no effort to cover herself. On the other side of the tent, Brian shifted uneasily in his chair and tried not to stare at the naked woman. In the hissing bluish light of the shine lanterns, she seemed like a dream, beautiful beyond words.

"Is the Angel…" Sandra croaked, the rush of words catching in her throat and causing a coughing fit.

Going to a table heavily laden with food, the teenager filled a wooden cup with water and rushed forward. Grasping it in both hands, the woman gulped the water down, then simply shoved the cup at him for more. He went back to refill the container, and returned also carrying the water bottle and a plate of smoked meats. Sandra emptied the cup again, a little excess running out of the corner of her mouth to dribble onto her breasts. Brian turned his head away as he held out the plate of food.

"How is my plane?" she demanded hoarsely,

grabbing a piece of fish and consuming it whole. The woman was irritated by his show of respect. Other men had chilled to see her like this, and he refused to look? Fool.

"Completely repaired and ready for flight, my lady," Brian said, shuffling closer.

Swinging her legs to the side of the bed, Sandra let the sheets slide to the floor, and for the first time noticed that her wound had been expertly wrapped, the bloody bandages still smelling faintly of shine.

"And where is Carter?" she demanded gruffly, stiffly raising a knee to wiggle her toes. Under the bandages, her thigh throbbed gently, but everything else worked.

"Guarding the Angel," Brian answered, as if surprised by the question.

She grunted in acknowledgment.

"But more importantly, how are you, Baron?" the teenager asked in concern, maintaining his position.

Brushing back her explosion of hair, Sandra felt a faint stirring between her legs as she studied the wide shoulders of the youthful sec man before answering. Young, healthy and strong, with a thick beard just starting to grow, Brian wasn't one of her eunuchs. Not yet, anyway, and Sandra began to wonder about the necessity of the mutilation. Her father had taken several wives before her mother yielded an heir, and her brother used to bed every willing girl he could find. So why should she be celibate and suffer? Why not take a lover, and when he was no longer amusing, or useful, he would join the ranks of her eunuchs with at least a memory of what it meant to be a real man. Plus, he was young and inexperienced. As his first, and last bed partner, she could control the boy like a mule in harness. Sex, pain, jolt, fear, she had to always have a handle of control of those near to her. Any other way meant betrayal, and death. Like Karl.

"Baron?" Brian repeated, turning slightly.

Resting a hand on his arm, Sandra eased herself to the rocky floor. The ground was chilly to her bare feet, and her skin became covered with gooseflesh, both nipples instantly hardening.

"I am fine," Sandra stated, patting his arm before letting go.

His face burned red at the friendly contact, and the woman experimentally arched her back as if stretching. The action thrust out her breasts and she caught Brian glancing at them briefly. So you are interested, eh? Good.

Suddenly, his glance moved to her legs and Sandra felt a rush of dampness at the frank look of approval from the strapping teen. But then his face darkened into a scowl.

"My lady, you're bleeding again!" Brian gasped, kneeling to touch her bandage.

Looking down, Sandra scowled at the sight of

crimson stain spreading across the white strips of cloth covering her thigh.

"Whoever stitched the wound shut will be whipped," she snapped angrily. "This kind of incompetence is not be to tolerated!"

"B-but we did not close the wound, my lady," Brian said, cringing slightly.

"Why not?" she snapped, privately enjoying the sight of the submissive teen.

"That was my decision, my lady," Carter said from the opening of the tent.

Releasing the flap, the sec chief walked in carrying an old porcelain bowl filled with steaming towels, and a small wooden box. "I thought you needed the rest and decided to wait until you awoke naturally."

The fleeting moment of passion fading away, Sandra snorted at that, then nodded.

"Very smart," she acknowledged, sitting on the edge of the bed. "As usual, you did the correct thing." Then she shivered again from the evening breeze that came from the opening.

"Brian, fetch me some clothing and get a brazier in here to warm this place," she ordered brusquely. "Carter, start working."

"Of course, my lady," Brian said eagerly, and rushed from the tent.

"As you can see, I did not alter the child as you asked, my lady," Carter said, placing the bowl on a chair. The box went on the floor and, extracting a key from his clothing, the sec chief carefully unlocked the lid.

"It is well that you didn't," Sandra said sternly, pulling a blanket across her exposed lap. "Make sure he isn't bothered by any of the others until I say so. His role in the ville will be different from that of yours."

"Whatever you command," Carter muttered, lowering his head to hide his expression.

Opening the wooden box, the sec chief started removing pale blue lengths of nylon fishing line and an assortment of curved needles. His grandfather had told tales about looting furniture stores in distant ruins to find the curved needles. After skydark, most of the hospitals had been destroyed in an orgy of hatred toward all tech. But such simple tools as these had been missed completely in the predark shops that made furniture. Designed for working on fabric, the steel needles were overly large, but the tips were still sharp and they made neat rows that would keep even the worst of wounds tightly closed.

"This is going to hurt," Carter said, offering the woman a piece of used leather.

"Then work quickly," Sandra said, sliding the piece of leather between her teeth and biting down hard.

When Brian returned several minutes later, he paused at the opening of the tent, confused by the sounds of what seemed to be a man and woman having sex. How could this be?

After a moment Brian stepped inside the tent. He was vastly relieved at the sight of Sandra grunting through the leather strap in her mouth as a kneeling Carter stitched the wound in her thigh shut. The woman shook slightly every time the needle went in, the reaction making her breasts sway.

As Brian went closer, he noticed Carter glancing under the blanket covering the woman's lap, and felt himself grow irrationally angry. What could it possibly matter if the eunuch liked to sneak a harmless peek of what he could never have? Brian had done the exact same thing only a short while ago. Although, there were still bullets in his blaster, and that made all the difference.

"Your clothing, my lady," Brian said, placing a brazier full of glowing coals near the foot of the bed, and a pile of garments alongside the naked woman.

Grabbing a clean shirt, Sandra quickly pulled it on and started closing the buttons. "Talk to me," she commanded, trying to take her mind off the painful sewing. "Was there enough copper tubing to make another still?"

"I'm sorry, my lady." Brian faltered. "I rushed to get the things you requested and didn't stop to ask about such things."

"I did," Carter said with a smirk of satisfaction.

Dipping the bloody upholstery needle into a bowl of shine, he started on a new line. "If all goes well, within a week we'll have a second still in operation. In a month, we will start producing enough shine to fill every lantern in the ville."

"Excellent news!" Brian grinned happily.

"Bah. Not a drop goes to the ville," Sandra advised, doing up the cuffs. "I need it all for fuel. Every drop."

"My lady?" the teenager asked, confused.

"How are the new Demons coming along?" Sandra asked the kneeling man, completely ignoring Brian for the moment.

"Very well, my lady," the sec chief replied, tugging the needle through her skin one last time and tying off the end in a neat bow knot.

"When will the first be ready to have an engine installed?"

Carter took a warm cloth from the ceramic bowl and wiped the bloody skin clean, his fingertips stroking her flesh for reasons he couldn't readily put to words.

"A month," he said, starting to pack away the needles and fishing line. "Mebbe more. The work of bending the wood is very delicate, and—"

"Unacceptable," she interrupted. "You have two weeks."

"I would need more workers," the sec chief replied hesitantly, placing the dirty towels into the bowl.

"Then get them!" Sandra commanded, rising stiffly. The leg trembled but supported her full weight.

"You have two weeks!" she repeated. "Fail me, and you shall lose more than just your life." Taking a pair of pants from the pile on the bed, the woman proceeded to tell them about the outlanders, and Karl.

"The dirty, little balless traitor," Brian growled, resting a hand on the holstered blaster at his side.

Gathering the locked box, Carter shot the young man a look of pure vitriolic hatred, and started to reach for his own weapon, when a breathless old man burst into the tent.

"What? How dare you enter this tent without permission!" Sandra raged, buckling a gunbelt around her waist.

"M-my l-lady!" the sweaty wrinklie panted. "I r-ran all the way…there are strangers in the ville!"

"So?" she demanded coldly, going to the table and choosing a choice cut of meat. Daintily, the woman began to nibble on the food. "Why tell me?"

"They have brought gifts for the ruler of Thunder ville!" the man gushed. "Not for your father, my lady, but for you. Gifts for the sky baron!"

Narrowing her eyes, Sandra put down the smoked fish. Slowly the woman began to check her blasters and derringers to make sure all of the weapons were properly loaded and clean.

"All right," she said at last. "Take me to them."

Chapter Fifteen

Dawn was just starting to break as Lady Tregart marched up the front steps of the blockhouse. Six armed eunuchs walked behind the woman, blasters on their hips and longblasters in their hands. Every person on the streets and in the courtyard smiled and waved at Tregart, and tried not to look at her plump, smooth-faced guards.

Stopping in front of the great iron-bound front door of the blockhouse, Sandra was pleased to see the sec men on duty had lost their haggard look of starvation. They were both terribly thin, but their eyes were no longer dull, and they stood straight with strength in their bodies.

"Door," she commanded, waving an impatient hand.

The two sec men lost their smiles and hurried to open the thick portal. They stood well aside as the woman and her entourage strode into the throne room.

As the crowd of ville folk parted in front of her like wheat to the wind, Sandra scowled darkly. Now what the nuking hell was going on here?

The throne room was packed full of people moving around piles of wicker baskets filled with bread, cans of predark food and entire wheels of gray cheese. There was a table stacked high with barbed arrows and dozens of longbows.

A second table was filled with bottles of shine in every color imaginable. Gallons of shine! And nestled in a small wicker basket, one lone bottle of predark liquor, resting on a silk cloth. Sandra lifted the container to marvel at the raised design on the glass. Incredible! The label was faded to nothing more than a suggestion, but the seal around the cap was intact.

At first, she didn't know what to make of this display of treasure. It was the wealth of a ville! Then comprehension came and she realized it was the wealth of several villes. So they had all paid, eh? She smirked with some satisfaction. She knew flying the Angel over the neighboring villes would strike terror to their hearts!

Then Sandra corrected herself. No, terror of me.

"Welcome, my daughter!" Baron Tregart called, waving a hand. "Over here!"

Placing the bottle of liquor down, Sandra turned to approach the head of the huge room.

Sitting in his throne, her father was in his robes of state, the heavy velvet cloak edged with ratty white fur that had seen much better days. Moved back inside again, the two wooden thrones were side by side on a raised dais. But now the splintery platform was covered with soft rugs of animal skins, and surrounding the elaborately carved chairs were a dozen iron braziers, the red-hot coals sending out waves of heat that drove away the chill of the night.

Covering the entire wall behind the thrones was a huge tapestry. Alternating layers of red and white stretched across the fabric, except for the upper left corner, which was a blue box filled with stars. The tapestry was burned in a few small spots, and there were several bullet holes, but its bright colors still seemed to fill the throne room. Some of the wrinkles claimed it was the symbol of what had once been America. To Baron Tregart, it was a priceless heirloom of the old days. Sandra Tregart considered it merely a decoration, and a rather poor one at that.

Stopping at the foot of the dais, Sandra gave a small head bob that served her as a bow.

"It seems that news of your machine has spread to the other villes," Baron Tregart said, smiling, stroking the head of a dog sitting by his side. Another dog lay the foot of the throne gnawing and slobbering on a wet bone. "All of this just arrived from Black Rock and Boar Head as tribute to the authority of Thunder ville!"

"Did it now?" Sandra muttered. That was when she noticed a line of people across the room. Dressed in rags and wearing heavy chains, the backs of the men were covered with old scars, and the bellies of the woman were sagging folds of loose skin, their fat breasts heavy and distended.

"Breeder slaves," Sandra said in disgust, shying away slightly.

Still smiling, Baron Tregart waved that aside. "Of course we shall set them free," he declared. "Thunder ville does not condone slavery!"

Surreptitiously, Sandra looked sideways at her armed eunuchs, but they didn't seem to find any glaring holes in that declaration. Her mother had been right, males only heard what they wanted and ignored everything else. Especially the truth.

"They also sent us a dozen horses. With saddles!" the baron added eagerly, leaning forward in the throne. "Wealth, my daughter! Riches beyond imagination!"

Coldly, Sandra scanned the crowd of excited civies and somber sec men to find Zane. The sec chief was leaning against the granite block wall near the iron door that led to the private apartments of the baron and baroness. The big man was unshaved, his hair tussled and unruly, but the blaster in his hand gleamed with oil as he slowly rotated the cylinder checking the black-powder load in the weapon as if he was about to go into battle.

"Report," Sandra ordered crisply.

"Everything your father has said is true, my lady," Zane said in a clear voice, holstering the piece. Pushing away from the wall, he strolled closer. "The horses are in good health, and the saddles are all aged leather, not green that will shrink. We even fed some of the bread and cheese to the dogs…" The animals perked up their heads at that, and turned to face their master. When no orders were issued, the beasts went back to nosily sharpening their teeth on the mutie bones.

"No signs of poisons or tox chems yet," Zane finished, sounding almost disappointed at not being betrayed.

"And these…" Sandra said, sweeping a hand across the line of chained slaves shivering on the bare floor.

"Useless," Zane stated bluntly. "Utter drek sent to make us feel sorry and set them free. In a month they'll eat ten times the tribute that was sent to us and weaken the entire ville. The men can't be trusted to walk the wall, and the women." The sec chief made a sour face. "I'd rather bed the horses."

"Yes, we must set them free," Baron Tregart said, rising to his full height in the throne. "You there, guard! Remove those chains!"

The slaves looked up at that, their faces a mixture of fear and disbelief. Only one male slave took a full second before reacting with a hopeful smile. Sandra noted that, and marked the man's position. So that was the game, eh?

"Hold!" Sandra's voice boomed as she raised a hand.

The sec man walked toward the slaves stopped in

his tracks, and looked first at Lady Tregart, then the baron, and then Zane.

"You heard Lady Tregart," Zane said ominously, crossing his arms.

"What? You dare to counter my orders?" Baron Tregart roared, standing from the throne. "I am the leader here, Daughter, not you! This is my ville!"

"Then defend it properly!" Sandra snarled, pulling out her blaster and firing.

A male slave cried out as his chest exploded in blood. Reeling backward, he slammed into the wall, dragging several other slaves along with him. His head hit the granite with an audible crunch, and the man went limp, sliding to the floor while leaving a gory trail behind on the wall.

The other slaves began to wail in terror, and the ville folk in the throne room talked excitedly among themselves at the unexpected chilling. Then everybody went silent as Lady Tregart fired again. The chained man shook violently, and went still.

"What is the meaning of this?" the baron demanded, walking to the edge of the dais. "Have you gone mad, Daughter? What possible harm could—"

"Harm?" Sandra shot back. "Watch and learn, my baron."

The last two words were said dripping in sarcasm, and the crowd grew nervous over the woman's open defiance of her father.

Walking to the corpse, Sandra turned it over. "See there," she said, ripping the garment off. "Look at his back!"

Shuffling closer, Baron Tregart scowled in disbelief, but there was no denying his own sight. The flesh was clean and unmarked. Without a sign of scar or welts.

"But…how…" the baron started, only to stop in confusion.

"He was a spy, my lord," Zane said. "Sent by our new 'friends' to learn what he could, and then escape to pave the way for an attack."

"Attack?" the old baron whispered, all of his earlier show of strength and vitality gone in a heartbeat. As they watched, the baron seemed to age in front of their eyes, growing weaker by the heartbeat.

"Invasion and enslavement!" Sandra shouted across the room to the crowd, who immediate responded in murmurs and grumblings.

Drawing their blasters, the sec men moved closer to the trembling slaves, while the ville folk stepped back, giving them room to move freely.

"The other barons would dare?" the baron asked softly, putting out to a hand to steady himself on the armrest of the throne. "But I gave them my word! The tribute in exchange for their safety."

"Honor means nothing to animals." Sandra spit, holstering her blaster. "Now do you see, Father? Now do you finally understand that there can never be peace with any other villes? We are alone. We stand, or fall, alone!"

The old man lowered his head to his chest, his aged-spotted hands tightening on the armrest. For several minutes nobody in the throne room dared to speak, and there was only the sound of the crackling torches and the faint jingling of the chains of the terrified slaves.

"I have been a fool." Hugh Tregart spoke slowly, facing the woman. "I didn't want to believe that the America of my mother was completely aced. No more than dust blew away in the wind."

"We can bring it back, Father," Sandra implored, kneeling on the steps. The position brought a wave of pain from the fresh stitching in her leg, and the woman forced herself to give no sign of discomfort. "I can bring it back and give it to you. Let me, Father. Let me save our people."

"At any cost?" the baron said in a suddenly powerful voice.

Her breath coming fast, Sandra pulled out a knife and closed a hand around the blade.

"Yes, my lord, at any cost." She spoke the ritual words and pulled the knife free. Blood began to drop from her fist onto the dais. "So I swear by the blood of my fathers."

"So be it," Baron Tregart said, rising stiffly. Carefully, as if he were afraid of breaking it, the old man slipped off his purple robe and draped it across the armrest. "I am too old to wage war. I was too old before you were born, Daughter."

Unable to speak, Sandra stared at her father. Could it be? Was this really happening? Women were forbidden to rule in this ville. Thus it had ever been. Only males of pure blood could sit on the throne.

"The ville is yours, my child," the baron said, gesturing to the empty chair.

Feeling as if she were flying, Sandra slowly walked toward the wooden chair. Not the one on the right for wives, but the chair on the right, reserved exclusively for the baron. It seemed to loom in front of her as if in a dream.

"Quiet please!" Sandra spoke loudly, her words echoing slightly off the stone walls. "Obviously, the first matter to resolve is what to do with the slaves."

As the crowd became quiet, the new baron studied the anxious people shivering in their dirty rags. There were many options available, but only one choice.

"This ville does not keep slaves," she declared at last. "Americans do not keep slaves!"

The faces of the chained people brightened at that, hope flickering in their weary eyes.

"But, my lady, we cannot let them go," her father said softly. "If one was a spy, there may be others."

She seemed surprised that he understood that. How odd.

"Yes, I know, dear Father. Zane!"

The big sec man stepped forward, his weapons jingling softly. "Yes, Baron Tregart?" he said, saluting.

"Kill them all," Sandra ordered calmly, leaning on the armrest. "But make it quick and as painless a possible."

With that, the slaves burst into hysterical screams, begging for their lives and swearing eternal fidelity to the baron and her throne.

"It shall be done, my lady," Zane said in a flat voice.

"And save the chains," she added after a moment. "We made need those again."

As the sec men pulled out iron cudgels and advanced upon the cringing slaves, Hugh Tregart turned his back on the sight.

"With your permission, I shall go and see your mother now," her father said. "And afterward, I shall stay out of your way as much as possible."

"No, I always want you in the throne room," Sandra replied unexpectedly, shifting position to take the weight off her bad leg. "When I am flying, there must be a Tregart here to rule."

"But that isn't the old way," he started to mutter.

She cut him off with a gesture. "It's my way," she corrected harshly. "As the baron, I so command."

"And I obey, my lady." Turning, the former baron shuffled across the dais. A sec man opened the iron door for the deposed man to leave, and then locked it tightly behind him.

Done and done.

"Sec chief Zane?" Sandra called, wiggling a finger. "Come here, please."

"My lady?" he said as a question.

Lowering her voice to a whisper, the baron said, "That was just for the ville folk, and my father. I need those slaves alive, so send them directly to my airfield."

The man arched an eyebrow. "It will be done, my lady," he replied.

Watching him closely for any signs of disobedience, Sandra saw none. Good. "And if your men wish to use the female slaves once or twice before delivering them to me," she added. "I have no objections."

"By the blood of my fathers, you're stone cold," Zane replied in a guttural whisper. "The men probably would have done it anyway, but now that ride comes as a gift from the throne, and buys their loyalty. You know them well."

"And is their loyalty for sale?" Sandra demanded harshly.

"Not anymore," Zane said, flashing a grin. "By

god, our ville will flourish under you! I look forward to serving you for many years, Baron Tregart."

Dismissing the sec chief with a gesture, Sandra settled back into the throne and watched as Zane joined his men. The wailing slaves were forced to carry the dead spy in their arms as the sec men drove them out of the throne room. As they departed, the civies began heading off to start their morning chores. Even as some died, life went on for the rest.

Like sheep being culled, she observed in disdain. They were all mindless sheep.

"Oh, yes, you and your men will all serve me well for many years to come," Sandra Tregart whispered softly, pulling a sharp knife from her belt and testing the edge of the blade with a thumb. "After I have made a few…alterations, that is."

Chapter Sixteen

Sliding a brass key into the heavy padlock, Hugh Tregart undid the lock on the hallway door. The hinges squeaked softly as he pushed the wooden door open and walked into the dim bedroom.

Thick velvet tapestries covered the walls and an oil lantern burned on top of a heavy oak table. In the flickering yellow light, the former baron could see the still form lying under the covers of the four-poster. Locking the door behind him, Tregart walked across the dim room and gazed down upon his wife.

The fever had taken her mind away ten years ago, and now she slept, unable to wake. A servant fed her broth and cleaned the sheets, but he no longer pretended that Hannah was still alive. This was merely her shell, breathing, eating, but empty as a spent brass cartridge.

Her once lovely face was lined and creased with the passage of time, her skin dabbled with age spots. Only her long hair was still coppery-red, the thick filaments almost seeming to move as if they were alive. His heart skipped a beat at the memory of when he had first seen Hannah, bathing in a pool of clean rainwater behind the ville tavern. Hugh had just turned a man that year, but she had clearly been a woman for much longer. He'd remained silent as Hannah stood to dry herself with a patched towel, then she slowly turned to smile at him, neither condemning nor enticing, before wrapping the towel around her body and padding away on bare feet.

Hugh had sought out her father, the ville blacksmith, that very day, and they were married by the next moon.

For thirty long years they ruled the ville side by side, fighting muties, and coldhearts, and that terrible night when a howler got past the gate. Hugh had been hacking at the thing while trying not to look directly at it, when Hannah had come out of nowhere and smashed a lantern at the feet of the thing. The howler went insane as the burning oil set its body on fire, and Hugh had rushed forward to hack the mutie in two. That was when the dogs converged and torn the howler apart.

He sighed at that memory. The dogs all died the next day, but they had helped save the ville, and he swore to never let one of them die again. The famine had almost made him break that vow, but then Sandra… Ah, Sandra…

"I really had no choice, dearest," Hugh whispered to the unconscious woman, the words catching in his throat. "Our daughter has gone insane. She wants to declare war on the world. If I stand in her way, she would have us both aced in our sleep. Blame it on a spy, or a coldheart, or trip me down the stairs. Oh gods, if only Edmund had lived!"

The woman seemed to stir at those words, a breeze moving her hair around her face like mist on a mountain. Hugh could never get over that effect. It was the triple-strangest thing he had ever seen.

"Well, now her fondest wish has come true and Sandra is the baron," he said, brushing a lock of hair off the wizened face. It seemed to clung to his fingers before settling back into place. "Which means I am no longer a threat. I can kill her now. She won't expect such a thing from me. Old and feeble, too weak to walk."

Releasing his wife's hand, the old man shuffled to an armoire and opened the doors. Clean clothes hung from a wooden pole. Moving them aside revealed a shelf at the rear of the cabinet. Lying on the piece of oily cloth was a brace of blasters and a pair of binocs.

Taking the blaster on the left, Hugh dropped the clip to inspect the four fat brass rounds inside. They were enormous .50-caliber cartridges, the soft lead tips cut into a crisscross pattern, turning them into deadly hellflowers. The bullets went into a person like a finger, but came out the back spread larger than a fist. Even a stickie dropped from being hit with a hellflower. Dum-dums, his grandfather had called them, but that word had a new meaning these days. Besides, hellflower was much more accurate. When these rounds flowered, you went straight to hell.

Then he lifted the binocs and turned to glance at his wife.

"Forgive me, darling," Hugh whispered, tucking the binocs inside his clothing. "We gave her life, now I must take it back for the good of the ville."

Turning toward the door, the old man never saw the woman on the bed struggle to raise a feeble hand in warning, then collapse from the tremendous strain of the effort.

Stepping into the hallway, Hugh locked the bedroom door again, and Hannah Tregart was left alone with the gently hissing oil lantern. Nobody remained to see the single tear roll down her cheek.

WATCHING FROM THE SHADOWS of an outcropping, Ryan was grudgingly forced to agree. It looked hopeless. The walls of the crater were impassable, the one entrance heavily guarded, and there was only flat empty ground for a good mile around the ridged crater. There was no way to get close without being seen.

"Any underground caverns, tunnels, predark sewer pipes?" Ryan asked, rubbing his unshaved chin.

Massaging his bandaged shoulder, Karl frowned. "No, Ryan," he said after a moment. "The ground is hard rock. My grandmother said it used to glow at night when she was a little girl, but that went away many snows ago."

A blast pit formed by a nuke? Instantly both Ryan and J.B. checked the rad counters on their shirt collars. The two men relaxed slightly as they saw the counters were silent. If the crater had once been hot, that was long gone.

"Look there," Krysty said, pointing to the gate. "We've seen those things before. Arbelists, I think Mildred called them."

"Giant crossbows," Mildred said with a frown. "This Lady Tregart is no fool. She has the place designed to fight an aerial attack, probably in case somebody stole one of her planes and came back to settle the score."

"Those things have a greater range than a hand-blaster, and would punch straight through anything we could get into the air."

"Pretty much seriously ace a wag, too," J.B. noted, taking half of a cigar out of a pocket and tucking it into the corner of his mouth. Setting the tobacco between his back teeth, J.B. inhaled around the cigar, relishing its rich, dark aroma. He longed to light the battered stogie, but Mildred would have come down on him like ugly on an ape.

"How long before your baron could get another Angel made?" Ryan demanded gruffly, resting a boot on a lump of broken concrete. There were some remnants of predark ruins mixed with the lava and tumbled boulders. But he had seen this before. The earth had rebelled at skydark and unleashed a thousand volcanoes across the continent. Sometimes when he considered the level of destruction, the man was surprised that anybody had survived the nuclear shitstorm that had scorched the planet.

"How long?" Karl repeated, "A moon, mebbe less."

"Fireblast!"

"And she's making several. Our stickies are juicy, and there is a lot of the ancient cloth she calls silk."

Mildred raised her head at that remark. Juicy? Ah, for glue. Clever.

Placing both hands on top of his ebony stick, Doc leaned forward and squinted at the distant front gate of the blast crater. "Indeed," he mumbled thoughtfully. "It truly seems that our esteemed sky baron has established a perimeter defense of formidable proportions."

"Still think your plan will work?" Mildred asked.

Ryan continued to watch the gate. "If you've got a better idea," he muttered, "I'm ready to listen. Trader always said if you're ever absolutely sure about something, what that really means is you don't know shit."

"On that, we agree," Mildred relented, glancing at the BMW motorcycle parked nearby. It was a chancy scheme, foolhardy really, but if it worked...

"Get hard, people," J.B. announced, lowering the longeyes. "There's company coming."

There were some specks on the desert floor moving toward the gate in the crater wall. Several men on horses were herding a line of people who moved with the classic shuffle of chained slaves, heads bent and shoulders hunched. On top of the gate, the sec men were cupping hands to their mouths as they shouted down orders, and the sec man with the longblaster started pulling the rope of a bell, the sheer distance neutralizing the ringing to a noise.

As the gate opened, the men on horseback forced the people in chains through the tiny door. The riders followed, each squeezing through individually, and then the opening in the gate was closed.

"Slaves." Jak scowled and spit on the ground.

"But where did all of these come from?" Karl asked in awe, almost moving into the sunlight. "Thunder ville does not use slaves! And all of those horses!"

"Tribute from other villes," Ryan guessed. "Ransom paid to keep Lady Tregart from skybombing them."

"So, she's already taking over villes," J.B. growled. "Dark night, she moves fast."

"We can always leave," Mildred said bluntly. She cast a look in the direction of the redoubt. A single jump in the mat-trans and the companions could be a thousand miles away. More. Maybe this Tregart would be happy with only a couple of villes under her heel. But if not, unchecked, this woman would soon have an empire. Piloted by her eunuchs, soon more and more biplanes would fill the skies. Bombs falling from stars to finish the job that the Nuke War had started.

The physician hung her head. The world was too savage, civilization too delicate right now for this new type of warfare. There was only one thing to do. Stop her now. Destroy the planes and burn her journals. Erase all knowledge of the Angel until it was no more than another Deathlands myth, like the Trader.

"Any idea who Tregart might have squeezed for the jack?" J.B. asked, tucking away the longeyes.

Biting a lip, Karl squatted on his heels. "No," he said. "Aside from rumors and whispers. Lord Tregart always tried to stay friendly with the other barons if he could. Some would trade, others..." He made a vague gesture.

"Doesn't matter," Ryan stated, pushing himself off the rock. "The sun is about to set. It's time to start."

"Yeah, guess so," J.B. said, straightening his fedora. "Come on, get in, Karl."

Turning, the man stared at the black Hummer as if it were filled with hooting stickies.

"I..." Karl swallowed, stepping away from the vehicle. "No, I can't. This is too much. I cannot betray my mistress any further."

As the man reached down to unbuckle his gunbelt and give it back to the others, Ryan stepped alongside him, the bulbous silencer of the SiG-Sauer digging into his neck.

"Was hoping to do this the easy way," Ryan said, taking the man's blaster with his free hand. "We need you in that wag, but we don't need ya breathing."

For a moment, it almost seemed as if Karl was going to challenge that ultimatum, then he slumped and got listlessly into the front seat of the Hummer. Ryan kept a careful watch on the man as Krysty buckled the seat belt good and tight.

"Tie hands?" Jak asked, pulling some twine from the pocket of his leather jacket.

"That shouldn't be necessary," Mildred started to say, feeling a rush of guilt at Karl's betrayed expression.

"Lash his throat to the head rest," Ryan ordered. "If he wants to jump out the door after that, he'll only choke himself."

As the work was done, Karl stared at the Deathlands warrior with open hatred. "So, you're just another outlander," the man muttered through clenched teeth. "I thought you were my friend! I thought—"

"You thought wrong," Ryan replied bluntly, holstering his blaster. "Karl, you're either with us or against us. Only the dead are neutral. You just made your choice."

Breathing heavily, Karl gave no reply, knowing that they would never understand.

Climbing into the rear seat, Jak double checked the knots and pulled out a blade. "In case," the albino teen said, resting a pale hand on the eunuch's shoulder.

Ignoring the threatening blade, Karl closed his eyes and leaned backward in the seat.

"Okay, everybody get razor," Ryan said, turning away from the vehicle. "When they come back, all hell is gonna break loose."

"More for you than us, lover," Krysty said, glancing toward the crater. "Last chance to change your mind."

Starting the Hummer with a roar, J.B. threw the wag into gear and peeled away in a spray of gravel.

"Too late," Ryan said, and started for the Beamer.

Chapter Seventeen

The sun was low behind the orange clouds on the horizon as Sandra Tregart rode her horse along the street of the ville. Incredibly, there was still a smell of mule soup in the air, and the ville folk all respectfully bowed as the woman passed. Wisely, Sandra knew that response was partially for her family name, and partially for the six armed sec men that rode just behind. Her eunuchs were known for having little patience with anybody that behaved badly toward their mistress.

Nearing the ville gate, the woman was pleased to see the old guards had been replaced. The new sec men were younger, and skeletally lean from the famine. But the brown heels of bread stuck out of their pockets, and the guards smartly saluted at her approach.

At last, Sandra chuckled internally. Everything is under control. The ville is mine! Nothing can stop me now.

As the guards pushed open the gate, the woman started riding through. But then Sandra quickly reined in her horse and placed a hand on the longblaster slung over the pommel. There was a figure racing toward the ville at breakneck speed.

"My lady, why did you stop?" a sec man asked, walking his mount alongside her own stallion. "Is everything all right?" Then he saw the oncoming runner and immediately pulled his blaster. "Should we sound the alarm?"

"Not yet," Sandra cautioned, releasing the longblaster. The sprinting man was only Carter. There was no sign of blood on the man, but his face was a mask of fear.

"Mist…ress, s-stop!" Carter wheezed, stopping a few yards away. "Get…get back inside!"

"Why?" she demanded hotly, craning her neck to see if anybody was following. The desert was clear to the Ohi and the low foothills beyond. But the setting sun was causing the mesas to throw long shadows across the landscape, a dark purple swatch that could be hiding anything.

"There…" The sec chief gulped for air. "There was a war wag that come out of the desert! It circled about the airfield, and even stopped to study the gate. We shot at the driver with the big crossbows, but missed. Then it roared off into the foothills, over there!"

Shifting in her saddle, Sandra scowled in the direction the man pointed. Who would dare to recce the crater? Perhaps the baron who sent the spies disguised as slaves? Was this a two-side attack? Then she saw the hesitation in the eunuch's face and knew there was more.

"Tell me the rest," Sandra demanded, leaning closer. "Out with it, man!"

Carter swallowed hard. "Karl was in the wag," he said simply.

"Stinkin' traitor!" she jeered, tightening the reins so hard the horse whinnied in fear. Easing the reins, she patted the muscular neck of the beast to calm it down.

"That yellowbelly has probably told them everything about our defenses!" Sandra stormed. She jerked her head toward the eunuch. "What color was the wag?"

"My lady?" Carter asked in confusion.

"What color was the wag, feeb!"

"Why, black, my lady. Is that important?"

"Oh, yes," she hissed, leaning back in the saddle, making the leather creak. "That's very important."

So they were back, the coldhearts from the riverbed. Without thinking, the woman rubbed the stiff wound in her bandaged thigh. Somebody in the black war wag had nearly chilled her yesterday with a longblaster. Mebbe she could return the favor this day.

Looking at the sky, Sandra frowned. Black dust, this was some sort of a trick. There was no way in hell that black wag randomly decided to recce the airfield at this part of the day, when it was just light enough for them to see, and only minutes before it was too dark for her to fly. The woman felt a rush of cold adrenaline flow into her stomach. The coldhearts from the river were planning an attack, a big one most likely.

"You there, guard!" she shouted, turning in the saddle. Her horse followed the press of her thigh, and shuffled around. "Front and center!"

A sec man left his post at the gate and rushed over. "Yes, baron?" he asked hesitantly. There was stubble on his chin, not from a lack of shaving, but the blossoming of manhood.

"Find Zane!" she barked at the teen. "Have him get the ville ready for an attack. Nobody is to enter, or leave, without my permission. Understood?"

"Yes, Baron!"

Then glancing over a shoulder, Sandra added, "And also have Zane send out a wag to check the foothills. Five men, twenty rounds each."

"Twenty!"

"Now, get moving, boy! This is why you became a sec man. Defend the ville!"

His eyes went wide at that, but the guard merely gave a salute and streaked through the open gate. As he raced around the corner heading toward the barracks, the teen was already shouting orders to the other sec men.

Tightening the reins to control her horse, Sandra

grunted in satisfaction at the sight. Okay, that took care of the ville. However, her real concern was the airfield.

"What should we do, my lady?" asked one of the mounted sec man nearby.

"Stay close to me. There may be snipers," Sandra said, starting her horse forward at a walk. "Carter, is the Angel ready to fly?"

"Yes, my lady," Carter replied, jogging to keep up with the animal. "But, mistress, soon it will be night—"

"And Karl knows that I don't fly at night," Sandra said, her voice dripping with hatred. "But this time, I will, and I'll blow that black war wag straight to hell!"

"Mistress, no!" Carter implored, grabbing the reins and trying to slow the stallion. "The danger is too great!"

"Coward!" she raged, jerking free. "When I cut off your balls, did I also cut out your heart?"

Shocked beyond words, Carter stepped backward at that, his face contorting into a feral mask of rage. The expression swiftly faded, but Sandra could see she had gone too far, and the man's open rebellion lay dangerously close to the surface.

"Carter, you stay here and help defend the ville!" she ordered, digging both heels into the horse. With a sharp whiny, the animal lurched forward into a gallop.

As the other mounted sec man started after their baron, Carter was suddenly left alone in a cloud of dust. For a long time, the chief eunuch watched them ride away. Then the man turned and started walking toward the ville, his own emotions a churning storm of indecision.

THE STARS WERE JUST beginning to appear in the evening sky as the war wag rolled out of the ville and across the desert plain.

Following the bank of the river, the armored station wagon swept past the airfield, the guard on the gate watching their progress closely.

"Damn muties," the driver of the wag muttered under his breath.

"Stuff it, Davis. They're norms," Zane replied, checking the clip in his Browning longblaster. "Just been snipped, is all."

"That makes 'em muties to me." Davis sneered.

Moving inland, the headlights washed over the rocky foothills far ahead of the vehicle. In the harsh illumination, the sec men could see a big wag parked under an escarpment, with several dark shapes sprawled on the ground nearby. Blasters lay strewed around everywhere, and smoke curled from inside the vehicle.

"Looks like they've been jacked," Zane said, working the bolt on the Browning. "Stay sharp, and look for any survivors. We may have two groups out here, and the baron will want some of them alive for questioning."

"We'll just tenderize 'em a bit first, Chief." Eagleson grinned, carefully closing the cylinder on his handcannon.

With the new shipment of tribute from the other villes, the guards all had extra ammo. Extra! It was unbelievable. They all still carried crossbows, but those were just for cheapjacks, muties and such, not important enough to waste a cartridge on. Along with the other trib, Davis had gotten a pair of homie boots, and Zane was wearing a predark gunbelt with enough loops around his waist to hold all the ammo in the world. And all because Lady Tregart—rad that, Baron Tregart—had flown over the other ville with her air wag.

Reaching into a pocket of his shirt, Eagleson pulled out a piece of jerky and ripped off a bite, then offered it around. Most of the other sec men took a chaw. Extra food, extra ammo, boots, slaves, if her father hadn't stepped down from the ville throne, the sec men would have taken over the ville to give it to her as a gift. Fuck peace. They were strong again! Eagleson and the others were itching for some way to show their loyalty to the lady, and stomping some outlanders who got too close to her private crater would do just fine.

With squealing brakes, Davis slowed the wag to a stop just outside the range of an arrow from the smoking wag.

"Don't like this," Zane quipped suspiciously. All

four of the doors were wide open on the wag, and there was nobody inside. Then he noticed the smoke wasn't coming from under the hood, but from something on the ground, partially hidden by a large rock. What was that, a rusty can? Nuking hell!

"It's a trap!" Zane bellowed, ducking low and throwing open the door.

As if in response, there came a flurry of blasterfire. The windshield shattered, a tire blew, and Davis rocked back with blood on his face.

Diving out of the wag, Zane hit the dirt and rolled away from the vehicle to come up firing his longblaster blindly. The rest of his sec men were only a split second behind their chief, and soon the night was alive with blasterfire.

Fanning the night with his handblaster, Eagleson cried out as blood erupted from his throat, spraying outward in an arc to wash across a couple of other sec men. As they turned, the dying man fell to his knees, his blaster triggering from the impact into the ground. Almost instantly there came two flashes of fire from the darkness above and a sec man reeled backward with most of his face removed.

"They're on top of the rock!" Zane screamed, racing behind the wag.

Crouching low, the sec chief feverishly worked the bolt to load a fresh ammo clip. Just then something landed with a thump on the ground and rolled beneath the station wagon. Bending, Zane tried to get a look under the vehicle when the night erupted with flame and thunder.

The wag was lifted off the ground by the detonation of the gren, then the fuel tanks ignited. The wag was blown apart from within, and it crashed back to the earth with a sound louder than doomsday.

AS THE WRITHING fireball rose upward, the companions on top of the rocky ledge hastily pulled back to safety.

"Move fast! We gotta get those crossbows out of the fire!" Ryan snarled, scrambling down to the desert floor again. They were going to need those. The next part of this attack was going to be tricky.

Chapter Eighteen

Climbing into the Angel, Sandra Tregart looked to the west just as something fiery rose like an atomic dawn above the jagged lava peaks. The writhing column hovered in the air for a moment, then faded away.

"That was an explosion," Brian said from the front of the biplane. Both of the teen's hands were on the propeller, poised to give it a starting shove.

"Yes, but who aced who is the question," Tregart huffed, slipping into the cockpit.

Brian removed his hands from the propeller. "I could check, my lady."

"Don't bother, I'll know soon enough." She set the choke and throttle. The wind was kicking up again, and her bandaged leg was throbbing like a cannie drum. Not a good night to fly. But there wasn't a sign of the tox chem clouds overhead. Visibility would be at a max.

Good hunting weather. There had been a lot of that lately, she knew. According to her father, it seemed to take longer and longer for the death clouds to return from the days when he was a small boy. Mebbe the world was finally healing itself from the aftereffects of the Nuke War. The world was taking back the sky, but then, so was she.

Checking the box at her side, Sandra counted a full complement of twelve skybombs, six Molotovs and six pipebombs, the stubby fuses jutting and ready to go. If she missed with one, the shrapnel in the other would do the job.

Standing near the biplane, a husky sec man held the rope attached to the chocks in his hands. "Is this flight wise, mistress?" René asked. "Even with the moonlight, it will be too dangerous for you to land in the desert. The ground is too soft. You'll never get airborne again."

Sandra stared at the man. Since when did he suddenly know so much about flying? She shook her head. No, calm down, she urged herself. René wasn't an enemy Flying was merely the dream of everybody, even these pitiful half-men.

"There are a few flattop mesas that I can use in an emergency," she explained, sliding on her sunglasses. Then, irritably, she yanked them off. Damn! Her vision would either be blurred from the wind, or everything would be tinted too dark to see. Some fragging choice!

"If you say so, mistress," René conceded, his hands worrying the thick rope.

"Just keep the new slaves sewing," she ordered, checking her hidden derringers. "I want those Demons ready to go in ten days."

"Ten!" Brian gasped.

His jaw dropping, René started to speak, but stopped, licking his lips in the effort to try to frame the question.

"Yes, you will receive a plane," Sandra said. "With Karl aced, you and Carter shall be the first of my new breed of sec men. Wingmen!"

"To fly," René whispered, his eyes taking on a dreamy quality.

"Check the feed," she said impatiently.

René snapped to attention and went to the rapid-fire attached to the front of the biplane and examined the belt of ammo. Even when the others got Sky wags, she knew that only the Angel would carry a rapid-fire. There were two more in the supply tent, but she carried the firing pins to the lightweight blasters in a pouch on her gunbelt. Ammo was scare, so every round was reserved for her. Someday though... Ah, someday when she ruled a dozen villes...a hundred!

Her leg started to throb again, and Sandra rubbed it through the bandage and loose pants. Those cold-hearts in the black wag had fired at her as if ammo grew on trees, so she had wisely taken some additional precautions for this flight. Wooden slats now lined the sides and bottom of the cockpit to serve as crude armor. To offset the additional weight, Sandra had ordered the rear seat removed, which would make the biplane light in the rear, and more difficult to do fast turns. But she felt it was more than worth the sacrifice. Once airborne, Sandra would be invulnerable. Unstoppable!

"Everything is ready, mistress," René reported, stepping clear of the wings.

She nodded and fed the engine some fuel. "Contact!"

"Contact!" Brian repeated, shoving with all of his strength. The wooden blades spun loosely for a tick, then the starter engaged and the motor roared into life.

"Baron! Wait! Baron!" someone shouted over the purr of the predark engine.

Scowling at the ground, the woman saw one of the servants from the blockhouse rush toward the machine, then stop in obvious fear. The norm was holding a heavy object wrapped in fine silk.

"What is that?" Sandra demanded, glaring at the servant. "More trib from another baron?"

"It is a gift from your father!" He practically gushed, sidling closer, and flinching every time the engine backfired or coughed.

"A gift? Open it," the woman commanded, setting the brake and leaning over the side for a better view.

Nodding agreement, the servant lovingly unfolded the thin silk to reveal a squat pair of predark longeyes, the kind called binocs.

"Excellent, mistress!" René said in delight. "Those will be a great help on your flight!"

Going still, Sandra kept her face expressionless. Yes, the binocs would be a tremendous help. However, as a child she had explored every inch of the ville, including her parents' bedroom and private cabinet. The lock had proved impossible to pick, but cuddling with her mother Tregart had stolen the key and gotten inside anyway. There had been a lot of blasters inside, along with a pair of binocs. Mebbe that exact pair. They certainly looked the same.

Her eyes narrowed. Except that the binocs in the cabinet had been useless. The glass at both ends was still intact, but there was something broken inside. She remembered that the view had been distorted and blurred. Those binocs were utterly useless. And there certainly wasn't another pair in the ville. Now why would her loving father send her a pair of drek binocs?

"Yes, a magnificent gift," she said in a voice of stone. "But I cannot see the peaks with these spinning propellers in the way. Would you check the rim of the crater for me?"

"Me?" the servant gasped.

"Please." She smiled coldly.

"Yes! At once, Baron!" Rushing away from the shaking biplane, the servant raised the binocs and pressed them to his face.

He frowned. "Baron, I must be doing something wrong because I can't see anything through these—" Then he started to shake all over, and lowered the heavy binocs. Steel shafts jutted from both of his eyes, blood mixing with a clear ichor to trickle like crimson tears down his cheeks. The servant turned to her, his mouth moving in gibberish. He settled to the ground, still holding the deadly binocs as death arrived.

"Black dust!" Brian snarled, drawing his blaster and looking around the airfield.

"A booby?" René cried in shock, almost dropping the rope. "You were sent a booby by your own father, the baron?"

"He may be my father," Sandra snarled, "but he is no longer my baron, remember? The old fool gave the throne to me."

"But still…" René started, unsure of what to say next.

Softly in the distance, thunder rumbled from the mountains to the far east. Slowly, Sandra turned to face Brian. The teen still had the blaster in his grip, and was looking for anything coming this way. The decision to use him was made in a heartbeat. "Brian!"

He turned and saluted. "Yes, Baron?"

"Go back to the ville and give my father the news of my death," she instructed. "Be sure to cry a lot. And then when they are not looking, chill him."

"The baron!"

"The former baron. I rule now."

Stupefied, the teen gazed at the blaster in his hand as if he had never seen one before, then he gently tucked the weapon into the holster at his side. As Brian lifted his head to look at the woman, she could see a new hard light in his eyes. She knew in that moment that he was no longer destined to join the ranks of her eunuchs, but to become the sec chief of Thunder ville.

"It shall be done, my lady," he whispered.

"Then get moving!" Sandra yelled, then added, "Captain Brian Stone!"

Swelling with pride, the sec man crisply saluted, then turned to run for the gate on the far side of the airfield.

"Chocks!" Sandra yelled, releasing the brake again.

"Chocks!" René shouted, yanking on the rope.

As the wooden wedges came free, the Angel started forward with a lurch, rapidly building speed and power until it was fairly skimming along the smooth rock floor of the ancient crater. Sandra would settle things in the ville upon her return, but first there were some outlanders to chill.

The woman thrilled to the almost sexual build of tension as she clicked off the safety on the big predark rapid-fire. Yes, first a little fun before she took care of ville biz. Blind Norad, she was going to enjoy this.

THE BIPLANE ROSE over the rim of the blast crater and moved about in a sweeping arc through the starry sky before slowly angling toward the foothills.

"Here she comes," Ryan said, kicking the BMW motorcycle into life. The bike shook slightly as the engine revved with power. Undoing his gunbelt, the man passed the SiG-Sauer to Mildred.

"Move fast, lover," Krysty urged.

"That is the plan," Ryan quipped, checking the Steyr SSG-70 longblaster across his shirt. The bolt-action was hanging in front of the man, and he worked the bolt to chamber a round.

As the buzz in the sky grew louder, Krysty and Mildred quickly joined the rest of the companions in the black Hummer safely out of view in front of the rocky escarpment. Only a few yards away, the smashed wag was still burning, the dancing flames making the rocks and corpses appear to move with nightmarish life.

Staying high, the Sky wag swept past the combat zone, then circled around to come in lower.

Shifting his combat boots on the ground, Ryan felt the urge to grab the Steyr to try to ace the bitch right now. But unless she was a total fool, she would have some sort of protection this time, a predark flak jacket or sheet iron. Hell, they weren't even sure that Mildred hit flesh that last time in the desert. For all Ryan knew the triple-damn thing was blasterproof, and stepping into view would only get his fragging head blown off.

"Softly, softly, catchee mutie," the Deathlands warrior whispered under his breath, butchering one of Doc's fav phrases.

Swooping in from the east, the Angel swept past the fiery wreckage of the wag, and for a split second, Ryan saw the profile of the woman in the moonlight.

Then, shoving back the kickstand, Ryan revved the engine and darted forward. The buzz of the Sky wag filled the air and he knew there was no way she could hear the subdued murmur of the Beamer. So he clicked on the headlight, the brilliant beam stabbing across the irregular ground of the foothills like a plasma beam.

Instantly the buzz of the Sky wag swelled and Tregart slipped sideways from the racing motorcycle. As he crested a hillock, the two machines ran parallel to each other for a breathless instant, and the drivers faced each other. Grabbing the Steyr, Ryan awkwardly lifted the longblaster and fired sideways at the Sky wag. The pilot jerked and suddenly the winged machine was dropping behind.

Had he actually hit Tregart? Then something fell from the sky to impact in his wake and erupt into a strident fireblast. If he had shot her, she was still alive.

Trying to work the bolt again, Ryan found the weapon jammed. The biplane flashed past him and started to circle around for another pass. Then from the starry heavens above, there came the loud chatter of a rapid-fire, and the ground to his left churned from the barrage of lead. Abandoning the effort, Ryan grabbed the handlebars tight as he streaked down the other side of the hillock, now concentrating fully on his driving.

Chapter Nineteen

Metal slid across metal as Brian Stone swung open the door in the airfield gate.

Instantly there was a blur of motion to his left. The teen started to turn when the wooden rifle butt cracked into his temple and he dropped to the ground without a noise. Several hands grabbed the unconscious sec man and dragged him out of the way, as Jak slipped through the door and into the crater.

Smoking a cig, a nearby sec man registered shock at the sight of the albino and inhaled to shout a warning. Jak flipped his hand and the man stumbled backward, the handle of a leaf-bladed throwing knife filling his mouth, the blade buried deep in the back of his throat. A wellspring of blood began to gush forth. Then Jak was upon him. A second knife flashed like silver in the light of the alcohol lanterns, and the sec men crumpled to the stony ground.

Retrieving his blades from the corpse, Jak turned to see J.B. and Krysty easing through the doorway with crossbows in their hands. Drawing his Colt

Python, the teen pointed upward and above them to the left and right. Quickly, the man and woman separated and walked backward into the crater until they could see the two guards standing on top of the gate. One was eating some kind of a crunchy vegetable, while the other was using a knife to dig a new hole in his gunbelt. Pitiful.

As the guard finished and sheathed the blade, J.B. gave a soft whistle. The two sec men turned in surprise at the noise, and there came the double twang of the crossbows firing. Grabbing their throats, the guards stumbled backward to go over the gate and out of sight.

As the bodies impacted on the ground outside in dull thumps, Mildred slipped in through the opening with the SiG-Sauer held tightly in both hands. Crackling torches were set on top of the gate, but none near the bottom, and the area was cast in murky shadows.

Cheap bitch was saving the shine for her planes and not wasting any on lanterns, the physician thought grimly. Thank goodness for overconfidence! New barons always seemed to think that their particular ville was impregnable. The damn fools. The only thing in the world impregnable was a woman who was already pregnant.

Closing the door behind her, Mildred moved stealthily through the darkness, scanning the vast open expanse of the airfield. The layout was pretty much as

Karl had said. She soon found her targets and knelt as if at a gun range to take careful aim with her crossbow.

At the gate, J.B. passed his crossbow to Jak, who immediately started reloading the weapon. Krysty already had another arrow inserted into her crossbow and was watching the shadows for any movements, her hair a flexing riot of curls around her tense face. The woman hated doing a nightcreep, even when there was no other choice.

Meanwhile, J.B. was attaching two of his most powerful pipebombs to the main timbers supporting the wall. He could hear Doc grunting softly from outside as the old man labored to remove as many of the dirt-filled tires as possible. The bodies he left where they landed.

J.B. eased up behind Mildred and tapped her twice on the shoulder to let her know that the others were ready. In response, she pulled the trigger once, quickly inserted another arrow and fired again. The move took all of five seconds.

A hundred yards away, a steaming pipe dented and fermenting mash sprayed out in a boiling stream. The man working the pressurized still began to shout in warning when the alcohol-rich brew reached the banked fire underneath and sluggishly ignited. The workers started to run as blue flames raced up the stream and entered the metal container. Just then, a pipe on the new still dented and also spurted an alcohol leak.

A tongue of flame shot out of the hole in the first punctured pipe, just as the second stream caught fire. One eunuch was shoveling wet garbage onto the cookfire, trying to kill the blaze, when the heated container burst apart in a deafening blast, chunks of metal, man and flaming mash spraying out in every direction. The blast was still echoing across the airfield when the new larger still exploded with twice the force, a halo of burning debris shot-gunning into the sky to rain back upon the screaming eunuchs and tents.

Moving fast, the companions spread out across the airfield, keeping safely inside the shadows of the tents not ablaze. As the conflagration spread, they could see dark shapes in the other tents, but they were all a jumbled blur and there was no way to tell what any individual tent contained.

Suddenly the door to a shitter slammed open and a man stepped into the firelight, tugging up his pants.

"What the nuking hell is going on!" he demanded in the squeaky voice of a child.

Shooting from the hip, Krysty fired her crossbow and the man staggered back into the wooden shack, clawing at the arrow sticking through his throat.

"Any sign of them?" Mildred asked in a guttural whisper.

"No—yes, over there!" Krysty said, dropping the spent crossbow and pulling out her S&W wheelgun. "The big tent on the end near the horse corral."

There was a rag tied around the barrel of the revolver to hold down any shine from the polished metal. The time for fancy, long-range crossbow chilling was done. From here on, all of the chilling would be up-close and dirty.

"Seen 'em," Jak replied, launching his last arrow at a man loading a longblaster. The bolt whizzed away and hit nothing.

As the teen tossed away the crossbow and pulled out his Colt, J.B. squeezed off a short burst from the Uzi just as the sec man brought up the longblaster and fired. Something big hummed past the companions, and the sec man dropped the blaster to clutch his belly before toppling over sideways.

"Close," Jak snarled, easing the pressure on the trigger of his blaster.

"Too close," Mildred added, firing two rounds at something moving in the shadows. But there was no answering cry of pain. Damnation, the firelight was throwing off her aim!

"Jak, you and J. B. go free the slaves and get them out of here!" Krysty ordered, firing into the night. A man cried out in pain. "Mildred and I will find Tregart's tech journal."

The men grunted in acknowledgment and moved off into the night.

By now, blasters were starting to sound all across the airfield and somebody was shouting near the gate.

Mildred glanced that way just as the night was split by thunderous flame and the shouting abruptly stopped.

"No mistaking Doc's LeMat." Krysty snorted, starting forward at an easy lope. "With him covering our back, just watch for the crossfire, and we may get out of here still breathing."

"That is the plan," Mildred replied, trying to imitate Ryan's deep voice.

Women screamed in one of the tents, followed by the sound of the hooting of stickies. Both Krysty and Mildred prayed the cages holding the muties were made of metal, and not wood.

A secondary explosion came from behind the line of tents, and a shrieking man dashed into view dripping flames. Ignoring the human torch, Krysty ducked to fan her blaster a fast three times at the silhouette of another man aiming a crossbow their way. He staggered from the .38 bone shredders, but still launched his weapon. The arrow appeared out of the darkness to violently slam against the rocky ground directly between the two women, the shaft breaking into splinters.

Cursing, Krysty grabbed her bloody cheek and Mildred fired twice. This time, he dropped permanently.

"You okay?" Mildred asked, easing out the spent clip from Ryan's borrowed blaster and inserting the only spare.

"I'll live," Krysty said tersely, looking at her wet

fingers, then wiping them dry on her pants. "Just a scratch."

Cracking open the cylinder of her blaster, she took out the spent shells to insert live rounds, then almost dropped the weapon as something painfully lanced through her head, going from ear to ear. Gaia!

"What the frag was that?" she demanded, looking frantically around. Krysty gingerly touched her ear, half expecting to find more blood from additional splinters. But there was no damage that she could find.

"What happened?" Mildred demanded in confusion.

"Something went through my head like a big nail," the redhead said with a tight throat. "I've never felt anything like that before in my life."

"Well, I can take a guess," Mildred said, pulling out the Czech ZKR target pistol with her left hand. She turned in a fast circle, the two blasters sweeping for targets. "That must have been an ultrasonic whistle. Get ready, they'll be here any second!"

"What?" Krysty demanded, noticing something moving in the darkness of the open airfield. No, several things.

"Dogs!" Mildred cried, firing both of her blasters at the slavering killers.

As THE HOT LEAD from the biplane chewed a double line of destruction along the ground, Ryan veered sharply to the right, arcing around a pile of loose rocks and weeds. The Beamer slipped in the gravel for a moment, and the one-eyed man tasted fear before the tires bit into solid earth again and he lurched ahead.

Already past him, the Sky wag was circling around once more to make another strafing run. As Sandra moved alongside, Ryan savagely braked to a halt and worked the jam out of the breech of the Steyr. Raising the longblaster, he put a shot into the tail of the machine with no visible results.

Grunting in annoyance, Ryan worked the bolt to chamber a fresh round. Yeah, he expected that. Ryan didn't even know where the fuel tank was on the biplane! On the crashed drone, the tank had been on the upper wing. But on this predark machine, the wings were clear of anything like that.

Wheeling to the right, Ryan ducked under some trees, braked, turned and shot again on an angle. Reaching open sky, he couldn't see the Sky wag anywhere, and so just sat there pretending to fiddle with the engine until she returned and he darted away again.

Being the bait in this trap was a bitch-risky gambit. The problem was to keep Tregart just interested enough to stay after him, but farther enough behind that the woman didn't nuke his ass. Or worse, go back to the airfield and ace his friends. It was a walk on razors either way, but the only way anybody had been able to figure out how to get Tregart to the kill zone. If it was still there!

Reaching a patch of level sand, Ryan stayed his course for several dangerous seconds, taking advantage of the precious stability to reload the Steyr. That gave him five rounds in the longblaster, with two more clips in his jacket, along with six loose rounds. He had also taken along a gren in case he needed a diversion, but a fat lot of good the mil charge would be against a fragging Sky wag!

Passing a clump of juniper bushes, Ryan gained a good mile before locating a rotten tree stump. Heading past it, he crouched over the hot engine to lower the wind resistance and gain more speed. In spite of the rough terrain, the speedometer hit 60 mph as the Beamer went straight over the edge of a gully. Flying above the ravine, Ryan caught a brief glimpse of a babbling creek below before he landed hard on the other side. Yes! But then the front wheel of the bike slipped out from underneath the man on a patch of green grass and he almost went over the handlebars.

The Sky wag started hammering lead again, as Ryan struggled to bring the wobbling bike under control. Turning into the skid, he got the wheels aligned and poured on the juice. The rpm hit the red line on the dashboard as he outran the hail of lead and then banked the wheels hard. Kicking out a leg, his boot hit the ground with a jarring impact, but Ryan kept the tilting Beamer angled away from the gully. If he took a spill now, it was the last train west without a doubt. Tregart was out for the chill this night, and he was the target in her scope.

A spreading tree loomed directly ahead of Ryan and he ducked low. But a branch banged his elbow, sending pain shooting through his arm from the glancing impact. Momentarily his hand went numb, and Ryan fought to control the runaway motorcycle with only one hand. He was almost to the edge of the gully again, when he regained control and shot back toward the original course.

Gaining another mile, Ryan risked a fast look upward and scowled when there was no sign of the Sky wag. Damn! Where had the bitch gone? This whole fragging deal was going straight into the shitter unless Ryan could keep the woman constantly on his tail. Time for a recce.

Heading for a hillock, Ryan bounced along the ground, dodging holes and fallen tree limbs until reaching the crest. Squealing to a halt, the man quickly scanned the sky with his good eye. And there she was! Diving straight out of the moon, using the silvery light to hide her approach. Nuking hell!

As Ryan frantically peeled away, the biplane swooped down along the hillock, its rapid-fire delivering short bursts. Streaking down the sloped ground, Ryan veered to the right and a second later a Molotov

exploded just where he had been. Glass shrapnel
peppered the man's jacket, and he felt the wave of
heat on his neck for a long moment before he went
out of range. Darting between two boulders, Ryan
jounced over a fallen tree and splashed through a
shallow creek before reaching the flat grassland. In
the sideview mirror, Ryan could see the hillock
coated with flames. Tregart was getting bastard good
at tossing those bombs.

Accelerating to full speed, Ryan climbed on top of
the mesa as the Beamer flashed through the night, the
bright headlight giving him only seconds to dodge
exposed roots or chunks of predark ruins that would
have sent the bike and rider tumbling to the death.

The buzz of her engine rising and falling on the
wind, Tregart winged around in a graceful circle to
swoop down once more, the rapid-fire chattering in
short bursts. As the Sky wag went past, there came a
whistling sound and the top of a nearby tree stri-
dently exploded as if hit by lightning. TNT!

A hail of splinters peppered his back with
stinging force, and Ryan braced himself for the
fenderless rear tire to blow. But as he gained another
mile and nothing happened, he eased the tension in
his arms and looked around to find the Sky wag. A
mile went by through the sparse grasslands with no
sign of the machine anywhere. Slowing his speed,
Ryan started to worry the woman had lost him,

when he caught the sound of the engine again. Nuking hell, was she leaving?

"Oh, no, you don't," Ryan growled, braking to a halt. Bringing up the Steyr, he cut loose three fast rounds, and then two more. As if she had been waiting to see the flashes of his longblaster, Tregart rolled the Sky wag over and came out of the aerial maneuver heading straight for him again.

Reloading for the last time, Ryan checked the dashboard, noting that the engine temperature was running dangerously high. But there was nothing he could do about that right now. Flexing his hands, the man revved the engine and rolled forward to build speed until the ground was only a blur beneath the purring bike.

Switching tactics, Tregart moved ahead of the man and tried attacking from directly in front. That almost worked, and Ryan had to switch off the headlight to dodge her bombs and bullets. But escape wasn't the plan. The moment he was in the clear, Ryan turned on the light again and sent two 7.62 mm hollowpoint rounds at the machine as it passed by the moon.

Incredibly small-caliber blasterfire was returned from Tregart as she shot at him with a handblaster.

He shouted a laugh at that, hoping that she might hear and get even more angry. It seemed to work because suddenly the Sky wag was flying only yards off the ground, the rapid-fire chattering nonstop.

Letting go of the handlebars, Ryan used both hands to steady the Steyr and gave her back two directly between the muzzle-flashes of the predark rapid-fire. Instantly she did a barrel roll and climbed into the air. Her handblaster fired away, but no bombs fell this time. Mebbe she was out? Ryan scowled in disbelief. More likely, Tregart just wanted him to think that she was out to lure him closer.

As the Angel circled, Ryan rummaged in his jacket pocket for the loose rounds and started thumbing them into an empty clip. Five miles remained, and the bike was getting low on fuel. Less than half a tank. But that would just have to be enough.

Removing the partially used clip and inserting the full one, Ryan tucked the old clip into his shirt pocket, along with the last live round. Just then the hairs on Ryan's neck stood up as he heard a scuffle in the dirt from nearby. Instantly he turned and fired. A man cried out, dropping his spear, but another threw his and the wooden shaft flashed by to smash into the windshield, breaking it to pieces.

Swinging the barrel of the Steyr to the new target, Ryan fired again just as two more spears came out of the darkness, one grazing his neck and the other slamming harmlessly against the engine block of the Beamer.

In the brief illumination of muzzle-flash, Ryan saw several half-naked men coming his way. Each was wearing a necklace of white bones, their heads were shaved, their muscular bodies covered with swirling tattoos. What the… It was the desert cannies! They had to have been following the tracks of the Hummer all of this distance to get revenge. Unfortunately, Ryan was using the same tracks as a guide to take him back to the forest!

Even as Ryan fired twice more, he could see the cannies were carrying blunt spears, the sharp stone tips removed. His blood went cold when he realized why. These spears weren't for chilling, but to knock a victim unconscious and take them alive. Alive for the cooking pot.

As the cannies broke into a rush and converged on the man, the buzz of the Sky wag began to get louder as Tregart started to commence another strafing run, bullets impacting everywhere.

Chapter Twenty

Writhing flames from the burning tents illuminated the night as the guard dogs attacked.

"Gaia!" Krysty shouted, firing from the hip as the animals spread out to circle the two women. "Quick! Go back-to-back!"

Shooting both of her blasters, Mildred rushed to join the other woman. The booming round from the ZKR missed, but the 9 mm slug from Ryan's SiG-Sauer grazed a dog across the belly. Yelping from the pain, the animal seemed puzzled how it got injured, and Mildred fired both weapons again. This time she got a double strike into the face of the beast and the dog's head literally exploded.

The rest of the dogs began to snarl savagely and race faster around the two women, looking for an opportunity to strike. Already down to four rounds, Krysty pulled her knife and kept the blade swinging to distract the animals from rushing.

Something exploded in the distance and there came the telltale chatter of the Uzi.

"John's shotgun is what we need," Mildred stated, shifting her posture to try to keep facing the dogs. She chanced a shot from the SiG-Sauer and only hit the ground. Damn, they were fast! "Any chance you have a gren?"

"Gave it to Jak!"

"Shit!"

A dog started toward Krysty, and as she aimed her blaster, the animal froze and a different dog charged in from the side. Quickly the redhead ducked and thrust out the blade, catching the dog directly in the throat. Gushing blood, the dying beast jerked away and took the blade along just as the first dog eased a foot closer. Krysty brought her blaster up and the animal froze, but its eyes never left her face.

"Gaia, these are hunting dogs!" she said hoarsely. "Trained to attack prey as a group!"

"Any suggestions?" Mildred demanded, watching nervously as two of the animals started edging in for her from the sides while a third crouched low, ready to leap. Mildred knew that the moment she fired at the two, the third would go for her throat. She flicked her eyes to the left for just a second, then back again to see the middle dog was closer.

"Got a knife?" Krysty asked tersely.

Mildred nudged her with a hip. "My left side," she said.

Warily, Krysty changed hands on her blaster and

reached backward. She found the sheath and pulled the blade free. Instantly the dog began to growl deep in its throat, as if understanding what a blade could do.

"Get ready," Krysty said, flipping the knife over in her hand to grasp the blade instead of the handle.

As the middle dog started closer, Mildred crossed her arms to point at the animals at her sides again, went back to her original position, then crossed her hands at the wrists. The dogs shifted in response to the moves, and always kept their eyes on the women.

"On your right," Krysty said in forced calm. "Here it comes."

"Go," Mildred said, tightening her grip on the weapons.

Keeping her blaster pointed at the crouching dog, Krysty flipped the knife over a shoulder. The blade went tumbling through the night and landed with a metallic ring on the hard ground between two of the dogs facing Mildred. Both of the animals darted their heads toward the unexpected noise, and she instantly fired. One dog yipped as a 9 mm Parabellum round smacked it in the chest, the other merely crouched as blood starting arching from a hole in its muscular neck. The third dog leaped.

Bringing up both of her blasters, Mildred fired into the chest of the animal and it slammed into her, the paws raking strips off her denim jacket. Firing blindly, Mildred shoved the dog aside as it snapped for her face, its sharp teeth closing only inches away, its hot, fetid breath blowing into her open mouth.

Turning sideways, Krysty fired her S&W .38, scoring two blood hits before the last dog charged. Raising an elbow to protect her throat, Krysty slammed the animal down and it fell, sprawling, only to scramble back onto its paws to try again. The woman twirled to get out of the way and rammed a boot into the belly of the beast. The dog was lifted off the ground, landing hard to snarl in mindless fury. Taking the blaster in both hands, Krysty carefully took aim and pumped a single round into its head. The dog yipped as it dropped limply, and Krysty spun, seeking a fresh target.

The last dog had closed its jaws around the bulbous silencer of the SiG-Sauer, and Mildred was pistol-whipping the animal to no effect. As Krysty took aim again, Mildred shoved her Czech ZKR wheelgun into its ear and stroked the trigger. The animal released the silencer as brains and blood blew out the other ear into the dark night. Already chilled, the beast flopped to the rocky ground and exhaled once before going still.

Watching for any more dogs, the women quickly reloaded and then retrieved their knives.

"You okay?" Krysty asked, sheathing the blade.

"Only some scratches." Mildred panted, tucking away her own knife before drawing the SiG-Sauer once more. "How about you?"

"Been better." Krysty grunted, touching her side.

Reaching out with the blaster, Mildred swept back the shaggy fur coat and frowned at the crimson stain on the woman's shirt.

"Does it hurt?" Mildred demanded, holstering a blaster and reaching for her med kit.

"Like fire, which means it's only a flesh wound," Krysty replied, starting for the tents again. "Come on, minutes count. If Tregart returns to find us out in the open…" She left the sentence hanging.

By now the flames were rising high into the sky, and wild hooting was coming from one tent covered with flames. Mildred paused, wishing there was something she could do for the poor stickies. Nothing deserved to die like that. But if she sent the muties free, their first act would be to try to tear off her face. Turning her back on the death screams, the physician moved onward, feeling another small part of her humanity dying.

"Look!" Krysty cried, pointing with her blaster. "There's nobody defending that tent!" The woman's other hand was under her coat, pressing on the bleeding gash.

"Which means there's nobody there," Mildred said grimly. "So it's either the barracks or Tregart's private tent."

"Let's go."

The two women moved fast along the hard ground,

firing sporadically at any distant figure with a shaved head. Dodging around the body of a man holding a pair of predark binocs, the two companions reached the abandoned tent and drew their knives. Slashing vents in the cloth, they did a recce through the openings before rushing in through the flap.

The inside of the tent was sumptuously decorated with fur rugs on the floor and actual wood furniture. There was even a bed with a brass railing headboard that looked so normal it gave Mildred a touch of homesickness. Then a piercing scream cut the night, the flames rising to cast nightmarish shadows on the cloth walls, and she was all grim biz once more.

There were alcohol lanterns on the dining and bedside tables, but lighting those would only have announced their presence to everybody in the crater. Separating, the women began to ransack the place, turning over tables and yanking open chests to find only food, blasters and miscellaneous machine parts. The blasters all seemed to have parts missing, but the grens were good. Krysty grabbed two and tossed one to Mildred. The physician made the catch and tucked the explosive charge into a pocket of her military jacket.

"Check the bed next," Mildred said, watching the shadows on the cloth wall. Blaster shots were sounding regularly across the airfield, and there came the chatter of the Uzi, closely followed by the loud report of the Colt Python. Karl had said the airfield had only twenty workers, but there certainly seemed to be more. Had he lied? Or had the reinforcements already arrived from Thunder ville?

Ripping off the blankets, Krysty slashed the mattress, then flipped it over. There, on the box springs, was a small leather volume. Hastily grabbing it, Krysty angled the book to try to read by the flickering firelight.

The math and the diagrams made no sense to her, but Tregart described her problems in duplicating the Angel in exquisite detail.

"This is it," Krysty said, pulling out her butane lighter and thumbing it alive. For a split second the woman paused, knowing she was destroying an invaluable wealth of technological information. Then reality came back hard and she placed the flame to the ancient paper. It caught easily and soon the manual was burning freely.

"Goodbye, yellow brick road," Mildred said under her breath as the journal was tossed onto a table.

"Not quite yet," Krysty mused, grabbing a lantern and turning it upside down. The glass flue fell off with a crash and the alcohol poured out of the reservoir onto the journal. The red flames turned blue for a tick as they swelled in volume.

"My lady, is that you?" a sec man asked, throwing open the flap to the tent. "I heard your voice and—" Seeing the two women, his smooth face registered shock. "Outlanders!" he cried, going for the blaster on his belt.

Mildred and Krysty fired in unison, the barrage of lead punching the man outside.

"Back door," Mildred stated, pulling the SiG-Sauer to cover the entrance with her two blasters.

Slashing the tent with her knife, Krysty ripped apart the cloth and stepped through into the fiery night. She held the rent wide for Mildred, then the women took off into the billowing smoke.

Hot embers stung their faces, and it was difficult to see anything clearly through the flames. They stopped as a crackle of blasters came from behind, then the women understood it was only the ammo in the burning tent starting to cook off.

Moving away from the area, they ran over more chilled sec men, and arched around a bonfire of what seemed to be the skeletons of giant birds.

"That the Sky wags?" Krysty demanded, squinting against the heat and smoke.

"That's them," Mildred said, studying the fire. There were six frameworks for biplanes in the heart of the blaze. Six! With those, Tregart had planned to rule the world.

"Look good and chilled to me," Krysty said resolutely.

"They're nuked," Mildred agreed.

"Thank Gaia!"

"Gaia?" a voice repeated.

The women turned with their weapons at the ready as two figures came out of the smoke. Krysty and Mildred almost fired when the men raised blasters, then the thick fumes parted for a moment and everybody relaxed.

"You okay, Millie?" J.B. asked, blood dripping off his face. There was a new hole in his fedora and a piece missing from his leather jacket.

"Just battered and bruised," Mildred replied with a weary smile. "Are the slaves free?"

"Gone," Jak stated, a slash along one cheek crusted with dried blood. "Run fast with chains off."

"Get the book?"

"It's ashes."

With the firelight dancing on his glasses, J.B. looked around. "Then we're done," he stated. "Let's get back to the wag."

"Freeze!" a screaming voice interrupted.

The companions turned and fired all of their weapons at the same time. There was a startled cry and two arrows shot by harmlessly. Warily moving closer, the four found a man lying on the ground. Still alive, his chest was pumping crimson and there were two empty crossbows in his twitching hands.

"Ya…fragging outies may have got me…" René said in a low wheeze, "but you'll still get aced… My dogs will—" The man trembled and expired.

"Dogs?" Jak demanded suspiciously, cocking back the hammer on his Colt Magnum.

"They're already on the last train west," Krysty stated, reaching down to yank off the whistle hanging from a rawhide cord around the neck of the corpse. Might come in handy someday.

Leaving the burning tents behind, the cool desert wind deliciously washed over the companions. Getting their bearings, the four started at a run back toward the distant gate. A few bodies and windblown debris were scattered across the ground. As they dashed past a pile of wooden boxes, a sec man reached out of hiding to grab Jak by the collar. The man shrieked in agony as his fingers fell away from the razor blades hidden along the coat collar, then Jak slashed out with a knife, ending the matter.

A tent collapsed, blowing hot air and embers to the sky. But a sec man stumbled from the fiery heart of the inferno, horribly burned over most of his body, the blackened skin cracked and oozing in a network of gaping flesh. Shouting obscenities, the dying man started forward, firing a brace of revolvers. Stuttering lightning shook the night as J.B. cut loose with the Uzi machine pistol on full-auto, the hail of hot lead fanning the destruction to stitch the charred man across the chest. But already numb from the overload of his pain, the man didn't even feel the hits and turned to aim both blasters at the startled Armorer.

The black-powder weapons roared, and J.B. felt something hum past his cheek as he gave the sec man another long burst. The stream of 9 mm Parabellum rounds hammered the dying attacker back into the blazing ruins of the tent and he disappeared among the flame and smoke.

Without warning, a violent explosion echoed across the airfield. The companions pivoted to see the gate blow apart. The wreckage was still falling when the black Hummer smashed its way through the splintered timbers and started rolling their way.

Rushing from the darkness, a man fired a crossbow at the wag and missed. Behind the steering wheel, Doc veered the armored wag abruptly and clipped the sec man with the front fender. He went flying to land on the ground with a sickening crunch.

In a squeal of brakes, Doc stopped the Hummer near the companions. "Ten minutes exactly," he reported. "I do hope that I am not tardy."

"You're right on time," Mildred said, assisting Krysty into the wag. In the ceiling light of the Hummer, the physician could now see just how badly soaked was the redhead's shirt. The firelight had disguised the sheer volume of blood. Not good. This wasn't good, at all.

"Did you get the technical manual?" Doc asked as J.B. and Jak piled into the vehicle.

Her face a waxy color, Krysty grunted as she

leaned back in the seat. "Yes," she whispered through gritted teeth. "And the Demons are all burned."

"Exemplary," Doc declared, very displeased with the woman's appearance.

Throwing the wag into gear, Doc drove jerkily across the littered field, encountering no further resistance. But situated at the windows, J.B. and Jak tried to watch for trouble from every direction.

Reaching the smashed gate, the Hummer rolled over the assorted debris, and Krysty gave a pained expression at every jolt. Opening the woman's bearskin coat, Mildred finally saw the wound. A tooth was still buried in the ripped flesh.

As they pulled away from the crater, the wheels started humming softly as the big wag built speed across the smooth landscape. They could faintly hear an alarm bell ringing from the walled ville just to the north.

"Find me a level stretch," Mildred demanded, pulling items from her med kit. "And I'll need light. Lots of light."

"That's not advisable," J.B. warned, thumbing fresh rounds into an exhausted clip for the Uzi.

"Got no choice," Mildred said hoarsely, applying a compress. "She's dying."

"So be it," Doc said calmly, and he turned off the headlights. "Jak, be my guide."

"Got covered," the teen said, his ruby-red eyes staring ahead into the moonlight desert.

Racing for the safety of the foothills, behind them dozens of sec men on horseback poured out of Thunder ville, led by a grim and bloody-faced Captain Brian Stone.

SNARLING A CURSE, Ryan dived off the BMW motorcycle, firing the Steyr. A cannie screamed as blood erupted from his knee and he crumpled holding the shattered limb.

Then a spear slammed into a boulder alongside Ryan and exploded into splinters that sprayed across his face. Instinctively jerking away to protect his good eye, the big man worked the bolt to chamber a fresh round, and shot another cannie in the heart. Then a third spear rammed him in the stomach.

The breath exploded from his lungs at the blow, and Ryan doubled over, just as the hail of bullets from the Angel racked across the landscape. One cannie yelled in shock and threw a spear into the air. Another turned and ran. Fighting to drag air into his lungs, Ryan fired the Steyr at the remaining cannies as he reclaimed the bike. The Angel was circling for another run. He had no time for this drek! Seconds counted right now. He had to keep moving, or everything was lost!

As the one-eyed man started the Beamer, a cannie charged and Ryan used his panga to slash at the flesh-eater. Howling in anguish, the cannie fell away, trying to use both hands to hold in his guts, the ropy intestines slithering out of the gaping wound in his belly onto the grass.

Rolling forward, Ryan slammed into another cannie and sent the man tumbling. In the clear, Ryan fed the predark machine gas and roared away just as Angel peppered the crest of the hill with a long burst of blasterfire.

Bouncing down the slope, Ryan cursed as the headlight blinked out. Slowing his speed, the furious man smacked it with a fist and the light returned with a vengeance, even brighter than before. Yes!

The buzz from the Angel grew louder and with a whoosh a reddish glow filled the night as the hill exploded from an expertly dropped Molotov. Dripping fire, the cannies dashed around madly, screaming in their unknown language. Taking advantage of the distraction, Ryan streaked back to the Hummer tracks he had been following and took off for the nearby forest. Only a few more miles now…

Tregart tried another strafing run, and Ryan swung back to drive underneath the Sky wag before she could take aim. The Angel peeled away to the left, then swung back with its rapid-fire hammering the ground in a sideways pass.

Ryan's luck held, and he escaped injury, but the bike was hit several times. The dashboard was smashed, the dilly bar dented, and the rear tire had taken a hit. Ryan braced for the unexpected crash, but the predark mil tire didn't explode or even deflate at the puncture.

However, the man knew that he couldn't depend upon it surviving a second strike, so he poured on the gas, forcing the Beamer to full-speed across the wild grassland.

Minutes translated into miles and Ryan discovered that he could smell the blood long before he saw the mound of corpses.

This was it. Ground zero. Just before breaking camp that morning, the companions had gone hunting. Or rather, they did some chilling. A herd of deer eating the grass just outside the forest didn't seem to know what a human was, and had paid the companions no attention at all. Contentedly grazing, the animals watched placidly while Ryan and the others took aim with their blasters and then cut loose.

After the slaughter, the companions butchered the bodies, throwing the organs and meat around to make as big a mess as possible. Retreating to a safe distance, they waited and watched, hoping for the best. Their vigil was rewarded when the first stingwing arrived to investigate the wealth of fresh meat. Soon, there were dozens of the winged muties feasting on the aced deer, with more arriving every minute. That was what Ryan was heading for at sixty miles per hour. His secret weapon. A dozen dead deer covered with feasting stingwings.

As the headlight washed over the ragged skeletons, Ryan saw that a flock of stingwings was still there, tearing apart the rotting animals. Perfect. Sounding the horn, he saw the muties jerk their beaks in his direction, and then he plowed through the middle of the flock, crushing several stingwings under the spinning tires of the big bike. The headlight shattered, and a tumbling body hit the windshield, cracking the glass so bad Ryan thought it was going to come through. Crushed stingwings tumbled in every direction.

Rarely attacked alone, the stingwings were totally confused by the assault and took to the sky for safety. Whirling high above the grassland, they began to circle the rotting corpses, preparing to reclaim their food source, when a harsh buzzing sounded from the sky. The enraged muties saw something large flying their way and swarmed together to strike at the new enemy.

"MOTHER OF DOOM!" Sandra cried as the flock of stingwings rose from below and charged straight at her.

Slamming the joystick to the left, she tromped on the fuel pedal and the engine surged with power as the biplane slipped sideways across the deadly sky.

A stingwing darted past the woman, obviously misjudging the airstream, and went directly into the spinning propellers. The wooden blades only slowed for a moment as they annihilated the creature, blood and feathers spewing out in a grisly spray.

Another stingwing slammed into the guyline supporting the left wing and was beheaded. But a third punched straight through the right wing, leaving a hole in its wake.

Biting back a curse, Sandra shoved the stick forward and started heading for the ground, adding the pull of gravity to her engine to almost double her speed. So this was what the outlander had been heading for, a flock of stingwings! And she had been so sure that he'd been leading her back to his ville. The son of a bitch would pay for this! Her eunuchs would spend months torturing the man, and in the end Tregart would be wearing his tanned skin as a new pair of boots. Oh, yes, he'd pay!

As her speed increased, the wings began to shake, the wires humming musically from the strain of the dive. The stingwings were falling behind, but the earth was coming dangerously close. With no choice, Sandra eased up on the power and began to swoop upward.

Almost instantly the muties surrounded the Angel. Another died in the spinning propellers, but a third hit the rudder, going completely through the fabric covering the wooden frame.

Instantly, Sandra found the stability was gone, the biplane responding sluggishly to the stick. Blind norad! Dropping the wing flaps and shoving the stick sideways, the baron spun the biplane around in a barrel roll, the wings smacking the stingwings out of the sky and a dozen broken forms tumbled to earth.

Leveling out the biplane, Sandra saw a stingwing slam into the canvas cowling and rip off the stiff fabric to expose the working engine. As the crumpled body dropped away, black smoke began to pour from the machinery, the well of exhaust temporarily blinding her.

Snarling curses, Sandra started to reach for her sunglasses, then stopped and eased the flow of fuel to the engine. Drawing her blaster, the furious woman fired at the encircling stingwings. But it only seemed to enrage them more. The biplane confused them, but blasters they understood. Those were used by two-legs, and those were food.

A stingwing landed on the left wing, sunk its talons into the tough fabric and began to peck at the guylines holding the struts in place. Flying with one hand, Sandra leveled her blaster and fired. The stingwing exploded and fell away. But another slammed into her wrist and the blaster went flying. She saw it tumble only a few feet away, then drop behind and vanish.

Shitfire! Pulling one of her palmblasters, Sandra started to badly cough from breathing in the exhaust of the struggling engine. She unleashed both barrels at the stingwings, but only scored a single chill. The angry muties attacked again and again. Mostly striking the guylines, probably because of the high-pitched noise they were making. But a few were tearing at the fabric, exposing the inner framework of the biplane. In cold logic, Sandra knew that if enough of that was loosened or damaged, she would lose control of the Angel and death would swiftly follow.

Pulling out her last derringer, Sandra briefly debated trying to land and run for cover in the trees, but that would mean abandoning the Angel to the muties, and after they were done, it would never fly again. Visions of her ville cheering as the food arrived flashed through her mind, the new blaster in the hands of her father, the explosion that crushed Indera ville. Power, freedom, life, it all depended on the Angel. No. She could no longer leave it behind than her own beating heart.

"Mutie scum!" Sandra screeched, firing at the things and acing two more. Yes!

Working the controls, the woman swooped downward to suddenly bank back upward, twisting around in a loop. The bizarre maneuver confused the creatures for a moment and suddenly she was behind the flock.

"Die!" the woman screamed, squeezing the trigger on the joystick as she charged.

The heavy-duty combat rounds of the rapid-fire tore the stingwings apart, and then the props chewed through the core of the fluttering group like death itself. The spray of blood coated the windshield, completely blinding the woman, and the engine sputtered from the strain, nearly dying. She fed it maximum power and tightened the choke, thinning the air-shine mix to make it as rich as possible. Come on you, big bitch, don't chill on me now…she railed.

The engines roared back to life and the Angel shot through the scattering flock of stingwings. The fuselage was shaking all over from the massed damage, several of the guylines making pinging noises as the smaller strands began to snap under the accumulated strain and damage.

The sky around her was clear of stingwings, and Sandra risked a glance over a shoulder to try to find the muties. What was left of the flock was leaving, even the insane killers had finally had enough of the predark machine. Victory! She had won!

Then white-hot pain slammed into her back and side. Disorientated, Sandra fell onto the controls and barely heard the muted report of the longblaster from the ground below. Him! It had to have been him! The one-eye coldheart on the bike. Sandra had completely forgotten about the man during her battle with the winged muties.

There was a new mist in front of her eyes, and Sandra knew it had nothing to do with the smoking engine. Fighting to stay awake, Sandra knew she had no choice and started for the ground as gently as possible. But her speed was too fast, and suddenly the leafy treetops were flashing underneath the Angel only yards away.

By now, both of the wounds had gone numb, and she knew that was a very bad sign. She had to land soon, get to the med kit in the rear seat. A wave of cold seeped into her bones as Sandra felt the blood soak into her clothing and drip onto the floorboard. Pushing that from her mind, she struggled to maintain an even keel. *Adjust the throttle! Watch that oil pressure!* The engine was sputtering badly, the exhaust thicker than ever. Suddenly she remembered the bombs in the plane and started throwing them out so that the Molotovs and explosive charges wouldn't detonate if she crashed...when she crashed... *No! She was not going to wreck the Angel!*

Then a wing dipped too low and there was a violent jar. Everything became confused as she was hit from a hundred sides. The world turned upside down, there was the strong reek of shine filling the cockpit, and then everything went black.

Epilogue

About an hour later Ryan braked the softly purring BMW motorcycle to a halt on top of the rock ledge near the Hummer.

He could see that everybody in the wag was alive, although Krysty looked a lot paler than usual. Even her hair was hanging limply.

Pushing down the kickstand, Ryan climbed off the bike and started that way, but stopped. From the vantage point atop the ledge, he had a commanding view of the two villes in the distance. The airfield was dotted with fiery mounds, the distorted shadows of people and horses moving around the blazes doing who knew what, maybe scavenging for anything they could find. A lot of trib went into the crater, some of it had to still be useful.

"Glad to see you here," J.B. said. "So, did it work?"

"The stingwings tore her apart," Ryan stated. "And just to make sure, I pumped a couple of extra rounds into the Sky wag after it caught fire and was plummeting to the ground."

"Sounds aced," Jak said, cradling the S&W M-4000 shotgun.

There was dried blood on the teen's collar, but none of it seemed to be his. Ryan could guess the cause.

"Won't know for sure until I see her fragging corpse," Ryan said, cracking the knuckles on each hand. "But she was going so fast when she hit those trees I really don't see how anybody could have survived."

"Well done, my dear Ryan," Doc said from the edge of the rock ledge. "And we accomplished our own mission with equal aplomb. The technical journal is no more, Karl has been recovered and the slaves were set free."

Slaves? Ryan frowned, then shrugged. He really hadn't given them a lot of thought, but that had been done, too, so much the better.

"Found him easy enough, did they?" Ryan asked, going to the rear seat of the Hummer.

Mildred glanced up at his presence, then went right back to work stitching closed a jagged gash in Krysty's side. He could see that the redhead would be fine. Krysty was just asleep, her chest rising and falling in a regular pattern.

"Sure, they found Karl. No prob," J.B. said. "Just as we thought, the ville sec men went straight to the crater, giving us plenty of time to hide our tracks and get up here out of sight. Then they did a recce on the earlier war wag. Found Karl knocked out, lying with the aced sec men, an empty blaster in his hand." The man grinned behind the curling smoke. "Some stud named Brian thought Karl had to have escaped from the 'coldhearts' to warn the others. Real hero stuff."

"And he didn't mention us?"

"Not a word," J.B. stated.

"Good. Blaster or arrow?" Ryan asked, gesturing at Krysty's blood shirt.

"Dog bite," Mildred replied, using her knife to cut the fishing line. "There's a new scar for the collection."

"Better a scar than a pine box," Ryan said, reaching out to touch the cheek of the sleeping woman. She murmured something unintelligible and nodded off again.

"Another quote from the book of Trader?" Mildred asked, tucking away her medical tools.

Ryan shrugged. "Either him, or my father. Just something I heard once."

"Wise words."

"I know."

"Bullet holes, blood, stingwing feathers..." Jak stated, kneeling alongside the predark machine examining the damage. "Must been hell of a ride. Bike nuked."

"So's my ass." Ryan snorted, rubbing the back of his pants. "Leave it behind for the locals to scav. We don't need it anymore. Make better time back to the redoubt in the Hummer."

"Booby?" Jak asked, squinting an eye and reaching into his pocket to unearth a gren.

"No, just let it be. Let's roll."

Standing, the teenager tucked the mil charge away. Good. Grens were hard to come by, and he hated to waste one.

Climbing into the Hummer, Ryan caught a motion in the starry sky and grabbed for the longblaster still hung across his chest. Then he saw it was only a vulture, probably attracted by the smell of spilled blood and death in the crater. Ryan closed the door and leaned out the window, watching it circle the airfield like a plane getting ready to land. Damnedest thing.

Yeah, vultures first, Ryan scowled. Then the stingwings would be next, and after that, stickies. Mebbe even more of those triple-cursed howlers! But that was a prob for the locals, and had nothing to do with them anymore.

"Fly free, little sky raider," Doc said, looking dreamily at the heavens. "Enjoy it while you can. Because someday a wiser humanity will rise from these Stygian ashes to take back the sky. Indeed, perhaps to conqueror the very stars!"

"Just not tonight, okay?" J.B. suggested, starting the engine.

"Of course." Doc smiled, his eyes lost in the mists of time. "There is always tomorrow, my friend."

High above the Deathlands, the vulture called out a challenge to anything else in the air, and for the moment, the cry went unanswered.

DAWN WAS JUST STARTING to break as consciousness returned to Baron Sandra Tregart. She was lying on bare earth, smashed wood and bits of charred silk everywhere. At first Sandra couldn't comprehend where she was, then the events of the night came rushing back and the woman sat upright with a cry.

Only to find herself still trapped in the wreckage of the Angel. Broken tree limbs were everywhere, along with bits and pieces of the once magnificent machine. The frame was reduced to kindling, the silk only tattered strips, the controls smashed, the engine a fire-blackened lump, and there was no sign of the propeller.

"Gone," she whispered in dismay. "All gone…"

"Not all, my lady," a familiar voice exhorted.

Turning, Sandra saw a pair of shiny boots walk closer and she forced her stiff neck to look upward into the grinning face of Baron Jeffers.

"Hello, bitch," he said as several sec men came out of the bushes along the riverbank.

"Anybody else?" Jeffers asked over a shoulder.

"No, Baron," a sec man reported, clutching a bolt-action longblaster. "She's alone."

He chortled. "Excellent."

"Jeffers," Sandra wheezed, trying to extract herself from the heavy wreckage. "Free me, and we can cut a deal."

"Oh, but I have everything that I want right here," Jeffers said, a touch of madness creeping into his words.

The baron held out a hand and a sec man reached into a canvas bag hanging at his side to pull out a Molotov. Flicking a predark butane lighter alive, Jeffers ignited the rag around the neck of the glass bottle.

"Absolutely everything that I want!" Jeffers repeated, raising the bottle high.

Desperately, Sandra fumbled for the palmblasters hidden under her arms only to remember she had lost them in the battle with the stingwings.

"Time to fry, bitch," Jeffers cooed sweetly, and threw the bottle, which smashed against the Angel. The glass shattered and the liquid burst into flames.

Panic fueled her weak arms, and Sandra grabbed the splintery frame holding her in place and heaved with both hands. But the wood only shattered from the effort, the broken ends driving into her shoulders and pinning her even more firmly into place.

"Please!" she begged, feeling the rising heat of the fire spreading across the battered fuselage. "We can cut a deal! I'll teach you to fly! To fly! The sky will be yours!"

"Rather have you aced." Jeffers chuckled.

"You can't do this! I'm a fellow baron!" Sandra screamed in terror.

Jeffers gave a cold laugh as the sec man placed another Molotov into his waiting hand.

The flames were higher now, spreading rapidly along the wreckage, and in spite of the boots, both of her feet were starting to feel prickly from the growing heat.

"Then chill me!" she commanded, tears washing the shine from her eyes. "Cut my throat, or shoot me in the heart. But don't let me burn alive! Have mercy!"

"Did you show mercy to my ville?" Baron Jeffers chortled, lighting the rag around the Molotov

"They were aced fast! It was all over in a few ticks!"

"Ah, but there were so many people there. My friends and family, now all of those ticks combined make a lot of minutes." He reached down to tuck the lit Molotov behind the trapped woman, just out of her reach. "But you, ah, my little sky baron, you'll take a good long time to die."

"Please!"

"Maybe we'll even toss on some water to kill the flames," Jeffers whispered. "And then cover you with wood and start a new fire in a few days. But eventually you'll beg for death."

"I am begging!"

Jeffers smiled insanely. "Yes, you are," he said softly. "But not loudly enough, bitch. Oh, nowhere nearly loud enough."

The painful feeling in her feet was intolerable, and there was a hideous stink of roasting meat in the air. Writhing in torment, Sandra couldn't hold back the scream boiling in her throat. Then the Molotov behind her burst and liquid fire engulfed her world, bringing agony beyond comprehension. The screaming and the hellish pain seemed to last forever, but always in the background Tregart could still hear Baron Jeffers laughing in glee as he tossed more and more Molotovs onto the growing pyre...

TRAVELING NORTHWARD, the companions found the ford and crossed the Ohi without any trouble. Returning to the redoubt, they collapsed in their beds and slept for a full day. Eventually rising, the companions checked the base one more time for any supplies they could find, then went to the mat-trans chamber to make a blind jump to another redoubt. As always, they hoped it would be one stuffed full of food and weapons. But even more importantly, a redoubt located in lush farmland without any muties or villes in a thousand miles.

As the electronic mist hissed softly into existence, rose, and the weary travelers fell away into nothingness, something small moved in the shadows of the control room on the other side of the closed oval door. Rolling into the fluorescent light, the droid paused, several tiny antennas flexing in the air, giving it a decidedly insectlike appearance. The machine was about the size of a shoebox, its hull a bland neutral color, but deeply embossed into the metal was a symbol: a circle surrounded by an elliptic ring with a tiny five-pointed star set off-center.

Going around the mummified corpse of a dead tech on the floor, the droid went to the control board of the master computer and then rolled up the flat metal side of the console to reach the banks of twinkling controls on top. Carefully not touching any of the dials or buttons, the droid proceeded to a small access slot and settled down on top of it with a locking click.

Power surged into the droid, recharging its nuke batteries, and it began to send a report to its master about the companions: when they arrived in the redoubt, when they left, what they took, a detailed description of their physical status, especially any wounds or weapons, and finally, the precise location of the new redoubt the six people had just jumped to....

NEUTRON FORCE

The ultimate stealth weapon is in the hands
of an unknown enemy...

A grim presidential directive comes down to
Stony Man: an unknown entity is in possession of
one of the deadliest weapons known to man, and the
death toll across the globe is mounting. It's a silent
murdering machine, killing with no heat, no noise,
no radiation—just silent, invisible slaughter from
ultrafast, subatomic particles. With no nation able
to defend against it, Stony Man's only option is to
destroy it. But first, they must find it....

STONY® MAN

*Available
June 2007
wherever
you buy books.*

James Axler
Outlanders®

SATAN'S SEED

The Cerberus warriors must endure the most frightening tests of their ingenuity when they discover secrets linking alien technology, Nazi time-travel experiments and a 260-year-old nightmare time-trawled in a new quest for power. The Pacific is swarming with SS troopers led by a dangerous woman and her strange advisor whose capacity for evil is rooted in the dark energy of the occult....

Available August wherever you buy books.

Or order your copy now by sending your name, address, zip or postal code, along with a check or money order (please do not send cash) for $6.50 for each book ordered ($7.99 in Canada), plus 75¢ postage and handling ($1.00 in Canada), payable to Gold Eagle Books, to:

In the U.S.	In Canada
Gold Eagle Books	Gold Eagle Books
3010 Walden Avenue	P.O. Box 636
P.O. Box 9077	Fort Erie, Ontario
Buffalo, NY 14269-9077	L2A 5X3

Please specify book title with your order.
Canadian residents add applicable federal and provincial taxes.

GOLD
EAGLE®

GOUT42